A HOUSE
IN BLOOMSBURY

BY

MRS. OLIPHANT

First published in 1894

British Library Cataloguing-in-Publication Data
A catalogue record for this book is available
from the British Library

CONTENTS

MARGARET OLIPHANT

Margaret Oliphant was born in Wallyford, Scotland in 1828. When she was ten years old, her family moved to Liverpool, where she began to experiment with writing. She had her first novel, *Passages in the Life of Mrs. Margaret Maitlan* (1849), published when she was just 21. It was a moderate commercial success, and following her second novel (*Caleb Field,* published in 1851) Oliphant became a regular contributor to the famous *Blackwood's Magazine.*

By the 1860s, Oliphant was a popular and recognized author, and in order to support her family (she had become a widow in 1959) she became an incredibly prolific author. Oliphant eventually went on to write more than 120 works, including novels travelogues, histories and volumes of literary criticism. Two of her better-known fictional works are *Miss Marjoribanks* (1866) and *Phoebe Junior* (1876). Towards the end of her life, she wrote a well-received series of supernatural short stories called *Tales of the Seen and Unseen* (1885), which remains popular to this day. Oliphant died in 1897, aged 69.

CHAPTER I.

"Father," said Dora, "I am going upstairs for a little, to see Mrs. Hesketh, if you have no objection."

"And who is Mrs. Hesketh, if I might make so bold as to ask?" Mr. Mannering said, lifting his eyes from his evening paper.

"Father! I told you all about her on Sunday—that she's all alone all day, and sometimes her husband is so late of getting home. She is so lonely, poor little thing. And she is such a nice little thing! Married, but not so big as me."

"And who is—— her husband?" Mr. Mannering was about to say, but he checked himself. No doubt he had heard all about the husband too. He heard many things without hearing them, being conscious rather of the pleasant voice of Dora running on than of everything she said.

This had, no doubt, been the case in respect to the young couple upstairs, of whose existence he had become dimly sensible by reason of meeting one or other of them on the stairs. But there was nothing in the appearance of either which had much attracted him. They appeared to him a commonplace couple of inferior kind; and perhaps had he been a man with all his wits keenly about him, he would not have allowed his child to run wild about the little woman upstairs. But Mr. Mannering did not keep his wits about him sharpened to any such point.

Dora was a child, but also she was a lady, proof against any contamination of acquaintance which concerned only the letters of the alphabet. Her "h's" could take care of themselves, and so could her "r's". As for anything else, Mr. Mannering's dreamy yet not unobservant eyes had taken in the fact that the young woman, who was not a lady, was an innocent and good little woman; and it had never occurred to him to be afraid of any

7

chance influence of such a kind for his daughter. He acquiesced, accordingly, with a little nod of his head, and return of his mild eyes to his paper.

These two were the best of companions; but he was not jealous of his little girl, nor did he desire that she should be for ever in his sight. He liked to read his paper; sometimes he had a book which interested him very much. The thought that Dora had a little interest in her life also, special to herself, pleased him more than if she had been always hanging upon him for her amusement and occupation. He was not afraid of the acquaintance she might make, which was a little rash, perhaps, especially in a man who had known the world, and knew, or ought to have known, the mischief that can arise from unsuitable associates.

But there are some people who never learn; indeed, few people learn by experience, so far as I have ever seen. Dora had been an independent individuality to her father since she was six years old. He had felt, as parents often feel with a curious mixture of feelings, half pleasure, half surprise, half disappointment (as if there could be three halves! the reader will say; but there are, and many more), that she was not very much influenced by himself, who was most near to her. If such things could be weighed in any balance, he was most, it may be said, influenced by her. She retained her independence. How was it possible then that, conscious of this, he should be much alarmed by any problematical influence that could be brought to bear upon her by a stranger? He was not, indeed, the least afraid.

Dora ran up the stairs, which were dark at the top, for Mrs. Simcox could not afford to let her lodgers who paid so low a rent have a light on their landing; and the landing itself was encumbered by various articles, between which there was need of wary steering. But this little girl had lived in these Bloomsbury lodgings all her life, and knew her way about as well as the children of the house. Matters were facilitated, too, by the sudden opening of a door, from which the light and, sad to say, something of the smell of a paraffin lamp shone out, illuminating the rosy face of a young woman, with a piece of sewing in her hand, who looked out in bright expectation, but clouded over a little when she saw who it was. "Oh, Miss Dora!" she said; and added in an undertone, "I thought it was Alfred home a little sooner than usual," with a little sigh.

"I made such a noise," said Dora, apologetically. "I couldn't help it. Jane will leave so many things about."

"Oh, it's me, Miss Dora. I does my rooms myself; it saves a deal on the rent. I shouldn't have left that crockery there, but it saves trouble, and I'm not that used to housework."

"No," said Dora, seating herself composedly at the table, and resisting, by a strong exercise of self-control, her impulse to point out that the lamp could not have been properly cleaned, since it smelt so. "One can see," she added, the fact being incontestable, "that you don't know how to do many things. And that is a pity, because things then are not so nice."

She seemed to cast a glance of criticism about the room, to poor little Mrs. Hesketh's excited fancy, who was ready to cry with vexation. "My family always kep' a girl," she said in a tone of injury subdued. But she was proud of Dora's friendship, and would not say any more.

"So I should have thought," said Dora, critical, yet accepting the apology as if, to a certain extent, it accounted for the state of affairs.

"And Alfred says," cried the young wife, "that if we can only hold on for a year or two, he'll make a lady of me, and I shall have servants of my own. But we ain't come to that yet—oh, not by a long way."

"It is not having servants that makes a lady," said Dora. "We are not rich." She said this with an ineffable air of superiority to all such vulgar details. "I have never had a maid since I was quite a little thing." She had always been herself surprised by this fact, and she expected her hearer to be surprised. "But what does that matter?" she added. "One is oneself all the same."

"Nobody could look at you twice," said the admiring humble

friend. "And how kind of you to leave your papa and all your pretty books and come up to sit with me because I'm so lonely! It is hard upon us to have Alfred kep' so late every night."

"Can't he help it?" said Dora. "If I were you, I should go out to meet him. The streets are so beautiful at night."

"Oh, Miss Dora!" cried the little woman, shocked. "He wouldn't have me go out by myself, not for worlds! Why, somebody might speak to me! But young girls they don't think of that. I sometimes wish I could be taken on among the young ladies in the mantle department, and then we could walk home together. But then," she added quickly, "I couldn't make him so comfortable, and then——"

She returned to her work with a smile and a blush. She was always very full of her work, making little "things," which Dora vaguely supposed were for the shop. Their form and fashion threw no light to Dora upon the state of affairs.

"When you were in the shop, were you in the mantle department?" she asked.

"Oh, no. My figure isn't good enough," said Mrs. Hesketh; "you have to have a very good figure, and look like a lady. Some of the young ladies have beautiful figures, Miss Dora; and such nice black silks—as nice as any lady would wish to wear—which naturally sets them off."

"And nothing to do?" said Dora, contemptuously. "I should not like that."

"Oh, you! But they have a deal to do. I've seen 'em when they were just dropping down with tiredness. Standing about all day, and putting on mantles and things, and pretending to walk away careless to set them off. Poor things! I'd rather a deal stand behind the counter, though they've got the best pay."

"Have you been reading anything to-day?" said Dora, whose attention was beginning to flag.

Mrs. Hesketh blushed a little. "I've scarcely sat down all day till now; I've been having a regular clean-out. You can't think how the dust gets into all the corners with the fires and all that.

10

And I've just been at it from morning till night. I tried to read a little bit when I had my tea. And it's a beautiful book, Miss Dora, but I was that tired."

"It can scarcely take a whole day," said Dora, looking round her, "to clean out this one little room."

"Oh, but you can't think what a lot of work there is, when you go into all the corners. And then I get tired, and it makes me stupid."

"Well," said Dora, with suppressed impatience, "but when you become a lady, as you say, with servants to do all you want, how will you be able to take up a proper position if you have never read anything?"

"Oh, as for that," said Mrs. Hesketh in a tone of relief, "that can't be for a long time yet; and you feel different when you're old to what you do when you're young."

"But I am young," said Dora. She changed the subject, however, more or less, by her next question. "Are you really fond of sewing?" she said in an incredulous tone; "or rather, what are you most fond of? What should you like best to do?"

"Oh!" said the little wife, with large open eyes and mouth— she fell off, however, into a sigh and added, "if one ever had what one wished most!"

"And why not?" said inexperienced Dora. "At least," she added, "it's pleasant to think, even if you don't have what you want. What should you like best?"

"Oh," said Mrs. Hesketh again, but this time with a long-drawn breath of longing consciousness, "I should like that we might have enough to live upon without working, and Alfred and me always to be together,—that's what I should like best."

"Money?" cried Dora with irrepressible scorn.

"Oh, Miss Dora, money! You can't think how nice it would be just to have enough to live on. I should never, never wish to be extravagant, or to spend more than I had; just enough for Alfred to give up the shop, and not be bound down to those long hours any more!"

"And how much might that be?" said Dora, with an air of grand yet indulgent magnificence, as if, though scorning this poor ideal, she might yet perhaps find it possible to bestow upon her friend the insignificant happiness for which she sighed.

"Oh, Miss Dora, when you think how many things are wanted in housekeeping, and one's dress, and all that—and probably more than us," said Mrs. Hesketh, with a bright blush. She too looked at the girl as if it might have been within Dora's power to give the modest gift. "Should you think it a dreadful lot," said the young woman, "if I said two hundred a year?"

"Two hundred pounds a year?" said Dora reflectively. "I think," she added, after a pause, "father has more than twice as much as that."

"La!" said Mrs. Hesketh; and then she made a rapid calculation, one of those efforts of mental arithmetic in which children and simple persons so often excel. "He must be saving up a lot," she said admiringly, "for your fortune. Miss Dora. You'll be quite an heiress with all that."

This was an entirely new idea to Dora, who knew of heiresses only what is said in novels, where it is so easy to bestow great fortunes. "Oh no, I shall not be an heiress," she said; "and I don't think we save up very much. Father has always half a dozen pensioners, and he buys books and—things." Dora had a feeling that it was something mean and bourgeois—a word which Mr. Mannering was rather apt to use—to save up.

"Oh!" said Mrs. Hesketh again, with her countenance falling. She was not a selfish or a scheming woman; but she had a romantic imagination, and it was so easy an exercise of fancy to think of this girl, who had evidently conceived such a friendship for herself, as "left" rich and solitary at the death of her delicate father, and adopting her Alfred and herself as companions and guardians. It was a sudden and passing inspiration, and the young woman meant no harm, but there was a visionary disappointment in her voice.

"But," said Dora, with the impulse of a higher cultivation, "it

12

is a much better thing to work than to do nothing. When father is at home for a few days, unless we go away somewhere, he gets restless; and if he were always at home he would begin some new study, and work harder than ever."

"Ah, not with folks like us, Miss Dora," said Mrs. Hesketh. Then she added: "A woman has always got plenty to do. She has got her house to look after, and to see to the dinner and things. And when there are children——" Once more she paused with a blush to think over that happy prospect. "And we'd have a little garden," she said, "where Alfred could potter about, and a little trap that we could drive about in, and take me to see places, and oh, we'd be as happy as the day was long!" she cried, clasping her hands. The clock struck as she spoke, and she hastily put away her sewing and rose up. "You won't mind, Miss Dora, if I lay the table and get things ready for supper? Alfred will soon be coming now."

"Oh, I like to see you laying the table," said Dora, "and I'll help you—I can do it very well. I never let Jane touch our nice clean tablecloths. Don't you think you want a fresh one?" she said, looking doubtfully at the somewhat dingy linen. "Father always says clean linen is the luxury of poor people."

"Oh!" said little Mrs. Hesketh. She did not like criticism any more than the rest of us, nor did she like being identified with "poor people". Mr. Mannering's wise yet foolish aphorism (for how did he know how much it cost to have clean linen in Bloomsbury—or Belgravia either, for that matter?) referred to persons in his own condition, not in hers; but naturally she did not think of that. Her pride and her blood were up, however; and she went with a little hurry and vehemence to a drawer and took out a clean tablecloth. Sixpence was the cost of washing, and she could not afford to throw away sixpences, and the other one had only been used three or four times; but her pride, as I have said, was up.

"And where are the napkins?" said Dora. "I'll lay it for you. I really like to do it: and a nicely-laid table, with the crystal

13

sparkling, and the silver shining, and the linen so fresh and smooth, is a very pretty object to look at, father always says."

"Oh dear! I must hurry up," cried Mrs. Hesketh; "I hear Alfred's step upon the stairs."

Now Dora did not admire Alfred, though she was fond of Alfred's wife. He brought a sniff of the shop with him; which was disagreeable to the girl, and he called her "miss," which Dora hated. She threw down the tablecloth hurriedly. "Oh, I'll leave you then," she cried, "for I'm sure he does not like to see me here when he comes in."

"Oh, Miss Dora, how can you think such a thing?" cried her friend; but she was glad of the success of her expedient when her visitor disappeared. Alfred, indeed, did not come in for half an hour after; but Mrs. Hesketh was at liberty to make her little domestic arrangements in her own way. Alfred, like herself, knew that a tablecloth cost sixpence every time it went to the wash—which Dora, it was evident, did not do.

Dora found her father reading in exactly the same position as she had left him; he had not moved except to turn a leaf. He raised his head when she came in, and said: "I am glad you have come back, Dora. I want you to get me a book out of that bookcase in the corner. It is on the third shelf."

"And were you so lazy, father, that you would not get up to find it yourself?"

"Yes, I was so lazy," he said, with a laugh. "I get lazier and lazier every day. Besides, I like to feel that I have some one to do it for me. I am taking books out of shelves and putting them back again all the day long."

Dora put her arm on her father's shoulder, as she put down the book on the table before him. "But you like it, don't you, father? You are not tired of it."

"Of the Museum?" he said, with a laugh and a look of surprise. "No; I am not tired of it—any more than I am of my life."

This was an enigmatical reply, but Dora did not attempt to fathom it. "What the little people upstairs want is just to have money enough to live on, and nothing to do," she said.

"The little people? And what are you, Dora? You are not so very big."

"I am growing," said Dora, with confidence; "and I shouldn't like to have nothing to do all my life."

"There is a great deal to be said for that view of the question," said Mr. Mannering. "I am not an enthusiast for mere work, unless there is something to come out of it. 'Know what thou canst work at' does not apply always, unless you have to earn your living, which is often a very fortunate necessity. And even that," he said, with a smile, "has its drawbacks."

"It is surely far better than doing nothing," cried Dora, with her young nose in the air.

"Well, but what does it come to after all? One works to live, and consumes the fruits of one's work in the art of living. And what better is that than if you had never been? The balance would be much the same. But this is not the sort of argument for little girls, even though they are growing," Mr. Mannering said.

"I think the Museum must have been very stuffy to-day, father," was the remark which Dora made.

CHAPTER II.

The Mannerings lived in a house in that district of Bloomsbury which has so long meant everything that is respectable, mediocre, and dull,—at least, to that part of the world which inhabits farther West. It is possible that, regarded from the other side of the compass, Bloomsbury may be judged more justly as a city of well-sized and well-built houses, aired and opened up by many spacious breathing-places, set with stately trees. It is from this point of view that it is regarded by many persons of humble pretensions, who find large rooms and broad streets where in other districts they would only have the restricted space of respectable poverty, the weary little conventionality of the suburban cottage, or the dingy lodging-house parlours of town.

Bloomsbury is very much town indeed, surrounded on all sides by the roar of London; but it has something of the air of an individual place, a town within a town.

The pavements are wide, and so are the houses, as in the best quarter of a large provincial city. The squares have a look of seclusion, of shady walks, and retired leisure, which there is nothing to rival either in Belgravia or Mayfair. It is, or was—for it is many years since the present writer has passed over their broad pavements, or stood under the large, benignant, and stately shadow of the trees in Russell Square—a region apart, above fashion, a sober heart and centre of an older and steadier London, such as is not represented in the Row, and takes little part in the rabble and rout of fashion, the decent town of earlier days.

I do not mean to imply by this that the Mannerings lived in Russell Square, or had any pretensions to be regarded among the magnates of Bloomsbury; for they were poor people, quite poor, living the quietest life; not rich enough even to have a house of their own; mere lodgers, occupying a second floor in a house which was full of other lodgers, but where they retained the importance and dignity of having furnished their own rooms. The house was situated at the corner of a street, and thus gave them a glimpse of the trees of the Square, a view over the gardens, as the landlady described it, which was no small matter, especially from the altitude of the second floor. The small family consisted of a father and daughter—he, middle-aged, a quiet, worn, and subdued man, employed all day in the British Museum; and she, a girl very young, yet so much older than her years that she was the constant and almost only companion of her father, to whom Dora was as his own soul, the sharer of all his thoughts, as well as the only brightness in his life.

She was but fifteen at the time when this chapter of their history begins, a creature in short frocks and long hair slightly curling on her shoulders; taller, if we may state such a contradiction in words, than she was intended to be, or turned out in her womanhood, with long legs, long neck, long fingers, and something of the look of a soft-eyed, timid, yet playfully daring colt, flying up and down stairs as if she had wings on her shoulders, yet walking very sedately by the side of her father whenever they went out together, almost more steady and serious than he.

Mr. Mannering had the appearance of being a man who had always done well, yet never succeeded in life; a man with a small income, and no chance of ever bettering himself, as people say, or advancing in the little hierarchy of the great institution which he served meekly and diligently in the background, none of its promotions ever reaching him.

Scarcely any one, certainly none out of that institution, knew that there had been a period in which this gentle and modest life had almost been submerged under the bitterest wave, and in which it had almost won the highest honours possible to a man of such pursuits. This was an old story, and even Dora knew little of it. He had done so much at that forgotten and troubled time, that, had he been a rich man like Darwin, and able to retire and work in quiet the discoveries he had made, and the experiences he had attained, Robert Mannering's name might have been placed in the rolls of fame as high as that of his more fortunate contemporary.

But he was poor when he returned from the notable wanderings during the course of which he had been given up as dead for years, poor and heartbroken, and desiring nothing but the dimmest corner in which to live out his broken days, and just enough to live upon to bring up his little daughter, and to endure his existence, his duty to God and to Dora forbidding him to make an end of it.

It would be giving an altogether false idea of the man with whom this book is to be much occupied, to say that he had continued in this despairing frame of mind. God and Dora— the little gift of God—had taken care of that. The little girl had led him back to a way which, if not brilliant or prosperous, was like a field-path through many humble flowers, sweet with the air and breath of nature. Sooth to say, it was no field-path at all, but led chiefly over the pavements of Bloomsbury; yet the simple metaphor was not untrue.

Thus he lived, and did his work dutifully day by day. No headship of a department, no assistant keepership for him; yet much esteem and consideration among his peers, and a constant reference, whenever anything in his special sphere was wanted, to his boundless information and knowledge. Sometimes a foreign inquirer would come eager to seek him, as the best and highest authority on this subject, to the consternation of the younger men in other branches, who could not understand how anybody could believe "old Mannering" to be of consequence in the place; but generally his life was as obscure as he wished it to be, yet not any hard or painful drudgery; for he was still occupied with the pursuit which he had chosen, and which he had followed all his life; and he was wise enough to recognise and be thankful for the routine which held his broken existence together, and had set up again, after his great disaster, his framework as a man.

Dora knew nothing of any disaster; and this was good for him too, bringing him back to nature. "A cheerful man I am in life," he might have said with Thackeray, who also had good reason for being sad enough. A man who has for his chief society a buoyant, curious, new spirit, still trailing clouds of glory from her origin, still only making acquaintance with things of earth, curious about everything, asking a thousand penetrating questions, awakening a mood of interest everywhere, can scarcely be otherwise than cheerful.

The second floor at the corner of the Square which was inhabited by this pair consisted of three rooms, all good-sized and airy; the sitting-room being indeed spacious, larger than any two which could have been found in a fashionable nook in Mayfair. It was furnished, in a manner very unexpected by such chance visitors as did not know the character of the inhabitants, with furniture which would not have been out of place in Belgravia, or in a fine lady's drawing-room anywhere, mingled strangely with certain plain pieces put in for evident use.

A square and sturdy table occupied the portion of the room which was nearest to the door, with the clearest utility, serving for the meals of the father and daughter, while the other part of the room, partially separated by a stamped leather screen, had an air of subdued luxury, a little faded, yet unmistakable. The curtains were of heavy brocade, which had a little lost their colour, or rather gained those shadings and reflections which an artist loves; but hung with the softness of their silken fabric, profoundly unlike the landlady's nice fresh crimson rep which adorned the windows of the first floor. There was an Italian inlaid cabinet against the farther wall, which held the carefully prepared sheets of a herbarium, which Mr. Mannering had collected from all the ends of the earth, and which was of sufficient value to count for much in the spare inheritance which he meant for his only child. The writing-table, at which Dora had learned to make her first pothooks, was a piece of beautiful *marqueterie*, the oldest and most graceful of its kind.

But I need not go round the room and make a catalogue of the furniture. It settled quite kindly into the second floor in Bloomsbury, with that grace which the nobler kind of patrician, subdued by fortune, lends to the humblest circumstances, which he accepts with patience and goodwill. Mr. Mannering himself had never been a handsome man; and all the colour and brightness of youth had died out of him, though he was still in the fulness of middle age. But the ivory tone of his somewhat sharply cut profile and the premature stoop of his shoulders suited his surroundings better than a more vigorous personality would have done.

Dora, in her half-grown size and bigness, with her floating hair and large movements, seemed to take up a great deal more space than her father; and it was strange that she did not knock down more frequently the pretty old-fashioned things, and the old books which lay upon the little tables, or even those tables themselves, as she whisked about; but they knew Dora, and she knew them. She had spent a great part of every day alone with them, as long as she could remember, playing with those curiosities that lay upon them, while she was a child, in the long, silent, dreamy hours, when she was never without amusement, though as constantly alone.

Since she had grown older, she had taken pleasure in dusting them and arranging them, admiring the toys of old silver, and the carved ivories and trifles of all kinds, from the ends of the earth. It was her great pleasure on the Sunday afternoons, when her father was with her, to open the drawers of the cabinet and bring out the sheets of the herbarium so carefully arranged and classified. Her knowledge, perhaps, was not very scientific, but it was accurate in detail, and in what may be called locality in the highest degree. She knew what family abode in what drawer, and all its ramifications. These were more like neighbours to Dora, lodged in surrounding houses, than specimens in drawers. She knew all about them, where they came from, and their genealogy, and which were the grandparents, and which the children; and, still more interesting, in what jungle or marsh her father had found them, and which of them came from the African deserts in which he had once been lost.

By degrees she had found out much about that wonderful episode in his life, and had become vaguely aware, which was the greatest discovery of all, that it contained many things which she had not found out, and perhaps never would. She knew even how to lead him to talk about it, which had to be very skilfully done—for he was shy of the subject when assailed openly, and often shrank from the very name of Africa as if it stung him; while on other occasions, led on by some train of thought in his own mind, he would fall into long lines of recollections, and tell her of the fever attacks, one after another, which had laid him low, and how the time had gone over him like a dream, so that he never knew till long after how many months, and even years, he had lost.

Where was the mother all this time, it may be asked? Dora knew no more of this part of her history than if she had come into the world without need of any such medium, like Minerva from her father's head.

It is difficult to find out from the veiled being of a little child what it thinks upon such a subject, or if it is aware at all, when it has never been used to any other state of affairs, of the strange vacancy in its own life. Dora never put a single question to her father on this point; and he had often asked himself whether her mind was dead to all that side of life which she had never known, or whether some instinct kept her silent; and had satisfied himself at last that, as she knew scarcely any other children, the want in her own life had not struck her imagination. Indeed, the grandchildren of Mrs. Simcox, the landlady, were almost the only children Dora had ever known familiarly, and they, like herself, had no mother, they had granny; and Dora had inquired of her father about her own granny, who was dead long ago.

"You have only me, my poor little girl," he had said. But Dora had been quite satisfied.

"Janie and Molly have no papa," she answered, with a little pride. It was a great superiority, and made up for everything, and she inquired no more. Nature, Mr. Mannering knew, was by no means so infallible as we think her. He did not know, however, what is a still more recondite and profound knowledge, what secret things are in a child's heart.

I have known a widowed mother who wondered sadly for years why her children showed so little interest and asked no questions about their father; and then found out, from the lips of one grown into full manhood, what visions had been wrapt about that unknown image, and how his portrait had been the confidant of many a little secret trouble hidden even from herself. But Dora had not even a portrait to give embodiment to any wistful thoughts. Perhaps it was to her not merely that her mother was dead, but that she had never been. Perhaps—but who knows the questions that arise in that depth profound, the heart of a child?

It was not till Dora was fifteen that she received the great shock, yet revelation, of discovering the portrait of a lady in her father's room.

Was it her mother? She could not tell. It was the portrait of a young lady, which is not a child's ideal of a mother. It was hidden away in a secret drawer of which she had discovered the existence only by a chance in the course of some unauthorised investigations among Mr. Mannering's private properties.

He had lost something which Dora was intent on surprising him by finding; and this was what led her to these investigations. It was in a second Italian cabinet which was in his bedroom, an inferior specimen to that in the drawing-room, but one more private, about which her curiosity had never been awakened. He kept handkerchiefs, neckties, uninteresting items of personal use in it, which Dora was somewhat carelessly turning over, when by accident the secret spring was touched, and the drawer flew open. In this there was a miniature case which presented a very strange spectacle when Dora, a little excited, opened it. There seemed to be nothing but a blank at first, until, on further examination, Dora found that the miniature had been turned face downwards in its case. It may be imagined with what eager curiosity she continued her investigations.

The picture, as has been said, was that of a young lady—quite a young lady, not much older, Dora thought, than herself. Who could this girl be? Her mother? But that girlish face could not belong to any girl's mother. It was not beautiful to Dora's eyes; but yet full of vivacity and interest, a face that had much to say if one only knew its language; with dark, bright eyes, and a tremulous smile about the lips. Who was it; oh, who was it? Was it that little sister of papa's who was dead, whose name had been Dora too? Was it ——

Dora did not know what to think, or how to explain the little shock which was given her by this discovery. She shut up the drawer hastily, but she had not the heart to turn the portrait again as it had been turned, face downwards. It seemed too unkind, cruel almost. Why should her face be turned downwards, that living, smiling face? "I will ask papa," Dora said to herself; but she could not tell why it was, any more than she could explain her other sensations on the subject, that when the appropriate moment came to do so, she had not the courage to ask papa.

CHAPTER III.

There was one remarkable thing in Dora Mannering's life which I have omitted to mention, which is, that she was in the habit of receiving periodically, though at very uncertain intervals, out of that vast but vague universe surrounding England, which we call generally "abroad," a box. No one knew where it came from, or who it came from; at least, no light was ever thrown to Dora upon that mystery. It was despatched now from one place, now from another; and not a name, or a card, or a scrap of paper was ever found to identify the sender.

This box contained always a store of delights for the recipient, who, though she was in a manner monarch of all she surveyed, was without many of the more familiar pleasures of childhood. It had contained toys and pretty knick-knacks of many quaint foreign kinds when she was quite a child; but as she grew older, the mind of her unknown friend seemed to follow her growth with the strangest certainty of what would please these advancing youthful years.

The foundation of the box, if that word may be employed, was always a store of the daintiest underclothing, delicately made, which followed Dora's needs and growth, growing longer as she grew taller; so that underneath her frocks, which were not always lovely, the texture, form, and colour being chiefly decided by the dressmaker who had "made" for her as long as she could remember, Dora was clothed like a princess; and thus accustomed from her childhood to the most delicate and dainty accessories—fine linen, fine wool, silk stockings, handkerchiefs good enough for any fine lady. Her father had not, at first, liked to see these fine things; he had pushed them away when she spread them out to show him her treasures, and turned his back upon her, bidding her carry off her trumpery.

It was so seldom, so very seldom, that Mr. Mannering had an objection to anything done by Dora, that this little exhibition of temper had an extraordinary effect; but the interval between one arrival and another was long enough to sweep any such recollection out of the mind of a child; and as she grew older, more intelligent to note what he meant, and, above all, more curious about everything that happened, he had changed his tone. But he had a look which Dora classified in her own mind as "the face father puts on when my box comes".

This is a sort of thing which imprints itself very clearly upon the mind of the juvenile spectator and critic. Dora knew it as well as she knew the clothes her father wore, or the unchanging habits of his life, though she did not for a long time attempt to explain to herself what it meant. It was a look of intent self-restraint, of a stoical repression. He submitted to having the different contents of the box exhibited to him without a smile on his face or the least manifestation of sympathy—he who sympathised with every sentiment which breathed across his child's facile spirit. He wound himself up to submit to the ordeal, it seemed, with the blank look of an unwilling spectator, who has not a word of admiration for anything, and, indeed, hates the sight he cannot refuse to see.

"Who can send them, father? oh, who can send them? Who is it that remembers me like this, and that I'm growing, and what I must want, and everything? I was only a child when the last one came. You must know—you must know, father! How could any one know about me and not know you—or care for me?" Dora cried, with a little moisture springing to her eyes.

"I have already told you I don't know anything about it," said Mr. Mannering, oh, with such a shut-up face! closing the shutters upon his eyes and drawing down all the blinds, as Dora said.

"Well, but suppose you don't know, you must guess; you must imagine who it could be. No one could know me, and not know you. I am not a stranger that you have nothing to do with. You

25

must know who is likely to take so much thought about your daughter. Why, she knows my little name! There is 'Dora' on my handkerchiefs."

He turned away with a short laugh. "You seem to have found out a great deal for yourself. How do you know it is 'she'? It might be some old friend of mine who knew that my only child was Dora—and perhaps that I was not a man to think of a girl's wants."

"It may be an old friend of yours, father. It must be, for who would know about me but a friend of yours? But how could it be a man? It couldn't be a man! A man could never work 'Dora'——"

"You little simpleton! He would go to a shop and order it to be worked. I daresay it is Wallace, who is out in South America."

Such a practical suggestion made Dora pause; but it was not at all an agreeable idea. "Mr. Wallace! an old, selfish, dried-up ——" Then with a cry of triumph she added: "But they came long, long before he went to South America. No—I know one thing—that it is a lady. No one but a lady could tell what a girl wants. You don't, father, though you know me through and through; and how could any other man? But I suppose you have had friends ladies as well as men?"

His closed-up lips melted a little. "Not many," he said; then they shut up fast again. "It may be," he said reluctantly, with a face from which all feeling was shut out, which looked like wood, "a friend—of your mother's."

"Oh, of mamma's!" The girl's countenance lit up; she threw back her head and her waving hair, conveying to the man who shrank from her look the impression as of a thing with wings. He had been of opinion that she had never thought upon this subject, never considered the side of life thus entirely shut out from her experience, and had wondered even while rejoicing at her insensibility. But when he saw the light on her face he shrank, drawing back into himself. "Oh," cried Dora, "a friend of my mother's! Oh, father, she must have died long, long ago, that I never remember her. Oh, tell me, who can this friend be?"

He had shut himself up again more closely than ever—not only were there shutters at all the windows, but they were bolted and barred with iron. His face was more blank than any piece of wood. "I never knew much of her friends," he said.

"Mother's friends!" the girl cried, with a half shriek of reproachful wonder. And then she added quickly: "But think, father, think! You will remember somebody if you will only try."

"Dora," he said, "you don't often try my patience, and you had better not begin now. I should like to throw all that trumpery out of the window, but I don't, for I feel I have no right to deprive you of —— Your mother's friends were not mine. I don't feel inclined to think as you bid me. The less one thinks the better—on some subjects. I must ask you to question me no more."

"But, father ——"

"I have said that I will be questioned no more."

"It wasn't a question," said the girl, almost sullenly; and then she clasped her hands about his arm with a sudden impulse. "Father, if you don't like it, I'll put them all away. I'll never think of them nor touch them again."

The wooden look melted away, his features quivered for a moment. He stooped and kissed her on the forehead. "No," he said, making an effort to keep his lips firmly set as before. "No; I have no right to do that. No; I don't wish it. Keep them and wear them, and take pleasure in them; but don't speak to me on the subject again."

This conversation took place on the occasion of a very special novelty in the mysterious periodical present which she had just received, about which it was impossible to keep silence. The box—"my box," as Dora had got to call it—contained, in addition to everything else, a dress, which was a thing that had never been sent before.

It was a white dress, made with great simplicity, as became Dora's age, but also in a costly way, a semi-transparent white, the sort of stuff which could be drawn through a ring, as happens in fairy tales, and was certainly not to be bought in ordinary

English shops. To receive anything so unexpected, so exciting, so beautiful, and not to speak of it, to exhibit it to some one, was impossible. Dora had not been able to restrain herself. She had carried it in her arms out of her room, and opened it out upon a sofa in the sitting-room for her father's inspection. There are some things which we know beforehand will not please, and yet which we are compelled to do; and this was the consciousness in Dora's mind, who, besides her delight in the gift, and her desire to be able to find out something about the donor, had also, it must be allowed, a burning desire to make discoveries as to that past of which she knew so little, which had seized upon her mind from the moment when she had found the portrait turned upon its face in the secret drawer of her father's cabinet. As she withdrew now, again carrying in her arms the beautiful dress, there was in her mind, underneath a certain compunction for having disturbed her father, and sympathy with him so strong that she would actually have been capable of sacrificing her newly-acquired possessions, a satisfaction half-mischievous, half-affectionate, in the discoveries which she had made. They were certainly discoveries; sorry as she was to "upset father," there was yet a consciousness in her mind that this time it had been worth the while.

The reader may not think any better of Dora for this confession; but there is something of the elf in most constitutions at fifteen, and she was not of course at all sensible at that age of the pain that might lie in souvenirs so ruthlessly stirred up. And she had indeed made something by them. Never, never again, she promised herself, would she worry father with questions; but so far as the present occasion went, she could scarcely be sorry, for had not she learned much—enough to give her imagination much employment? She carried away her discoveries with her, as she carried her dress, to realise them in the shelter of her own room. They seemed to throw a vivid light upon that past in which her own life was so much involved. She threw the dress upon her bed carelessly, these other new thoughts having momentarily taken the interest out of even so exciting a novelty as that; and arranged in shape and sequence what she had found out. Well, it was not so much, after all. What seemed most clear in it was that father had not been quite friends with mother, or at least with mother's friends. Perhaps these friends had made mischief between them—perhaps she had cared for them more than for her husband; but surely that was not possible. And how strange, how strange it was that he should keep up such a feeling so long!

As Dora did not remember her mother, it was evident that she must have been dead many, many years. And yet her father still kept up his dislike to her friends! It threw a new light even upon him, whom she knew better than any one. Dora felt that she knew her father thoroughly, every thought that was in his mind; and yet here it would seem that she did not know him at all. So good a man, who was never hard with anybody, who forgave her, Dora, however naughty she might have been, as soon as she asked pardon; who forgave old Mr. Warrender for contradicting him about that orchid, the orchid that was called Manneringii, and which father had discovered, and therefore must know best; who forgave Mrs. Simcox when she swept the dust from the corners upon the herbarium and spoilt some of the specimens; and yet who in all these years had never forgiven the unknown persons, who were mother's friends, some one of whom must be nice indeed, or she never would go on remembering Dora, and sending her such presents. What could he have against this unknown lady,—this nice, nice woman? And how was it possible that he should have kept it up in his mind, and never forgiven it, or forgotten all these years? It made Dora wonder, and feel, though she crushed the feeling firmly, that perhaps father was not so perfect as she had thought.

And then there was this lady to think of—her mother's friend, who had kept on all this time thinking of Dora. She would not have been more than a baby when this benefactress saw her last, since Dora did not remember either mother, or mother's friend; yet she must recollect just how old Dora was, must have guessed just about how tall she was, and kept count how she had grown from one time to another. The beautiful dress was just almost long enough, almost fitted her in every way. It gave the girl a keen touch of pleasure to think that she was just a little taller and slighter than her unknown friend supposed her to be—but so near; the letting down of a hem, the narrowing of a seam, and it would be a perfect fit. How foolish father must be to think that Mr. Wallace, or any other man, would have thought of that! Her mother's friend—what a kind friend, what a constant friend, though father did not like her!

It overawed Dora a little to think if ever this lady came home, what would happen? Of course, she would wish to see the girl whom she had remembered so long, whom she had befriended so constantly; and what if father would not permit it? It would be unkind, ungrateful, wrong; but what if father objected, if it made him unhappy? Dora did not see her way through this dreadful complication. It was sufficiently hard upon her, a girl at so early an age, to become the possessor of a beautiful dress like this, and have no one to show it to, to talk it over with; nobody even to tell her exactly how it fitted, to judge what was necessary for its perfection, as Dora herself, with no experience, and not even a good glass to see herself in, could scarcely do. To hide a secret of any kind in one's being at fifteen is a difficult thing; but when that secret is a frock, a dress!—a robe, indeed, she felt it ought to be called, it was so exquisite, so poetical in its fineness and whiteness. Dora had no one to confide in; and if she had possessed a thousand confidants, would not have said a word to them which would seem to involve her father in any blame. She put her pretty dress away, however, with a great sense of discomfiture and downfall. Perhaps he would dislike to see her wear it, even if she had ever any need for a beautiful dress like that. But she never had any need. She never went anywhere, or saw anybody. A whole host of little grievances came up in the train of that greater one. She wondered if she were to spend all her life like this, without ever tasting those delights of society which she had read of, without ever knowing any one of her own age, without ever seeing people dance, or hearing them sing. As for performing in these ways herself, that had not come into Dora's mind. She would like, she thought, to look on and see how they did it, for once, at least, in her life.

When she had come to this point, Dora, who was a girl full of natural sense, began to feel instinctively that she was not in a good way, and that it would be better to do something active to clear away the cobwebs. It was evening, however, and she did not know exactly what to do. To go back to the sitting-room where her father was reading, and to sit down also to read at his side, seemed an ordeal too much for her after the excitement of their previous talk; but it was what probably she would have been compelled to do, had she not heard a heavy step mounting the stairs, the sound of a knock at the door, and her father's voice bidding some one enter.

She satisfied herself presently that it was the voice of one of Mr. Mannering's chief friends, a colleague from the Museum, and that he was safe for a time not to remark her absence or to have urgent need for her. What now should Dora do? The openings of amusement were small. Mrs. Hesketh had been exhausted for the moment. It must be said that Dora was free of the whole house, and that she used her *petites entrées* in the most liberal and democratic fashion, thinking no scorn of going downstairs sometimes to the funny little room next to the kitchen, which Mrs. Simcox called the breakfast-room, and used as her own sanctum, the family centre where her grandchildren and herself found refuge out of the toils of the kitchen. The kitchen itself remained in the possession of Jane; and Jane, like her mistress, occasionally shared the patronage of Miss Dora. To-night perhaps she wanted solace of another kind from any which could be given her on the basement story. It is not often that a young person in search of entertainment or sympathy has all the gradations of the social system to choose from. The first floor represented the aristocracy in the establishment at Bloomsbury.

31

It was occupied by a Scotch lady, a certain Miss Bethune, a somewhat harsh-featured and angular person, hiding a gentle heart under a grim exterior; but a little intolerant in her moods, and not always sure to respond to overtures of friendship; with a maid not much less unlike the usual denizens of Bloomsbury than herself, but beaming with redness and good humour, and one of Dora's chief worshippers in the house. When the girl felt that her needs required the sympathy of a person of the highest, *i.e.*, her own class, she went either boldly or with strategy to the drawing-room floor. She had thus the power of drawing upon the fellowship of her kind in whatever way the temper of the time adapted it best for her.

Mrs. Simcox and the girls downstairs, and Mrs. Hesketh above, would have been lost in raptures over Dora's new dress. They would have stared, they would perhaps have touched with a timid finger, they would have opened their eyes and their mouths, and cried: "Oh!" or "La!" or "Well, I never!" But they would not have understood. One's own kind, Dora felt, was necessary for that. But as it was evening, and Miss Bethune was not always gracious, she did not boldly walk up to her door, but lingered about on the stairs, coming and going, until, as was pretty sure to occur, Gilchrist, the maid, with her glowing moon face and her sandy locks, came out of the room. Gilchrist brightened immediately at the sight of the favourite of the house.

"Oh, is that you, Miss Dora? Come in and see my lady, and cheer her up. She's not in the best of spirits to-night."

"Neither am I—in the best of spirits," said Dora.

"You!" cried Gilchrist, with what she herself would have called a "skreigh" of laughter. She added sympathetically: "You'll maybe have been getting a scold from your papaw".

"My father never scolds," said Dora, with dignity.

"Bless me! but that's the way when there's but wan child," said Miss Bethune's maid: "not always, though," she added, with a deep sigh that waved aloft her own cap-strings, and caught Dora's hair like a breeze. The next moment she opened the door and said, putting her head in: "Here's Miss Dora, mem, to cheer you up a bit: but no' in the best of spirits hersel'".

"Bless me!" repeated Miss Bethune from within: "and what is wrong with her spirits? Come away, Dora, come in." Both mistress and maid had, as all the house was aware, curious modes of expressing themselves, which were Scotch, though nobody was aware in Bloomsbury how that quality affected the speech—in Miss Bethune's case at least. The lady was tall and thin, a large framework of a woman which had never filled out. She sat in a large chair near the fire, between which and her, however, a screen was placed. She held up a fan before her face to screen off the lamp, and consequently her countenance was in full shadow. She beckoned to the girl with her hand, and pointed to a seat beside her. "So you are in low spirits, Dora? Well, I'm not very bright myself. Come and let us mingle our tears."

"You are laughing at me, Miss Bethune. You think I have no right to feel anything."

"On the contrary, my dear. I think at your age there are many things that a girl feels—too much; and though they're generally nonsense, they're just as disagreeable as if they were the best of sense. Papa a little cross?"

"Why should you all think anything so preposterous? My father is never cross," cried Dora, with tears of indignation in her eyes.

"The better for him, my dear, much the better for him," said Miss Bethune; "but, perhaps, rather the worse for you. That's not my case, for I am just full of irritability now and then, and ready to quarrel with the tables and chairs. Well, you are cross yourself, which is much worse. And yet I hear you had one of your grand boxes to-day, all full of bonnie-dies. What a lucky little girl you are to get presents like that!"

"I am not a little girl, Miss Bethune."

"No, I'll allow you're a very big one for your age. Come, Dora, tell me what was in the box this time. It will do you good."

Dora hesitated a little to preserve her dignity, and then she said almost with awe: "There was a dress in it".

"A dress!" cried Miss Bethune, with a little shriek of surprise; "and does it fit you?"

"It's just a very, very little bit too short," said Dora, with pride, "and just a very, very little bit too wide at the waist."

"Run and bring it, and let me see it," cried the lady. "I've no doubt in the world it fits like a glove. Gilchrist, come in, come in, and see what the bairn's got. A frock that fits her like a glove."

"Just a very, very little too short, and a very, very little too wide in the waist," said Dora, repeating her formula. She had flown upstairs after the first moment's hesitation, and brought it back in her arms, glad in spite of herself to be thus delivered from silence and the sense of neglect.

"Eh, mem," cried Gilchrist, "but it must be an awfu', awfu' faithful woman that has minded how a lassie like that grows and gets big, and just how big she gets, a' thae years."

"There ye are with your moral!" cried the mistress; and to Dora's infinite surprise tears were on her cheeks. "It's just the lassie that makes all the difference," said Miss Bethune. She flung the pretty dress from her, and then she rose up suddenly and gave Dora a hasty kiss. "Put it on and let me see it," she said; "I will wager you anything it just fits like a glove."

CHAPTER IV.

"That is a very strange business of these Mannerings, Gilchrist," said Miss Bethune to her maid, when Dora, excited by praise and admiration, and forgetting all her troubles, had retired to her own habitation upstairs, escorted, she and her dress, by Gilchrist, who could not find it in her heart, as she said, to let a young thing like that spoil her bonnie new frock by not putting it properly away. Gilchrist laid the pretty dress lovingly in a roomy drawer, smoothing out all its creases by soft pats of her accustomed hands, and then returned to her mistress to talk over the little incident of the evening.

Miss Bethune's spirits were improved also by that little exhibition. What a thing it is to be able to draw a woman softly out of her troubles by the sight of a pretty child in a pretty new dress! Contemptible the love of clothes, the love of finery, and so forth, let the philosophers say. To me there is something touching in that natural instinct which relieves for a moment now and then the heaviest pressure. Dora's new frock had nothing to do with any gratification of Miss Bethune's vanity; but it brought a little dawning ray of momentary light into her room, and a little distraction from the train of thoughts that were not over bright. No man could feel the same for the most beautiful youth ever introduced in raiment like the day. Let us be thankful among all our disabilities for a little simple pleasure, now and then, that is common to women only. Boy or girl, it scarcely matters which, when they come in dressed in their best, all fresh and new, the sight pleases the oldest, the saddest of us—a little unconsidered angel-gift, amid the dimness and the darkness of the every-day world. Miss Bethune to outward aspect was a little grim, an old maid, as people said, apart from the sympathies of life. But the dull evening and the pressure of many thoughts had been made bright to her by Dora's new frock.

"What business, mem?" asked Gilchrist.

"If ever there was a living creature slow at the uptake, and that could not see a pikestaff when it is set before your eyes!" cried Miss Bethune. "What's the meaning of it all, you stupid woman? Who's that away in the unknown that sends all these bonnie things to that motherless bairn?—and remembers the age she is, and when she's grown too big for dolls, and when she wants a frock that will set her off, that she could dance in and sing in, and make her little curtesy to the world? No, she's too young for that; but still the time's coming, and fancy goes always a little before."

"Eh, mem," said Gilchrist, "that is just what I have askit mysel'—that's just what I was saying. It's some woman, that's the wan thing; but what woman could be so thoughtful as that, aye minding just what was wanted?" She made a gesture with her hands as if in utter inability to divine, but her eyes were fixed all the time very wistfully on her mistress's face.

"You need not look at me like that," the lady said.

"I was looking at you, mem, not in any particklar way."

"If you think you can make a fool of me at the present period of our history, you're far mistaken," said Miss Bethune. "I know what you were meaning. You were comparing her with me, not knowing either the one or the other of us—though you have been my woman, and more near me than anybody on earth these five-and-twenty long years."

"And more, mem, and more!" cried Gilchrist, with a flow of tears, which were as natural to her as her spirit. "Eh, I was but a young, young lass, and you a bonnie ——"

"Hold your peace!" said Miss Bethune, with an angry raising of her hand; and then her voice wavered and shook a little, and a tremulous laugh came forth. "I was never a bonnie—anything, ye auld fool! and that you know as well as me."

"But, mem——"

"Hold your peace, Gilchrist! We were never anything to brag

36

of, either you or me. Look in your glass, woman, if you don't believe me. A couple of plain women, very plain women, mistress and maid."

This was said with a flash of hazel eyes which gave a half-humorous contradiction at the same moment to the assertion. Gilchrist began to fold hems upon the apron with which she had just dried her tears.

"I never said," she murmured, with a downcast head, "a word about mysel',—that's no' a woman's part. If there's nobody that speaks up for her she has just to keep silence, if she was the bonniest woman in the world."

"The auld fool! because there was once a silly lad that had nobody else to come courting to! No, Gilchrist, my woman, you were never bonnie. A white skin, I allow, to go with your red hair, and a kind of innocent look in your eyes,—nothing, nothing more! We were both plain women, you and me, not adapted to please the eyes of men."

"They might have waited long afore we would have tried, either the wan or the other of us," cried Gilchrist, with a flash of self-assertion. "No' that I would even mysel' to you, mem," she added in an after breath.

"As for that, it's a metaphysical question," said Miss Bethune. "I will not attempt to enter into it. But try or no', it is clear we did not succeed. And what it is that succeeds is just more than I can tell. It's not beauty, it's a kind of natural attraction." She paused a moment in this deep philosophical inquiry, and then said quickly: "All this does not help us to find out what is this story about the Mannerings. Who is the woman? Is it somebody that loves the man, or somebody that loves the girl?"

"If you would take my opinion, mem, I would say that the man—if ye call Mr. Mannering, honest gentleman, the man, that has just every air of being a well-born person, and well-bred, and not a common person at all——"

"You haveral! The king himself, if there was a king, could be no more than a man."

"I would say, mem, that it was not for him—oh, no' for him, except maybe in opposition, if you could fancy that. Supposing," said Gilchrist, raising her arm in natural eloquence, "supposin' such a thing as that there should be a bonnie bairn like Miss Dora between two folk that had broken with one another—and it was the man, not the woman, that had her. I could just fancy," said the maid, her brown eyes lighting, her milky yet freckled complexion flushing over,—"I could just fancy that woman pouring out everything at the bairn's feet—gold and silver and grand presents, and a' the pomps of this world, partly out of an adoration for her hersel', partly just to make the man set his teeth at her that was away—maybe, in the desert—unknown!"

Gilchrist stood like a sibyl making this picture flash and gleam before her own inward vision with a heat and passion that seemed quite uncalled for in the circumstances. What was Hecuba to her, or she to Hecuba, that she should be so inspired by the possibilities of a mystery with which she had nothing to do? Her eloquence brought a corresponding glow, yet cloud, over the countenance of her mistress, who sat and listened with her head leaning on her hand, and for some time said nothing. She broke the silence at last with a laugh in which there was very little sound of mirth.

"You are a limited woman," she said—"a very limited woman. You can think of no state of affairs but one, and that so uncommon that perhaps there never was a case in the world like it. You will never be done, I know that, taking up your lesson out of it—all to learn one that has neither need to learn nor wish to learn—a thing that is impossible. Mind you what I say, and be done with this vain endeavour. Whatever may be the meaning of this Mannering business, it has no likeness to the other. And I am not a person to be schooled by the like of you, or to be taught in parables by my own woman, as if I was a person of no understanding, and her a mistress of every knowledge."

Miss Bethune rose hurriedly from her seat, and made a turn about the room with an air of high excitement and almost passion. Then she came and stood before the fire, leaning on the mantelpiece, looking down upon the blaze with a face that seemed to be coloured by the reflection. Finally, she put out a long arm, caught Gilchrist by the shoulders, who stood softly crying, as was her wont, within reach, and drew her close. "You've been with me through it all," she said suddenly; "there's nobody that knows me but you. Whatever you say, it's you only that knows what is in my heart. I bear you no ill-will for any word you say, no' for any word you say; and the Lord forgive me if maybe all this time it is you that has been right and me that has been wrong!" Only a moment, scarcely so much, Miss Bethune leant her head upon Gilchrist's shoulder, then she suddenly pushed her away. And not a second too soon, for at that moment a knock came to the door. They both started a little; and Miss Bethune, with the speed of thought, returned to the chair shaded by a screen from the lamplight and firelight in which she had been sitting, "not in good spirits," at the time of the interruption of Dora. "Go and see who it is," she said, half in words, half by the action of her hand. Nothing could have been more instantaneous than this rapid change.

When Gilchrist, scarcely less rapid though so much heavier than her mistress, opened the door, there stood before it a little man very carefully dressed, though in morning costume, in a solemn frock coat, with his hat in his hand. Though professional costume no longer exists among us, it was impossible not to feel and recognise in a moment that nothing but a medical man, a doctor to the tips of his fingers, could have appeared in just that perfect neatness of dress, so well brushed, so exactly buttoned, so gravely clothed in garments which, though free of any peculiarity of art or colour, such as that which distinguishes the garb of a clergyman, were yet so completely and seriously professional. His whiskers, for it was in the days when these ornaments were still worn, his hair, brown, with a slight crisp and upturning, like lining, of grey, the watch-chain that crossed his waistcoat, as well as the accurate chronometer of a watch to which so many eager and so many languid pulses had beat, were all in perfect keeping; even his boots—but we must not pursue too far this discussion of Dr. Roland's personal appearance. His boots were not the polished leather of the evening; but they were the spotless boots of a man who rarely walked, and whose careful step from his carriage to a patient's door never carried in any soil of the outside to the most delicate carpet. Why, being one of the inhabitants of this same house in Bloomsbury, he should have carried his hat in his hand when he came to the door of Miss Bethune's drawing-room from his own sitting-room downstairs, is a mystery upon which I can throw no light.

The ideas of a man in respect to his hat are indeed unfathomable. Whether he carries it as a protection or a shield of pretence, whether to convey to you that he is anxiously expected somewhere else, and that you are not to calculate upon anything but a short appearance upon your individual scene, whether to make it apparent by its gloss and sheen how carefully he has prepared for this interview, whether it is to keep undue familiarity at arm's length, or provide a becoming occupation for those hands with which many persons, while in repose, do not know what to do, it is impossible to tell. Certain it is that a large number of men find consolation and support in the possession of that article of apparel; and though they may freely abuse it in other circumstances, cling to it on social occasions as to an instrument of salvation. Dr. Roland held it fast, and bowed over it with a little formality, as he came into his neighbour's presence. They met on the stairs or in the hall sometimes three or four times in a day, but they were not the less particular in going through all the forms of civility when the doctor came to pay a call, as if they had not seen each other for a week before. He was a man of very great observation, and he did not miss a single particular of the scene. The screen drawn round the lady, defending her not only from the fire but from inspection, and a slight glistening upon the cheek of Gilchrist, which, as she did not paint or use any cosmetic, had but one explanation. That he formed a completely wrong conclusion was not Dr. Roland's fault. He did so sometimes from lack of material on which to form his judgment, but not often. He said to himself, "There has been a row," which, as the reader is aware, was not the case; but then he set himself to work to smooth down all agitation with a kindness and skill which the gentlest reader, knowing all about it, could not have surpassed.

"We have just been doing a very wrong thing, Gilchrist and me," said Miss Bethune; "a thing which you will say, doctor, is the way of ladies and their maids; but that is just one of your generalisings, and not true—except now and then. We have been wondering what is the strange story of our bonnie little Dora and that quiet, learned father of hers upstairs."

"Very natural, I should say," said the doctor. "But why should there be any story at all? I don't wonder at the discussion, but why should there be any cause for it? A quiet, learned man, as you say, and one fair daughter and no more, whom he loves passing well."

"Ah, doctor," said Miss Bethune, "you know a great deal about human nature. You know better than that."

The doctor put down his hat, and drew his chair nearer the fire. "Should you like to hear the story of poor Mannering?" he said.

CHAPTER V.

There is nothing more usual than to say that could we but know the life history of the first half-dozen persons we meet with on any road, we should find tragic details and unexpected lights and shadows far beyond the reach of fiction, which no doubt is occasionally true: though probably the first half-dozen would be found to gasp, like the knife-grinder: "Story? Lord bless you! I have none to tell, sir." This, to be sure, would be no argument; for our histories are not frequently unknown to, or, at least, unappreciated by ourselves, and the common human sense is against any accumulation of wonders in a small space. I am almost ashamed to say that the two people who inhabited one above the other two separate floors of my house in Bloomsbury, had a certain singularity and unusualness in their lives, that they were not as other men or women are; or, to speak more clearly, that being as other men and women are, the circumstances of their lives created round them an atmosphere which was not exactly that of common day. When Dr. Roland recounted to Miss Bethune the story of Mr. Mannering, that lady shut her lips tight in the partial shadow of the screen, to restrain the almost irrepressible murmurs of a revelation equally out of the common which belonged to herself. That is, she was tempted to utter aloud what she said in her soul, "Oh, but that is like me!" "Oh, but I would never have done that!"—comparing the secret in her own life, which nobody in this place suspected, with the secret in her neighbour's, which, at least to some few persons, was known.

Poor Mr. Mannering! there was a strange kind of superiority and secret satisfaction in pitying his fate, in learning all the particulars of it, in assuring herself that Dora was quite ignorant, and nobody in the house had the least suspicion, while at the same time secure in the consciousness that she herself was wrapt in impenetrable darkness, and that not even this gossip of a doctor could divine her. There is an elation in knowing that you too have a story, that your own experiences are still more profound than those of the others whom you are called upon to pity and wonder over, that did they but know!—which, perhaps, is not like the more ordinary elation of conscious superiority, but yet has its sweetness. There was a certain dignity swelling in Miss Bethune's figure as she rose to shake hands with the doctor, as if she had wrapped a tragic mantle round her, as if she dismissed him like a queen on the edge of ground too sacred to be trodden by any vulgar feet. He was conscious of it vaguely, though not of what it was. He gave her a very keen glance in the shadow of that screen: a keener observer than Dr. Roland was not easily to be met with,—but then his observations were generally turned in one particular way, and the phenomena which he glimpsed on this occasion did not come within the special field of his inquiries. He perceived them, but he could not classify them, in the scientific narrowness of his gaze.

Miss Bethune waited until the well-known sound of the closing of Dr. Roland's door downstairs met her ear; and then she rang violently, eagerly for her maid. What an evening this was, among all the quiet evenings on which nothing happened,—an evening full of incidents, of mysteries, and disclosures! The sound of the bell was such that the person summoned came hurrying from her room, well aware that there must be something to be told, and already breathless with interest. She found her mistress walking up and down the room, the screen discarded, the fan thrown down, the very shade on the lamp pushed up, so that it had the tipsy air of a hat placed on one side of the head. "Oh, Gilchrist!" Miss Bethune cried.

Dr. Roland went, as he always went, briskly but deliberately downstairs. If he had ever run up and down at any period of his life, taking two steps at a time, as young men do, he did it no longer. He was a little short-sighted, and wore a "pince-nez," and was never sure that between his natural eyes, with which he looked straight down at his feet, and his artificial ones, which had a wider circle, he might not miss a step, which accounted for the careful, yet rapid character of his movements. The door which Miss Bethune waited to hear him close was exactly below her own, and the room filled in Dr. Roland's life the conjoint positions of waiting-room, dining-room, and library. His consulting-room was formed of the other half looking to the back, and shut off from this by folding-doors and closely-drawn curtains. All the piles of *Illustrated News*, *Graphic*, and other picture papers, along with various well-thumbed pictorial volumes, the natural embellishments of the waiting-room, were carefully cleared away; and the room, with Dr. Roland's chair drawn near a cheery blazing fire, his reading-lamp, his book, and his evening paper on his table, looked comfortable enough. It was quite an ordinary room in Bloomsbury, and he was quite an ordinary man. Nothing remarkable (the reader will be glad to hear) had ever happened to him. He had gone through the usual studies, he had knocked about the world for a number of years, he had seen life and many incidents in other people's stories both at home and abroad. But nothing particular had ever happened to himself. He had lived, but if he had loved, nobody knew anything about that. He had settled in Bloomsbury some four or five years before, and he had grown into a steady, not too overwhelming practice. His specialty was the treatment of dyspepsia, and other evils of a sedentary life; and his patients were chiefly men, the men of offices and museums, among whom he had a great reputation. This was his official character, not much of a family adviser, but strong to rout the liver fiend and the demons of indigestion wherever encountered. But in his private capacity Dr. Roland's character was very remarkable and his scientific enthusiasm great.

He was a sort of medical detective, working all for love, and nothing for reward, without fee, and in many cases without even the high pleasure of carrying out his views. He had the eye of a hawk for anything wrong in the complexion or aspect of those who fell under his observation. The very postman at the door, whom Dr. Roland had met two or three times as he went out for his constitutional in the morning, had been divined and cut open, as it were, by his lancet of a glance, and saved from a bad illness by the peremptory directions given to him, which the man had the sense (and the prudence, for it was near Christmas) to obey. In that case the gratuity passed from doctor to patient, not from patient to doctor, but was not perhaps less satisfactory on that account. Then Dr. Roland would seize Jenny or Molly by the shoulders when they timidly brought a message or a letter into his room, look into the blue of their eyes for a moment, and order a dose on the spot; a practice which made these innocent victims tremble even to pass his door.

"Oh, granny, I can't, I can't take it up to the doctor," they would say, even when it was a telegram that had come: little selfish things, not thinking what poor sick person might be sending for the doctor; nor how good it was to be able to get a dose for nothing every time you wanted it.

But most of the people whom he met were less easily manageable than the postman and the landlady's little granddaughters. Dr. Roland regarded every one he saw from this same medical point of view; and had made up his mind about Miss Bethune, and also about Mr. Mannering, before he had been a week in the house. Unfortunately, he could do nothing to impress his opinion upon them; but he kept his eyes very wide open, and took notes, attending the moment when perhaps his opportunity might occur. As for Dora, he had nothing but contempt for her from the first moment he had seen her. Hers was a case of inveterate good health, and wholly without interest. That girl, he declared to himself scornfully, would be well anywhere. Bloomsbury had no effect upon her. She was neither anæmic or dyspeptic, though the little things downstairs were both. But her father was a different matter. Half a dozen playful demons were skirmishing around that careful, temperate, well-living man; and Dr. Roland took the greatest interest in their advances and withdrawals, expecting the day when one or other would seize the patient and lay him low. Miss Bethune, too, had her little band of assailants, who were equally interesting to Dr. Roland, but not equally clear, since he was as yet quite in the dark as to the moral side of the question in her case.

He knew what would happen to these two, and calculated their chances with great precision, taking into account all the circumstances that might defer or accelerate the catastrophe. These observations interested him like a play. It was a kind of second sight that he possessed, but reaching much further than the vision of any Highland seer, who sees the winding-sheet only when it is very near, mounting in a day or two from the knees to the waist, and hence to the head. But Dr. Roland saw its shadow long before it could have been visible to any person gifted with the second sight. Sometimes he was wrong—he had acknowledged as much to himself in one or two instances; but it was very seldom that this occurred. Those who take a pessimistic view either of the body or soul are bound to be right in many, if not in most cases, we are obliged to allow.

But it was not with the design of hunting patients that Dr. Roland made these investigations; his interest in the persons he saw around him was purely scientific. It diverted him greatly, if such a word may be used, to see how they met their particular dangers, whether they instinctively avoided or rushed to encounter them, both which methods they constantly employed in their unconsciousness. He liked to note the accidents (so called) that came in to stave off or to hurry on the approaching trouble. The persons to whom these occurred had often no knowledge of them; but Dr. Roland noted everything and forgot nothing. He had a wonderful memory as well as such excessively clear sight; and he carried on, as circumstances permitted, a sort of oversight of the case, even if it might be in somebody else's hands. Sometimes his interest in these outlying patients who were not his, interfered with the concentration of his attention on those who were—who were chiefly, as has been said, dyspeptics and the like, affording no exciting variety of symptoms to his keen intellectual and professional curiosity. And these peculiarities made him a very serviceable neighbour. He never objected to be called in in haste, because he was the nearest doctor, or to give a flying piece of advice to any one who might be attacked by sudden pain or uneasiness; indeed, he might be said to like these unintentional interferences with other people's work, which afforded him increased means of observation, and the privilege of launching a new prescription at a patient's head by way of experiment, or confidential counsel at the professional brother whom he was thus accidentally called upon to aid.

On the particular evening which he occupied by telling Miss Bethune the story of the Mannerings,—not without an object in so doing, for he had a strong desire to put that lady herself under his microscope and find out how certain things affected her,—he had scarcely got himself comfortably established by his own fireside, put on a piece of wood to make a blaze, felt for his cigar-case upon the mantelpiece, and taken up his paper, when a knock at his door roused him in the midst of his preparations for comfort. The doctor lifted his head quickly, and cocked one fine ear like a dog, and with something of the thrill of listening with which a dog responds to any sound. That he let the knock be repeated was by no means to say that he had not heard the first time. A knock at his door was something like a first statement of symptoms to the doctor. He liked to understand and make certain what it meant.

"Come in," he said quickly, after the second knock, which had a little hurry and temerity in it after the tremulous sound of the first.

The door opened; and there appeared at it, flushed with fright and alarm, yet pallid underneath the flush, the young and comely countenance of Mrs. Hesketh, Dora's friend on the attic floor.

"Oh!" Dr. Roland said, taking in this unexpected appearance, and all her circumstances, physical and mental, at a glance. He had met her also more than once at the door or on the stairs. He asked kindly what was the little fool frightened about, as he rose up quickly and with unconscious use and wont placed a chair in the best light, where he should be able to read the simple little alphabet of her constitution and thoughts.

"Oh, doctor, sir! I hope you don't mind me coming to disturb you, though I know as it's late and past hours."

"A doctor has no hours. Come in," he said.

Then there was a pause. The agitated young face disappeared, leaving Dr. Roland only a side view of her shoulder and figure in profile, and a whispering ensued. "I cannot—I cannot! I ain't fit," in a hoarse tone, and then the young woman's eager pleading. "Oh, Alfred dear, for my sake!"

"Come in, whoever it is," said Dr. Roland, with authority. "A doctor has no hours, but either people in the house have, and you mustn't stay outside."

Then there was a little dragging on the part of the wife, a little resistance on the part of the husband; and finally Mrs. Hesketh appeared, more flushed than ever, grasping the sleeve of a rather unwholesome-looking young man, very pink all over and moist, with furtive eyes, and hair standing on end. He had a fluttered clandestine look, as if afraid to be seen, as he came into the full light of the lamp, and looked suspiciously around him, as if to find out whether anything dangerous was there.

"It is my 'usband, sir," said Mrs. Hesketh. "It's Alfred. He's been off his food and off his sleep for I don't know how long, and I'm not happy about him. I thought perhaps you might give him a something that would put him all straight."

"Off his food and off his sleep? Perhaps he hasn't been off his drink also?" said the doctor, giving a touch to the shade of the lamp.

"I knew," said the young man, in the same partially hoarse voice, "as that is what would be said."

"And a gentleman like you ought to know better," said the indignant wife. "Drink is what he never touches, if it isn't a 'alf pint to his supper, and that only to please me."

"Then it's something else, and not drink," said the doctor. "Sit down, and let me have a look at you." He took into his cool grasp a somewhat tremulous damp hand, which had been hanging down by the patient's side, limp yet agitated, like a thing he had no use for. "Tell me something about him," said Dr. Roland. "In a shop? Baxter's?—yes, I know the place. What you call shopman,—no, assistant,—young gentleman at the counter?"

"Oh, no," said Mrs. Hesketh, with pride; "book-keeper, sir— sits up in his desk in the middle of the costume department, and——"

"Ah, I see," said the doctor quickly. He gave the limp wrist, in which the pulse had suddenly given a great jump, a grip with his cool hand. "Control yourself," he said quietly. "Nerves all in a whirl, system breaking down—can you take a holiday?"

"Oh, yes," said the young man in a sort of bravado, "of course I can take a holiday! and an express ticket for the workhouse after it. How are we to live if I go taking holidays? We can't afford no holidays," he said in his gruff voice.

"There are worse places than the workhouse," said the doctor, with meaning. "Take this, and to-morrow I'll give you a note to send to your master. The first thing you want is a good night's sleep."

"Oh, that is the truth, however you know it," cried Mrs. Hesketh. "He hasn't had a night's sleep, nor me neither, not for a month back."

"I'll see that he has one to-night," said Dr. Roland, drawing back the curtain of his surgery and opening the folding-doors.

"I won't take no opiates, doctor," said the young man, with dumb defiance in his sleepy eyes.

"You won't take any opiates? And why, if I may ask?" the doctor said, selecting a bottle from the shelf.

"Not a drop of your nasty sleepy stuff, that makes fellows dream and talk nonsense in their sleep—oh, not for me!"

"You are afraid, then, of talking nonsense in your sleep? We must get rid of the nonsense, not of the sleep," said the doctor. "I don't say that this is an opiate, but you have got to swallow it, my fine fellow, whether or not."

"No," said the young man, setting his lips firmly together.

"Drink!" cried Dr. Roland, fully roused. "Come, I'll have no childish, wry faces. Why, you're a man—with a wife—and not a naughty boy!"

"It's not my doing coming here. She brought me, and I'll see her far enough——"

"Hold your tongue you young ass, and take your physic! She's a capital woman, and has done exactly as she ought to have done. No nonsense, I tell you! Sleep to-night, and then to-morrow you'll go and set yourself right with the shop."

"Sir!" cried the young man, with a gasp. His pulse gave a jump under the strong cool grip in which Dr. Roland had again taken it, and he fixed a frightened imploring gaze upon the doctor's face.

"Oh, doctor!" cried the poor wife, "there's nothing to set right with the shop. They think all the world of Alfred there."

"They'll think all the more of him," said Dr. Roland, "after he has had a good night's sleep. There, take him off to bed; and at ten o'clock to-morrow morning I expect to see him here."

"Oh, doctor, is it anything bad? Oh, sir, can't you make him all right?" she cried, standing with clasped hands, listening to the hurried yet wavering step with which her husband went upstairs.

"I'll tell you to-morrow morning," Dr. Roland said.

When the door was closed he went and sat down again by his fire; but the calm of his mind, the pleasure of his cigar, the excitement of his newspaper, had gone. Truth to tell, the excitement of this new question pleased him more than all these things together. "Has he done it, or is he only going to do it?" he asked himself. Could the thing be set right, or could it never be set right? He sat there for perhaps an hour, working out the question in both directions, considering the case in every light. It was a long time since he had met with anything so interesting.

He only came to himself when he became conscious that the fire was burning very low, and the chill of the night creeping into the air. Then Dr. Roland rose again, compounded a drink for himself of a different quality from that which he had given to his patient, and selected out of his bookcase a yellow novel. But after a while he pitched the book from him, and pushed away the glass, and resumed his meditations. What was grog, and what was Gaboriau, in comparison with a problem like this?

CHAPTER VI.

The house in Bloomsbury was, however, much more deeply troubled and excited than it would have been by anything affecting Alfred Hesketh, when it was known next morning that Mr. Mannering had been taken ill in the night, and was now unable to leave his bed. The doctor had been sent for early—alas! it was not Dr. Roland—and the whole household was disturbed. Such a thing had not been known for nearly a dozen years past, as that Mr. Mannering should not walk downstairs exactly at a quarter before ten, and close the door behind him, forming a sort of fourth chime to the three-quarters as they sounded from the church clock. The house was put out for the day by this failure in the regularity of its life and movement; all the more that it was very soon known that this prop of the establishment was very ill, that "the fever" ran very high, and that even his life was in danger. Nobody made much remark in these circumstances upon the disappearance of the humble little people on the upper floor, who, after much coming and going between their habitation and that of Dr. Roland downstairs, made a hurried departure, providentially, Mrs. Simcox said—thus leaving a little available room for the nurse who by this time had taken possession of the Mannering establishment, reducing Dora to the position which she had never occupied, of a child, and taking the management of everything. Two of these persons, indeed, had been ordered in by the doctor—a nurse for the day, and a nurse for the night, who filled the house with that air of redundant health and cheerfulness which seem to belong to nurses, one or other of them being always met on the stairs going out for her constitutional, going down for her meals, taking care of herself in some methodical way or other, according to prescription, that she might be fit for her work. And no doubt they were very fit for their work, and amply responded to the confidence placed in them: which was only not shared by Dora, banished by them out of her father's room—and Miss Bethune, a woman full of prejudices, and Gilchrist, whose soft heart could not resist the cheerful looks of the two fresh young women, though their light-heartedness shocked her a little, and the wrongs of Dora filled her heart with sympathy.

Alas! Dora was not yet sixteen—there was no possibility, however carefully you counted the months, and showed her birthday to be approaching, to get over that fact. And what were her love and anxious desire to be of service, and devotion to her father, in comparison with these few years and the superior training of the women, who knew almost as much as the doctor himself? "Not saying much, that!" Dr. Roland grumbled under his breath, as he joined the anxious circle of malcontents in Miss Bethune's apartment, where Dora came, trying proudly to restrain her tears, and telling how she had been shut out of Mr. Mannering's room—"my own father's room!" the girl cried in her indignation, two big drops, like raindrops, falling, in spite of her, upon her dress.

"It's better for you, my bonnie dear,—oh, it's better for you," Gilchrist whispered, standing behind her, and drying her own flowing eyes with her apron.

"Dora, my darling," said Miss Bethune, moved to a warmth of spirit quite unusual to her, "it is quite true what Gilchrist says. I am not fond of these women myself. They shall never nurse me. If I cannot have a hand that cares for me to smooth my pillow, it shall be left unsmoothed, and none of these good-looking hussies shall smile over me when I'm dying—no, no! But it is different; you're far too young to have that on your head. I would not permit it. Gilchrist and me would have taken it and done every justice to your poor papa, I make no doubt, and been all the better for the work, two idle women as we are—but not you. You should have come and gone, and sat by his bedside and cheered him with the

53

sight of you; but to nurse him was beyond your power. Ask the doctor, and he will tell you that as well as me."

"I have always taken care of my father before," said Dora. "When he has had his colds, and when he had rheumatism, and when——that time, Dr. Roland, you know."

"That was the time," said the doctor, "when you ran down to me in the middle of the night and burst into my room, like a wise little girl. We had him in our own hands then, and we knew what to do with him, Dora. But here's Vereker, he's a great swell, and neither you nor I can interfere."

It comforted Dora a little to have Dr. Roland placed with herself among the outsiders who could not interfere, especially when Miss Bethune added: "That is just the grievance. We would all like to have a finger in the pie. Why should a man be taken out of the care of his natural friends and given into the charge of these women, that never saw him in their lives before, nor care whether he lives or dies?"

"Oh, they care—for their own reputation. There is nothing to be said against the women, they'll do their duty," said the doctor. "But there's Vereker, that has never studied his constitution—that sees just the present symptoms, and no more. Take the child out for a walk, Miss Bethune, and let's have her fresh and fair for him, at least, if"—the doctor pulled himself up hastily, and coughed to swallow the last alarming syllable,—"fresh and fair," he added hastily, "*when* he gets better, which is a period with which no nurses can interfere."

A colloquy, which was silent yet full of eager interest and feeling, sprang up between two pairs of eyes at the moment that *if*—most alarming of conjectures—was uttered. Miss Bethune questioned; the doctor replied. Then he said in an undertone: "A constitution never very strong,—exhausting work, exhausting emotions, unnatural peace in the latter life."

Dora was being led away by Gilchrist to get her hat for the proposed walk; and Dr. Roland ended in his ordinary voice.

"Do you call that unnatural peace, with all the right

circumstances of his life round him, and—and full possession of his bonnie girl, that has never been parted from him? I don't call that unnatural."

"You would if you were aware of the other side of it lopped off—one half of him, as it were, paralysed."

"Doctor," said Miss Bethune, with a curious smile, "I ought to take that as a compliment to my sex, as the fools say—if I cared a button for my sex or any such nonsense! But there is yourself, now, gets on very well, so far as I can see, with that side, as you call it, just as much lopped off."

"How do you know?" said the doctor. "I may be letting concealment, like a worm in the bud, feed on my damask cheek. But I allow," he said, with a laugh, "I do get on very well: and so, if you will permit me to say it, do you, Miss Bethune. But then, you see, we have never known anything else."

Something leaped up in Miss Bethune's eye—a strange light, which the doctor could not interpret, though it did not escape his observation. "To be sure," she said, nodding her head, "we have never known anything else. And that changes the case altogether."

"That changes the case. I say nothing against a celibate life. I have always preferred it—it suits me better. I never cared," he added, again with a laugh, "to have too much baggage to move about."

"Do not be uncivil, doctor, after being more civil than was necessary."

"But it's altogether a different case with poor Mannering. It is not even as if his wife had betrayed him—in the ordinary way. The poor thing meant no harm."

"Oh, do not speak to me!" cried Miss Bethune, throwing up her hands.

"I know; it is well known you ladies are always more severe— but, anyhow, that side was wrenched away in a moment, and then there followed long years of unnatural calm."

"I do not agree with you, doctor," she said, shaking her

head. "The wrench was defeenitive." Miss Bethune's nationality betrayed itself in a great breadth of vowels, as well as in here and there a word or two. "It was a cut like death: and you do not call calm unnatural that comes after death, after long years?"

"It's different—it's different," the doctor said.

"Ay, so it is," she said, answering as it were her own question.

And there was a pause. When two persons of middle age discuss such questions, there is a world lying behind each full of experiences, which they recognise instinctively, however completely unaware they may be of each other's case.

"But here is Dora ready for her walk, and me doing nothing but haver," cried Miss Bethune, disappearing into the next room.

They might have been mother and daughter going out together in the gentle tranquillity of use and wont,—so common a thing!—and yet if the two had been mother and daughter, what a revolution in how many lives would have been made!—how different would the world have been for an entire circle of human souls! They were, in fact, nothing to each other—brought together, as we say, by chance, and as likely to be whirled apart again by those giddy combinations and dissolutions which the head goes round only to think of. For the present they walked closely together side by side, and talked of one subject which engrossed all their thoughts.

"What does the doctor think? Oh, tell me, please, what the doctor thinks!"

"How can he think anything, Dora, my dear? He has never seen your father since he was taken ill."

"Oh, Miss Bethune, but he knew him so well before. And I don't ask you what he knows. He must think something. He must have an opinion. He always has an opinion, whatever case it may be."

"He thinks, my dear, that the fever must run its course. Now another week's begun, we must just wait for the next critical moment. That is all, Dora, my darling, that is all that any man can say."

"Oh, that it would only come!" cried Dora passionately. "There is nothing so dreadful as waiting—nothing! However bad a thing is, if you only know it, not hanging always in suspense."

"Suspense means hope; it means possibility and life, and all that makes life sweet. Be patient, be patient, my bonnie dear."

Dora looked up into her friend's face. "Were you ever as miserable as I am?" she said. Miss Bethune was thought grim by her acquaintances and there was a hardness in her, as those who knew her best were well aware; but at this question something ineffable came into her face. Her eyes filled with tears, her lips quivered with a smile. "My little child!" she said.

Dora did not ask any more. Her soul was silenced in spite of herself: and just then there arose a new interest, which is always so good a thing for everybody, especially at sixteen. "There," she cried, in spite of herself, though she had thought she was incapable of any other thought, "is poor Mrs. Hesketh hurrying along on the other side of the street."

They had got into a side street, along one end of which was a little row of trees.

"Oh, run and speak to her, Dora."

Mrs. Hesketh seemed to feel that she was pursued. She quickened her step almost into a run, but she was breathless and agitated and laden with a bundle, and in no way capable of outstripping Dora. She paused with a gasp, when the girl laid a hand on her arm.

"Didn't you hear me call you? You surely could never, never mean to run away from me?"

"Miss Dora, you were always so kind, but I didn't know who it might be."

"Oh, Mrs. Hesketh, you can't know how ill my father is, or you would have wanted to ask for him. He has been ill a month, and I am not allowed to nurse him. I am only allowed to go in and peep at him twice a day. I am not allowed to speak to him, or to do anything for him, or to know——"

Dora paused, choked by the quick-coming tears.

"I am so sorry, miss. I thought as you were happy at least: but there's nothing, nothing but trouble in this world," cried Mrs. Hesketh, breaking into a fitful kind of crying. Her face was flushed and heated, the bundle impeding all her movements. She looked round in alarm at every step, and when she saw Miss Bethune's tall figure approaching, uttered a faint cry. "Oh, Miss Dora, I can't stay, and I can't do you any good even if I could; I'm wanted so bad at home."

"Where are you going with that big bundle? You are not fit to be carrying it about the streets," said Miss Bethune, suddenly standing like a lion in the way.

The poor little woman leant against a tree, supporting her bundle. "Oh, please," she said, imploring; and then, with some attempt at self-defence, "I am going nowhere but about my own business. I have got nothing but what belongs to me. Let me go."

"You must not go any further than this spot," said Miss Bethune. "Dora, go to the end of the road and get a cab. Whatever you would have got for that where you were going, I will give it you, and you can keep your poor bits of things. What has happened to you? Quick, tell me, while the child's away."

The poor young woman let her bundle fall at her feet. "My husband's ill, and he's lost his situation," she said, with piteous brevity, and sobbed, leaning against the tree.

"And therefore you thought that was a fine time to run away and hide yourself among strangers, out of the reach of them that knew you? There was the doctor, and there was me. Did you think we would let harm happen to you? You poor feckless little thing!"

"The doctor! It was the doctor that lost Alfred his place," cried the young woman angrily, drying her eyes. "Let me go—oh, let me go! I don't want no charity," she said.

"And what would you have got for all that?"

"Perhaps ten shillings—perhaps only six. Oh, lady, you don't know us except just to see us on the stairs. I'm in great trouble, and he's heartbroken, and waiting for me at 'ome. Leave me alone and let me go."

"If you had put them away for ten shillings they would have been of no further use to you. Now, here's ten shillings, and you'll take these things back; but you'll mind that they're mine, though I give you the use of them, and you'll promise to come to me, or to send for me, and to take no other way. What is the matter with your husband? Let him come to the doctor, and you to me."

"Oh, never, never, to that doctor!" Mrs. Hesketh cried.

"The doctor's a good man, and everybody's friend, but he may have a rough tongue, I would not say. But come you to me. We'll get him another place, and all will go well. You silly little thing, the first time trouble comes in your way, to fall into despair! Oh, this is you, Dora, with the cab. Put in the bundle. And now, here's the money, and if you do not come to me, mind you will have broken your word."

"Oh, ma'am! Oh, Miss Dora!" was all the poor little woman could say.

"Now, Dora," said Miss Bethune cheerfully, "there's something for you to do—Gilchrist and you. You'll give an account to me of that poor thing, and if you let her slip through your fingers I'll never forgive you. There's something wrong. Perhaps he drinks, or perhaps he does something worse—if there's anything worse: but whatever it is, it is your responsibility. I'm an idle, idle person; I'm good for nothing. But you're young, and Gilchrist's a tower of strength, and you'll just give an account of that poor bit creature, soul and body, to me."

CHAPTER VII.

Mr. Mannering's illness ran on and on. Week after week the anxious watchers waited for the crisis which did not come. It was evident now that the patient, who had no violence in his illness any more than in his life, was yet not to be spared a day of its furthest length. But it was allowed that he had no bad symptoms, and that the whole matter turned on the question whether his strength could be sustained. Dr. Roland, not allowed to do anything else for his friend, regulated furtively the quality and quantity of the milk, enough to sustain a large nursery, which was sent upstairs. He tested it in every scientific way, and went himself from dairy to dairy to get what was best; and Mrs. Simcox complained bitterly that he was constantly making inroads into "my kitchen" to interfere in the manufacture of the beef tea. He even did, which was against every rule of medical etiquette, stop the great Dr. Vereker on the stairs and almost insist upon a medical consultation, and to give his own opinion about the patient to this great authority, who looked him over from the crown of his head to the sole of his foot with undisguised yet bewildered contempt. Who was this man who discoursed to the great physician about the tendencies and the idiosyncrasies of the sick man, whom it was a matter of something like condescension on Dr. Vereker's part to attend at all, and whom this little person evidently believed himself to understand better?

"If Mr. Mannering's friends wish me to meet you in consultation, I can have, of course, no objection to satisfy them, or even to leave the further conduct of the case in your hands," he said stiffly.

"Nothing of the kind—nothing of the kind!" cried poor Dr. Roland. "It's only that I've watched the man for years. You perhaps don't know——"

"I think," said Dr. Vereker, "you will allow that after nearly six weeks' attendance I ought, unless I am an ignoramus, to know all there is to know."

"I don't deny it for a moment. There is no practitioner in London certainly who would doubt Dr. Vereker's knowledge. I mean his past—what he has had to bear—the things that have led up——"

"Moral causes?" said the great physician blandly, raising his eyebrows. "My dear sir, depend upon it, a bad drain is more to be reckoned with than all the tragedies of the world."

"I shall not depend on anything of the kind!" cried Dr. Roland, almost dancing with impatience.

"Then you will permit me to say good-morning, for my time is precious," answered his distinguished brother—"unless," he added sarcastically, pausing to look round upon the poor doctor's sitting-room, then arrayed in its morning guise as waiting-room, with all the old *Graphics*, and picture books laid out upon the table—"Mr. Mannering's friends are dissatisfied and wish to put the case in your hands?"

"Do you know who Mr. Mannering's friends are?" cried Dr. Roland. "Little Dora, his only child! I know no others. Just about as little influential as are those moral causes you scorn, but I don't."

"Indeed!" said Dr. Vereker, with more consideration of this last statement. Little Dora was not much of a person to look to for the rapidly accumulating fees of a celebrated doctor during a long illness. But though he was a prudent man, he was not mercenary; perhaps he would have hesitated about taking up the case had he known at first, but he was not the man to retire now out of any fear of being paid. "Mr. Mannering is a person of distinction," he said, in a self-reassuring tone; "he has been my patient at long intervals for many years. I don't think we require to go into the question further at this moment." He withdrew with great dignity to the carriage that awaited him, crossing one or two of Dr. Roland's patients, whose appearance somewhat changed his idea of the little practitioner who had thus ventured to assail him; while, on the other hand, Roland for his part was mollified by the other's magnanimous reception of a statement which seemed to make his fees uncertain. Dr. Vereker was not in the least a mercenary man, he would never have overwhelmed an orphan girl with a great bill: at the same time, it did float across his mind that if the crisis were once over which professional spirit and honour compelled him to conduct to a good end if possible, a little carelessness about his visits after could have no bad result, considering the constant vicinity of that very keen-eyed practitioner downstairs.

A great doctor and two nurses, unlimited supplies of fresh milk, strong soup, and every appliance that could be thought of to alleviate and console the patient, by these professional persons of the highest class, accustomed to spare no expense, are, however, things that do not agree with limited means; and Dora, the only authority on the subject, knew nothing about her father's money, or how to get command of it. Mrs. Simcox's bills were very large in the present position of affairs, the rooms that had been occupied by the Heskeths being now appropriated to the nurses, for whom the landlady furnished a table more plentiful than that to which Mr. Mannering and his daughter had been accustomed. And when the crisis at last arrived, in the middle of a tardy and backward June, the affairs of the little household, even had there been any competent person to understand them, were in a very unsatisfactory state indeed—a state over which Dr. Roland and Miss Bethune consulted in the evenings with many troubled looks, and shakings of the head. She had taken all the necessary outgoings in hand, for the moment as she said; and Miss Bethune was known to be well off. But the prospect was rather serious, and neither of them knew how to interfere in the sick man's money matters, or to claim what might be owing to him, though, indeed, there was probably nothing owing to him until quarter day: and there were a number of letters lying unopened which, to experienced eyes, looked painfully like bills, as if quarter day would not have enough to do to provide for its own things without responding to this unexpected strain. Dora knew nothing about these matters. She recognised the letters with the frankest acquaintance. They were from old book shops, from scientific workmen who mounted and prepared specimens, from dealers in microscopes and other delicate instruments. "Father says these are our dressmakers, and carriages, and parties," said Dora, half, or indeed wholly, proud of such a distinction above her fellows.

Miss Bethune shook her head and said, "Such extravagance!" in Dr. Roland's ear. He was more tolerant. "They are all the pleasures the poor man has," he said. But they did not make the problem more easy as to how the present expenses were to be met when the quarter's pay came in, even if it could be made available by Dora's only friends, who were "no relations," and had no right to act for her. Miss Bethune went through a great many abstruse calculations in the mornings which she spent alone. She was well off,—but that is a phrase which means little or much, according to circumstances; and she had a great many pensioners, and already carried a little world on her shoulders, to which she had lately added the unfortunate little Mrs. Hesketh, and the husband, who found it so difficult to get another place. Many cares of a similar kind were on this lady's head. She never gave a single subscription to any of the societies: collectors for charities called on her in vain; but to see the little jottings of her expenses would have been a thing not without edification for those who could understand the cipher, or, rather, the combination of undecipherable initials, in which they were set down. She did not put M. for Mannering in her accounts; but there were a great many items under the initial W., which no one but herself could ever have identified, which made it quite sure that no stranger going over these accounts could make out who Miss Bethune's friends were. She shook her head over that W. If Dora were left alone, what relics would there be for her out of the future quarter's pay, so dreadfully forestalled, even if the pay did not come to a sudden stop at once? And, on the other hand, if the poor man got better, and had to face a long convalescence with that distracting prospect before him, no neighbour any longer daring to pay those expenses which would be quite as necessary for him in his weak state as they were now? Miss Bethune could do nothing but shake her head, and feel her heart contract with that pang of painful pity in which there is no comfort at all. And in the meantime everything went on as if poor Mannering were a millionaire, everything was ordered for him with a free hand which a prince could have had; and Mrs. Simcox excelled herself in making the nurses, poor things, comfortable. What could any one do to limit this full flowing tide of liberality? Of course, he must have everything that could possibly be wanted for him; if he did not use it, at least it must be there in case he might use it. What could people who were "no relations" do? What could Dora do, who was only a child? And indeed, for the matter of that, what could any one, even in the fullest authority, have done to hinder the sick man from having anything which by the remotest possibility might be of use to him? Thus affairs went on with a dreadful velocity, and accumulation of wrath against the day of wrath.

That was a dreadful day, the end of the sixth week, the moment when the crisis must come. It was in the June evening, still daylight, but getting late, when the doctor arrived. Mr. Mannering had been very ill all day, sleeping, or in a state of stupor nearly all the time, moving his head uneasily on his pillow, but never rousing to any consciousness of what was going on about him. The nurses, always cheerful, did not, however, conceal their apprehensions. He had taken his beef tea, he had taken the milk which they poured down his throat: but his strength was gone, and he lay with no longer any power to struggle, like a forsaken boat on the sea margin, to be drifted off or on the beach according to the pleasure of wind and tide.

Miss Bethune sat in her room holding Dora's hand, who,

however, did not realise that this was more important than any of the other days on which they had hoped that "the turn" might come, and a little impatient of the seriousness of the elder woman, who kept on saying tender words to her, caressing her hand,—so unnecessarily emotional, Dora thought, seeing that at all events it was not *her* father who was ill, and she had no reason to be so unhappy about it. This state of excitement was brought to a climax by the sound of the doctor's steps going upstairs, followed close by the lighter step of Dr. Roland, whom no etiquette could now restrain, who followed into the very room, and if he did not give an opinion in words, gave it with his eyes, and saw, even more quickly than the great Dr. Vereker, everything that was to be seen. It was he who came down a few minutes later, while they were both listening for the more solemn movements of the greater authority, descending with a rush like that of a bird, scarcely touching the steps, and standing in the last sunset light which came from the long staircase window behind, like something glorified and half angelic, as if his house coat, glazed at the shoulders and elbows, had been some sort of shining mail.

Tears were in Dr. Roland's eyes; he waved his hand over his head and broke forth into a broken hurrah. Miss Bethune sprang up to meet him, holding out her hands. And in the sight of stern youth utterly astonished by this exhibition, these two elderly people as good as rushed into each other's arms.

Dora was so astounded, so disapproving, so little aware that this was her last chance for her father's life, that she almost forgot her father in the consternation, shame, and horror with which she looked on. What did they mean? It could not have anything to do with her father, of whom they were "no relations". How dared they to bring in their own silly affairs when she was in such trouble? And then Miss Bethune caught herself, Dora, in her arms.

"What is the matter?" cried the girl. "Oh, let me alone! I can think of nothing but father and Dr. Vereker, who is upstairs."

"It is all right—it is all right," said Dr. Roland. "Vereker will take half an hour more to make up his mind. But I can tell you at once; the fever's gone, and, please God, he'll pull through."

"Is it only you that says so, Dr. Roland?" cried Dora, hard as the nether millstone, and careless, indeed unconscious, what wound she might give.

"You little ungrateful thing!" cried Miss Bethune; but a shadow came over her eyes also. And the poor practitioner from the ground floor felt that "only you" knock him down like a stone. He gave a laugh, and made no further reply, but walked over to the window, where he stood between the curtains, looking out upon the summer evening, the children playing on the pavement, all the noises and humours of the street. No, he had not made a name for himself, he had not secured the position of a man who has life and death in his nod. It was hard upon Dr. Roland, who felt that he knew far more about Mr. Mannering than half a hundred great physicians rolled into one, coming in with his solemn step at the open door.

"Yes, I think he will do," said Dr. Vereker. "Miss Mannering, I cannot sufficiently recommend you to leave everything in the hands of these two admirable women. It will be anxious work for some time yet; his strength is reduced to the very lowest ebb, but yet, I hope, all will come right. The same strenuous skilful nursing and constant judicious nourishment and rest. This young lady is very young to have such an anxiety. Is there really no one—no relation, no uncle—nor anything of that kind?"

"We have no relations," said Dora, growing very red. There seemed a sort of guilt in the avowal, she could not tell why.

"But fast friends," said Miss Bethune.

"Ah, friends! Friends are very good to comfort and talk to a poor little girl, but they are not responsible. They cannot be applied to for fees; whereas an uncle, though perhaps not so good for the child——" Dr. Vereker turned to Dr. Roland at the window. "I may be prevented from coming to-morrow so soon as I should wish; indeed, the patient should be looked at again to-night if I had time. But it is a long way to come back here. I am sure it will be a comfort to this young lady, Dr. Roland, if you, being on the spot, would kindly watch the case when I am not able to be here."

Dr. Roland cast but one glance at the doubting spectators, who had said, "Only you."

"With all my heart, and thank you for the confidence you put in me," he said.

"Oh, that," said the great doctor, with a wave of his hand, "is only your due. I have to thank you for one or two hints, and you know as well as I do what care is required now. We may congratulate ourselves that things are as they are; but his life hangs on a thread. Thank you. I may rely upon you then? Good-evening, madam; forgive me for not knowing your name. Good-night, Miss Mannering."

Dr. Roland attended the great man to the door; and returned again, taking three steps at a time. "You see," he cried breathlessly, "I am in charge, though you don't think much of me. He's not a mercenary man, he has stayed to pull him through; but we shan't see much more of Dr. Vereker. There's the fees saved at a stroke."

"And there's the women," said Miss Bethune eagerly, "taking real pleasure in it, and growing fatter and fairer every day."

"The women have done very well," said the doctor. "I'll have nothing said against them. It's they that have pulled him through." Dr. Roland did not mean to share his triumph with any other voluntary aid.

"Well, perhaps that is just," she said, regretfully; "but yet here is me and Gilchrist hungering for something to do, and all the good pounds a week that might be so useful handed over to them."

Dora listened to all this, half indignant, half uncomprehending. She had a boundless scorn of the "good pounds" of which Miss Bethune in her Scotch phraseology spoke so tenderly. And she did not clearly understand why this particular point in her father's illness should be so much more important than any other. She heard her own affairs discussed as through a haze, resenting that these other people should think they had so much to do with them, and but dimly understanding what they meant by it. Her father, indeed, did not seem to her any better at all, when she was allowed for a moment to see him as he lay asleep. But Dora, fortunately, thought nothing of the expenses, nor how the little money that came in at quarter day would melt away like snow, nor how the needs, now miraculously supplied as by the ravens, would look when the invalid awoke to a consciousness of them, and of how they were to be provided in a more natural way.

It was not very long, however, before something of that consciousness awoke in the eyes of the patient, as he slowly came back into the atmosphere of common life from which he had been abstracted so long. He was surprised to find Dr. Roland at his pillow, which that eager student would scarcely have left by day or night if he could have helped it, and the first glimmering of anxiety about his ways and means came into his face when Roland explained hastily that Vereker came faithfully so long as there was any danger. "But now he thinks a poor little practitioner like myself, being on the spot, will do," he said, with a laugh. "Saves fees, don't you know?"

"Fees?" poor Mannering said, with a bewildered consciousness; and next morning began to ask when he could go back to the Museum. Fortunately, all ideas were dim in that floating weakness amid the sensations of a man coming back to life. Convalescence is sweet in youth; but it is not sweet when a man whose life is already waning comes back out of the utter prostration of disease into the lesser but more conscious ills of common existence. Presently he began to look at the luxuries with which he was surrounded, and the attendants who watched over him, with alarm. "Look here, Roland, I can't afford all this. You must put a stop to all this," he said.

"We can't be economical about getting well, my dear fellow," said the doctor. "That's the last thing to save money on."

"But I haven't got it! One can't spend what one hasn't got," cried the sick man. It is needless to say that his progress was retarded, and the indispensable economies postponed, by this new invasion of those cares which are to the mind what the drainage which Dr. Vereker alone believed in is to the body.

"Never mind, father," Dora said in her ignorance; "it will all come right."

"Right? How is it to come right? Take that stuff away. Send these nurses away. I can't afford it. Do you hear me? I cannot afford it!" he began to cry night and day.

CHAPTER VIII.

Mr. Mannering's convalescence was worse than his illness had been to the house in Bloomsbury. Mrs. Simcox's weekly bill fell by chance into the patient's hands, and its items filled him with horror. When a man is himself painfully supported on cups of soup and wings of chicken, the details of roast lamb for the day-nurse's dinner, and bacon and eggs for the night-nurse's breakfast, take an exaggerated magnitude. And Mrs. Simcox was very conscientious, putting down even the parsley and the mint which were necessary for these meals. This bill put back the patient's recovery for a week, and prolonged the expenses, and brought the whole house, as Mrs. Simcox declared tearfully, on her comparatively innocent head.

"For wherever's the bill to go if not to the gentleman hisself?" cried the poor woman. "He's sittin' up every day, and gettin' on famous, by what I hears. And he always did like to see 'is own bills, did Mr. Mannering: and what's a little bit of a thing like Miss Dora to go to, to make her understand money? Lord bless you! she don't spend a shilling in a week, nor knows nothing about it. And the nurses, as was always to have everything comfortable, seeing the 'ard work as they 'as, poor things. And if it was a bit o' mint for sauce, or a leaf o' parsley for garnish, I'd have put it in out o' my own pocket and welcome, if I'd a thought a gentleman would go on about sich things."

"You ridiculous woman, why couldn't you have brought it to me, as you have done before? And who do you suppose cares for your parsley and your mint?" cried Miss Bethune. But nobody knew better than Miss Bethune that the bills could not now be brought to her; and it was with a sore heart, and that sense of the utter impossibility of affording any help, with which we look on impotent at the troubles of our neighbours, whom we dare not offend even by our sympathy, that she went downstairs in a morning of July, when London was hot and stifling, yet still, as ever, a little grace and coolness dwelt in the morning, to refresh herself with a walk under the trees in the Square, to which she had a privilege of entrance.

Even in London in the height of summer the morning is sweet. There is that sense of ease and lightness in it, which warm and tranquil weather brings, before it comes too hot to bear. There were smells in the streets in the afternoon, and the din of passing carts and carriages, of children playing, of street cries and shouts, which would sometimes become intolerable; but in the morning there was shade and softness, and a sense of trouble suspended for the moment or withdrawn, which often follows the sudden sharp realisation of any misfortune which comes with the first waking. The pavement was cool, and the air was (comparatively) sweet. There was a tinkle of water, though only from a water cart. Miss Bethune opened the door into this sweetness and coolness and morning glory which exists even in Bloomsbury, and found herself suddenly confronted by a stranger, whose hand had been raised to knock when the door thus suddenly opened before him. The sudden encounter gave her a little shock, which was not lessened by the appearance of the young man—a young fellow of three or four and twenty, in light summer clothes, and with a pleasant sunburnt countenance.

Not his the form, not his the eye,
That youthful maidens wont to fly.

Miss Bethune was no youthful maiden, but this sudden apparition had a great effect upon her. The sight made her start, and grow red and grow pale without any reason, like a young person in her teens.

"I beg your pardon," said the young man, making a step back, and taking off his hat. This was clearly an afterthought, and

71

due to her appearance, which was not that of the mistress of a lodging-house. "I wanted to ask after a ——"

"I am not the person of the house," said Miss Bethune quickly.

"Might I ask you all the same? I would so much rather hear from some one who knows him."

Miss Bethune's eyes had been fixed upon him with the closest attention, but her interest suddenly changed and dropped at the last word. "Him?" she said involuntarily, with a flash out of her eyes, and a look almost of disappointment, almost of surprise. What had she expected? She recovered in a moment the composure which had been disturbed by this stranger's appearance, for what reason she only knew.

"I came," he said, hesitating a little, and giving her another look, in which there was also some surprise and much curiosity, "to inquire about Mr. Mannering, who, I am told, lives here."

"Yes, he lives here."

"And has been ill?"

"And has been ill," she repeated after him.

The young man smiled, and paused again. He seemed to be amused by these repetitions. He had a very pleasant face, not intellectual, not remarkable, but full of life and good-humour. He said: "Perhaps I ought not to trouble you; but if you know him, and his child——"

"I know him very well, and his child,—who is a child no longer, but almost grown up. He is slowly recovering out of a very long dangerous illness."

"That is what we heard. I came, not for myself, but for a lady who takes a great interest. I think that she is a relation of—of Mr. Mannering's late wife."

"Is that woman dead, then?" Miss Bethune said. "I too take a great interest in the family. I shall be glad to tell you anything I know: but come with me into the Square, where we can talk at our ease." She led him to a favourite seat under the shadow of a tree. Though it was in Bloomsbury, and the sounds of town were in the air, that quiet green place might have been far in the country, in the midst of pastoral acres. The Squares of Bloomsbury are too respectable to produce many children. There were scarcely even any perambulators to vulgarise this retreat. She turned to him as she sat down, and said again: "So that woman is dead?"

The young stranger looked surprised. "You mean Mrs. Mannering?" he said. "I suppose so, though I know nothing of her. May I say who I am first? My name is Gordon. I have just come from South America with Mrs. Bristow, the wife of my guardian, who died there a year ago. And it is she who has sent me to inquire."

"Gordon?" said Miss Bethune. She had closed her eyes, and her head was going round; but she signed to him with her hand to sit down, and made a great effort to recover herself. "You will be of one of the Scotch families?" she said.

"I don't know. I have never been in this country till now."

"Born abroad?" she said, suddenly opening her eyes.

"I think so—at least—but, indeed, I can tell you very little about myself. It was Mrs. Bristow——"

"Yes, I know. I am very indiscreet, putting so many questions, but you reminded me of—of some one I once knew. Mrs. Bristow, you were saying?"

"She was very anxious to know something of Mr. Mannering and his child. I think she must be a relation of his late wife."

"God be thanked if there is a relation that may be of use to Dora. She wants to know—what? If you were going to question the landlady, it would not be much——"

"I was to try to do exactly what I seem to have been so fortunate as to have done—to find some friend whom I could ask about them. I am sure you must be a friend to them?"

"How can you be sure of that, you that know neither them nor me?"

He smiled, with a very attractive, ingenuous smile. "Because you have the face of a friend."

"Have I that? There's many, many, then, that would have been the better for knowing it that have never found it out. And you are a friend to Mrs. Bristow on the other side?"

"A friend to her?—no, I am more like her son, yet not her son, for my own mother is living—at least, I believe so. I am her servant, and a little her ward, and—devoted to her," he added, with a bright flush of animation and sincerity. Miss Bethune took no notice of these last words.

"Your mother is living, you believe? and don't you know her, then? And why should you be ward or son to this other woman, and your mother alive?"

"Pardon me," said the young man, "that is my story, and it is not worth a thought. The question is about Mrs. Bristow and the Mannerings. She is anxious about them, and she is very broken in health. And I think there is some family trouble there too, so that she can't come in a natural straightforward way and make herself known to them. These family quarrels are dreadful things."

"Dreadful things," Miss Bethune said.

"They are bad enough for those with whom they originate; but for those who come after, worse still. To be deprived of a natural friend all your life because of some row that took place before you were born!"

"You are a Daniel come to judgment," said Miss Bethune, pale to her very lips.

"I hope," he said kindly, "I am not saying anything I ought not to say? I hope you are not ill?"

"Go on," she said, waving her hand. "About this Mrs. Bristow, that is what we were talking of. The Mannerings could not be more in need of a friend than they are now. He has been very ill. I hear it is very doubtful if he'll ever be himself again, or able to go back to his occupation. And she is very young, nearly grown up, but still a child. If there was a friend, a relation, to stand up for them, now would be the very time."

"Thank you," he said. "I have been very fortunate in finding you, but I don't think Mrs. Bristow can take any open step. My idea is that she must be a sister of Mrs. Mannering, and thus involved in the dissension, whatever it was."

"It was more than a dissension, so far as I have heard," Miss Bethune said.

"That is what makes it so hard. What she wishes is to see Dora."

"Dora?"

"Indeed, I mean no disrespect. I have never known her by any other name. I have helped to pack boxes for her, and choose playthings."

Miss Bethune uttered a sudden exclamation.

"Then it was from Mrs. Bristow the boxes came?"

"Have I let out something that was a secret? I am not very good at secrets," he said with a laugh.

"She might be an aunt as you say:—an aunt would be a good thing for her, poor child:—or she might be—— But is it Dora only she wants to see?"

"Dora only; and only Dora if it is certain that she would entertain no prejudices against a relation of her mother."

"How could there be prejudices of such a kind?"

"That is too much to say: but I know from my own case that there are," the young man said.

"I would like to hear your own case."

He laughed again. "You are very kind to be so much interested in a stranger: but I must settle matters for my kind guardian. She has not been a happy woman, I don't know why,—though he was as good a man as ever lived:—and now she is in very poor health—oh, really ill. I scarcely thought I could have got her to England alive. To see Dora is all she seems to wish for. Help me, oh, help me to get her that gratification!" he cried.

Miss Bethune smiled upon him in reply, with an involuntary movement of her hands towards him. She was pale, and a strange light was on her face.

"I will do that if I can," she said. "I will do it if it is possible. If I help you what will you give me in return?"

The youth looked at her in mild surprise. He did not

understand what she could mean. "Give you in return?" he asked, with astonishment.

"Ay, my young man, for my hire; everybody has a price, as I daresay you have heard said—which is a great lie, and yet true enough. Mine is not just a common price, as you will believe. I'm full of fancies, a—whimsical kind of a being. You will have to pay me for my goodwill."

He rose up from the seat under the tree, and, taking off his hat again, made her a solemn bow. "Anything that is within my power I will gladly give to secure my good guardian what she wishes. I owe everything to her."

Miss Bethune sat looking up at him with that light on her face which made it unlike everything that had been seen before. She was scarcely recognisable, or would have been to those who already knew her. To the stranger standing somewhat stiffly before her, surprised and somewhat shocked by the strange demand, it seemed that this, as he had thought, plain middle-aged woman had suddenly become beautiful.

He had liked her face at the first. It had seemed to him a friend's face, as he had said. But now it was something more. The surprise, the involuntary start of repugnance from a woman, a lady, who boldly asked something in return for the help she promised, mingled with a strange attraction towards her, and extraordinary curiosity as to what she could mean. To pay for her goodwill! Such a thing is, perhaps, implied in every prayer for help; gratitude at the least, if nothing more, is the pay which all the world is supposed to give for good offices: but one does not ask even for gratitude in words. And she was in no hurry to explain. She sat in the warm shade, with all the greenness behind, and looked at him as if she found somehow a supreme satisfaction in the sight—as if she desired to prolong the moment, and even his curiosity and surprise. He on his part was stiff, disturbed, not happy at all. He did not like a woman to let herself down, to show any wrong side of her, any acquisitiveness, or equivocal sentiment. What did she want of him? What had he to give? The thought seemed to lessen himself by reason of lessening her in his eyes.

"I tell you I am a very whimsical woman," she said at length; "above all things I am fond of hearing every man's story, and tracing out the different threads of life. It is my amusement, like any other. If I bring this lady to speech of Dora, and show her how she could be of real advantage to both the girl and her father, will you promise me to come to me another time, and tell me, as far as you know, everything that has happened to you since the day you were born?"

Young Gordon's stiffness melted away. The surprise on his face, which had been mingled with annoyance, turned into mirth and pleasure. "You don't know what you are bringing on yourself," he said, "nothing very amusing. I have little in my own record. I never had any adventures. But if that is your fancy, surely I will, whenever you like, tell you everything that I know about myself."

She rose up, with the light fading a little, but yet leaving behind it a sweetness which was not generally in Miss Bethune's face. "Let your friend come in the afternoon at three any day—it is then her father takes his sleep—and ask for Miss Bethune. I will see that it is made all right. And as for you, you will leave me your address?" she said, going with him towards the gate. "You said you believed your mother was living—is your father living too?"

"He died a long time ago," said the young man, and then added: "May I not know who it is that is standing our friend?"

Perhaps Miss Bethune did not hear him; certainly she let him out; and turned to lock the gate, without making any reply.

CHAPTER IX.

Dora had now a great deal to do in her father's room. The two nurses had at last been got rid of, to the great relief of all in the house except Mrs. Simcox, whose bills shrank back at once to their original level, very different from what they had been, and who felt herself, besides, to be reduced to quite a lower level in point of society, her thoughts and imaginations having been filled, as well as those of Janie and Molly, by tales of the hospitals and sick-rooms, which made them feel as if translated into a world where the gaiety of perfect health and constant exercise triumphed over every distress. Janie and Molly had both determined to be nurses in the enthusiasm created by these recitals. They turned their little nightcaps, the only things they had which could be so converted, into imitation nurses' caps, and masqueraded in them in the spare moments when they could shut themselves into their little rooms and play at hospital. And the sitting-room downstairs returned for these young persons to its original dulness when the nurses went away. Dora was in her father's room all day, and required a great deal of help from Jane, the maid-of-all-work, in bringing up and taking away the things that were wanted: and Gilchrist watched over him by night. There was a great deal of beef tea and chicken broth to be prepared—no longer the time and trouble saving luxuries of Brand's Essence and turtle soup. He would have none of these luxuries now. He inquired into every expense, and rejected presents, and was angry rather than grateful when anything was done for him. What he would have liked would have been to have eaten nothing at all, to have passed over meal-times, and lived upon a glass of water or milk and a biscuit. But this could not be allowed; and Mrs. Simcox had now a great deal of trouble in cooking for him, whereas before she had scarcely any at all. Mr. Mannering, indeed, was not an amiable convalescent. The breaking up of all the habits of his life was dreadful to him. The coming back to new habits was more dreadful still. He thought with horror of the debts that must have accumulated while he was ill; and when he spoke of them, looked and talked as if the whole world had been in a conspiracy against him, instead of doing everything, and contriving everything, as was the real state of the case, for his good.

"Let me have my bills, let me have my bills; let me know how I stand," he cried continually to Dr. Roland, who had the hardest ado to quiet him, to persuade him that for everything there is a reason. "I know these women ought to be paid at once," he would say. "I know a man like Vereker ought to have his fee every time he comes. You intend it very kindly, Roland, I know; but you are keeping me back, instead of helping me to recover." What was poor Dr. Roland to say? He was afraid to tell this proud man that everything was paid. That Vereker had taken but half fees, declaring that from a professional man of such distinction as Mr. Mannering, he ought, had the illness not been so long and troublesome, to have taken nothing at all,—was a possible thing to say; but not that Miss Bethune's purse had supplied these half fees. Even that they should merely be half was a kind of grievance to the patient. "I hope you told him that as soon as I was well enough I should see to it," he cried. "I have no claim to be let off so. Distinction! the distinction of a half man who never accomplished anything!"

"Come, Mannering, come, that will not do. You are the first and only man in England in your own way."

"In my own way? And what a miserable petty way, a way that leads to nothing and nowhere!" he cried.

This mood did not contribute to recovery. After his laborious dressing, which occupied all the morning, he would sit in his chair doing nothing, saying nothing, turning with a sort of sickness of despair from books, not looking even at the paper, without a smile even for Dora. The only thing he would sometimes do was to note down figures with a pencil on a sheet of paper and add them up, and make attempts to balance them with the sum which quarter day brought him. Poor Mr. Mannering was refused all information about the sums he was owing; he put them down conjecturally, now adding something, now subtracting something. As a matter of fact his highest estimation was below the truth. And then, by some unhappy chance, the bills that were lying in the sitting-room were brought to him. Alas! the foolishest bills—bills which Dora's father, knowing that she was unprovided for, should never have incurred—bills for old books, for fine editions, for delicate scientific instruments. A man with only his income from the Museum, and his child to provide for, should never have thought of such things.

"Father," said Dora, thinking of nothing but to rouse him, "there is a large parcel which has never been opened, which came from Fiddler's after you were taken ill. I had not any heart to open it to see what was in it; but perhaps it would amuse you to look at what is in it now."

"Fiddler's?" he said, with a sick look of dismay. "Another—another! What do I want with books, when I have not a penny to pay my expenses, nor a place to hide my head?"

"Oh, father, don't talk so: only have patience, and everything will come right," cried Dora, with the facile philosophy of youth. "They are great big books; I am sure they are something you wanted very much. It will amuse you to look at them, at least."

He did not consent in words, but a half motion of his head made Dora bring in, after a little delay to undo the large parcel, two great books covered with old-fashioned gilding, in brown leather, frayed at the corners—books to make the heart of a connoisseur dance, books looked out for in catalogues, followed about from one sale to another. Mr. Mannering's eyes, though they were dim and sunken, gave forth a momentary blaze. He put out his trembling hands for them, as Dora approached, almost tottering under the weight, carrying them in her arms.

"I will put them beside you on the table, father. Now you can look at them without tiring yourself, and I will run and fetch your beef tea. Oh, good news!" cried Dora, flinging into Miss Bethune's room as she ran downstairs. "He is taking a little interest! I have just given him the books from Fiddler's, and he is looking a little like his own self."

She had interrupted what seemed a very serious conversation, perceiving this only now after she had delivered her tidings. She blushed, drew back, and begged Miss Bethune's pardon, with a curious look at the unknown visitor who was seated on the sofa by that lady's side. Dora knew all Miss Bethune's visitors by heart. She knew most of those even who were pensioners, and came for money or help, and had been used to be called in to help to entertain the few callers for years past. But this was some one altogether new, not like anybody she had ever seen before, very much agitated, with a grey and worn face, which got cruelly red by moments, looking ill, tired, miserable. Poor lady! and in deep mourning, which was no doubt the cause of her trouble, and a heavy crape veil hanging over her face. She gave a little cry at the sight of Dora, and clasped her hands. The gesture caused her veil to descend like a cloud, completely concealing her face.

"I beg your pardon, indeed. I did not know there was anybody here."

Miss Bethune made her a sign to be silent, and laid her hand upon her visitor's arm, who was tremulously putting up her veil in the same dangerous overhanging position as before.

"This is Dora—as you must have guessed," she said.

The lady began to cry, feebly sobbing, as if she could not restrain herself. "I saw it was—I saw it was," she said.

"Dora, come here," said Miss Bethune. "This lady is—a relation of yours—a relation of—your poor mamma."

The lady sobbed, and held out her hands. Dora was not altogether pleased with her appearance. She might have cried at home, the girl thought. When you go out to pay a call, or even to make inquiries, you should make them and not cry: and there was something that was ridiculous in the position of the veil, ready to topple over in its heavy folds of crape. She watched it to see when the moment would come.

"Why 'my poor mamma'?" said Dora. "Is it because mother is dead?"

"There are enough of reasons," Miss Bethune said hastily.

Dora flung back her head with a sudden resistance and defiance. "I don't know about mother. She has been dead ever since I remember; but she was my mother, and nobody has any right to be sorry for her, as though that were a misfortune."

"She is a little perverse thing," said Miss Bethune, "but she has a great spirit. Dora, come here. I will go and see about your papa's beef tea, while you come and speak to this lady." She stooped over the girl for a moment as she passed her going out. "And be kind," she whispered; "for she's very ill, poor thing, and very broken. Be merciful in your strength and in your youth."

Dora could not tell what this might mean. Merciful? She, who was still only a child, and, to her own consciousness, ordered about by everybody, and made nothing of. The stranger sat on the sofa, trembling and sobbing, her face of a sallow paleness, her eyes half extinguished in tears. The heavy folds of the crape hanging over her made the faded countenance appear as if looking out of a cave.

"I am afraid you are not well," said Dora, drawing slowly near.

"No, I am not at all well. Come here and sit by me, will you? I am—dying, I think."

"Oh, no," said Dora, with a half horror, half pity. "Do not say that."

The poor lady shook her head. "I should not mind, if perhaps it made people a little forgiving—a little indulgent. Oh, Dora, my child, is it you, really you, at last?"

Dora suffered her hand to be taken, suffered herself to be drawn close, and a tremulous kiss pressed upon her cheek. She did not know how to respond. She felt herself entangled in the great crape veil, and her face wet with the other's tears. She herself was touched by pity, but by a little contrariety as well, and objection to this sudden and so intimate embrace.

"I am very, very sorry if you are ill," she said, disengaging herself as gently as possible. "My father has been very ill, so I know about it now; but I don't know you."

"My darling," the poor lady said. "My darling, my little child! my Dora, that I have thought and dreamed of night and day!"

Dora was more than ever confused. "But I don't know you at all," she said.

"No, that is what is most dreadful: not at all, not at all!—and I dying for the sight of you, and to hold you in my arms once before I die."

She held the girl with her trembling arms, and the two faces, all entangled and overshadowed by the great black veil, looked into each other, so profoundly unlike, not a line in either which recalled or seemed to connect with the other. Dora was confounded and abashed by the close contact, and her absolute incapacity to respond to this enthusiasm. She put up her hands, which was the only thing that occurred to her, and threw quite back with a subdued yet energetic movement that confusing veil. She was conscious of performing this act very quietly, but to the stranger the quick soft movement was like energy and strength personified.

"Oh, Dora," she said, "you are not like me. I never was so lively, so strong as you are. I think I must have been a poor creature, always depending upon somebody. You could never be like that."

"I don't know," said Dora. "Ought I to have been like you? Are we such near relations as that?"

"Just as near as—almost as near as—oh, child, how I have longed for you, and thought of you! You have never, never been out of my mind—not a day, Dora, scarcely an hour. Oh, if you only knew!"

"You must then have been very fond of my mother," Dora said a little stiffly. She might have been less cold had this enthusiasm been less great.

"Your mother!" the stranger said. She broke out into audible weeping again, after comparative composure. "Oh, yes, I suppose I was—oh, yes, I suppose I was," she said.

"You only suppose you were, and yet you are so fond as this of me?—which can be only," said Dora, severely logical, "for her sake."

The poor lady trembled, and was still for a moment; she then said, faltering: "We were so close together, she and I. We were like one. But a child is different—you are her and yourself too. But you are so young, my dearest, my dearest! You will not understand that."

"I understand it partly," said Dora; "but it is so strange that I never heard of you. Were my mother's relations against my father? You must forgive me," the girl said, withdrawing herself a little, sitting very upright; "but father, you know, has been everything to me. Father and I are one. I should like very much to hear about mamma, who must have died so long ago: but my first thought must always be for father, who has been everything to me, and I to him."

A long minute passed, during which the stranger said nothing. Her head was sunk upon her breast; her hand—which was on Dora's waist—quivered, the nervous fingers beating unconsciously upon Dora's firm smooth belt.

"I have nothing, nothing to say to you against your father. Oh, nothing!—not a word! I have no complaint—no complaint! He is a good man, your father. And to have you cling to him, stand up for him, is not that enough?—is not that enough," she cried, with a shrill tone, "whatever failed?"

"Then," said Dora, pursuing her argument, "mamma's relations were not friends to him?"

The lady withdrew her arm from Dora's waist. She clasped her tremulous hands together, as if in supplication. "Nothing was done against him—oh, nothing, nothing!" she cried. "There was no one to blame, everybody said so. It was a dreadful fatality; it was a thing no one could have foreseen or guarded against. Oh, my Dora, couldn't you give a little love, a little kindness, to a poor woman, even though she was not what you call a friend to your father? She never was his enemy—never, never!—never had an evil thought of him!—never wished to harm him—oh, never, never, never!" she cried.

She swayed against Dora's breast, rocking herself in uncontrolled distress, and Dora's heart was touched by that involuntary contact, and by the sight of an anguish which was painfully real, though she did not understand what it meant. With a certain protecting impulse, she put her own arm round the weeping woman to support her. "Don't cry," she said, as she might have said to a child.

"I will not cry. I will be very glad, and very happy, if you will only give me a little of your love, Dora," the lady sobbed in a broken voice. "A little of your love,—not to take it from your father,—a little, just a little! Oh, my child, my child!"

"Are you my mother's sister?" the girl asked solemnly.

The stranger raised her head again, with a look which Dora did not understand. Her eyes were full of tears, and of a wistful appeal which said nothing to the creature to whom it was addressed. After a moment, with a pathetic cry of pain and self-abandonment, she breathed forth a scarcely intelligible "Yes".

"Then now I know," said Dora, in a more satisfied tone. She was not without emotion herself. It was impossible to see so much feeling and not to be more or less affected by it, even when one did not understand, or even felt it to be extreme. "Then I will call you aunt, and we shall know where we are," she added. "I am very glad to have relations, as everybody has them. May I mention you to father? It must be long since you quarrelled, whatever it was about. I shall say to him: 'You need not take any notice, but I am glad, very glad, to have an aunt like other girls'."

"No, no, no, no—not to him! You must not say a word."

"I don't know how I can keep a secret from father," Dora said.

"Oh, child," cried the lady, "do not be too hard on us! It would be hard for him, too, and he has been ill. Don't say a word to him—for his own sake!"

"It will be very strange to keep a secret from father," Dora said reflectively. Then she added: "To be sure, there have been other things—about the nurses, and all that. And he is still very weak. I will not mention it, since you say it is for his own sake."

"For we could never meet—never, never!" cried the lady, with her head on Dora's breast—"never, unless perhaps one of us were dying. I could never look him in the face, though perhaps if I were dying—— Dora, kiss your poor—your poor, poor—relation. Oh, my child! oh, my darling! kiss me as that!"

"Dear aunt," said Dora quietly. She spoke in a very subdued tone, in order to keep down the quite uncalled-for excitement and almost passion in the other's voice. She could not but feel that her new relation was a person with very little self-control, expressing herself far too strongly, with repetitions and outcries quite uncalled for in ordinary conversation, and that it was her, Dora's, business to exercise a mollifying influence. "This is for you," she said, touching the sallow, thin cheek with her young rosy lips. "And this is for poor mamma—poor young mamma, whom I never saw."

The lady gave a quick cry, and clutched the girl in her trembling arms.

CHAPTER X.

The meeting with her new relation had a great effect upon Dora's mind. It troubled her, though there was no reason in the world why the discovery that her mother had a sister, and she herself an aunt, should be painful. An aunt is not a very interesting relation generally, not enough to make a girl's heart beat; but it added a complication to the web of altogether new difficulties in which Dora found herself entangled. Everything had been so simple in the old days—those dear old days now nearly three months off, before Mr. Mannering fell ill, to which now Dora felt herself go back with such a sense of happiness and ease, perhaps never to be known again. Then everything had been above board: there had been no payments to make that were not made naturally by her father, the fountainhead of everything, who gave his simple orders, and had them fulfilled, and provided for every necessity. Now Dora feared a knock at the door of his room lest it should be some indiscreet messenger bringing direct a luxury or novelty which it had been intended to smuggle in so that he might not observe it, or introduce with some one's compliments as an accidental offering to the sick man. To hurry off Janie or Molly downstairs with these good things intended to tempt the invalid's appetite, to stamp a secret foot at the indiscretions of Jane, who would bring in the bill for these dainties, or announce their arrival loud out, rousing Mr. Mannering to inquiries, and give a stern order that such extravagances should be no more, were now common experiences to Dora. She had to deceive him, which was, Miss Bethune assured her, for his good, but which Dora felt with a sinking heart was not at all for her own good, and made her shrink from her father's eye. To account for the presence of some rare wine which was good for him by a little story which, though it had been carefully taught her by Dr. Roland or Miss Bethune, was not true—to make out that it was the most natural thing in the world that *patés de fois gras*, and the strongest soups and essence should be no more expensive than common beef tea, the manufacture of Bloomsbury, because the doctor knew some place where they were to be had at wholesale rates for almost nothing—these were devices now quite familiar to her.

It was no worse to conceal the appearance of this new and strange personage on the scene, the relation of whom she had never heard, and whose existence was to remain a secret; but still it was a bigger secret than any that concerned the things that were to eat or drink, or even Mrs. Simcox's bills. Concealment is an art that has to be carefully learnt, like other arts, and it is extremely difficult to some minds, who will more easily acquire the most elaborate handicraft than the trick of selecting what is to be told and what is not to be told. It was beyond all description difficult to Dora. She was ready to betray herself at almost every moment, and had it not been that her own mind was much perturbed and troubled by her strange visitor, and by attempts to account for her to herself, she never could have succeeded in it. What could the offence be that made it impossible for her father ever to meet the sister of his wife again? Dora had learned from novels a great deal about the mysteries of life, some which her natural mind rejected as absurd, some which she contemplated with awe as tragic possibilities entirely out of the range of common life. She had read about implacable persons who once offended could never forgive, and of those who revenged themselves and pursued a feud to the death. But the idea of her father in either of these characters was too ridiculous to be dwelt upon for a moment. And there had been no evil intended, no harm,—only a fatality. What is a fatality? To have such dreadful issues, a thing must be serious, very terrible. Dora was bewildered and overawed. She put this question to Miss Bethune, but received no light on the subject. "A fatality is a thing that is not intentional—that happens by accident—that brings harm when you mean nothing but good," that authority said.

"But how should that be? It says in the Bible that people must not do evil that good may come. But to do good that evil may come, I never heard of that."

"There are many things in the world that you never heard of, Dora, my dear."

"Oh yes, yes, I know," cried the girl impatiently. "You are always saying that, because I am young—as if it were my fault that I am young; but that does not change anything. It is no matter, then, whether you have any meaning in what you do or not?"

"Sometimes it appears as if it was no matter. We walk blindly in this world, and often do things unawares that we would put our hands in the fire rather than do. You say an unguarded word, meaning nothing, and it falls to the ground, as you think, but afterwards springs up into a poisonous tree and blights your life; or you take a turn to the right hand instead of the left when you go out from your own door, and it means ruin and death—that's fatality, and it's everywhere," said Miss Bethune, with a deep sigh.

"I do not believe in it," said Dora, standing straight and strong, like a young tree, and holding her head high.

"Nor did I, my dear, when I was your age," Miss Bethune said.

At this moment there was a light knock at the door, and there appeared suddenly the young man whom Miss Bethune had met in the Square, and who had come as the messenger of the lady who was Dora's aunt.

"She is asking me what fatality is," said Miss Bethune. "I wonder if you have any light to throw on the subject? You are nearer her age than I."

The two young people looked at each other. Dora, though she was only sixteen, was more of a personage than the young Gordon whom she had not seen before. She looked at him with the condescension of a very young girl brought up among elder people, and apt to feel a boundless imaginative superiority over those of her own age. A young man was a slight person to Dora. She was scarcely old enough to feel any of the interest in him which exists naturally between the youth and the maiden. She looked at him from her pedestal, half scornful beforehand of anything he might say.

"Fatality?" he said. "I think it's a name people invent for anything particularly foolish which they do, when it turns out badly: though they might have known it would turn out badly all the time."

"That is exactly what I think," cried Dora, clapping her hands.

"This is the young lady," said young Gordon, "whom I used to help to pack the toys for. I hope she will let me call her Miss Dora, for I don't know her by any other name."

"To pack the toys?" said Dora. Her face grew blank, then flashed with a sudden light, then grew quite white and still again, with a gasp of astonishment and recognition. "Oh!" she cried, and something of disappointment was in her tone, "was it—was it *she* that sent them?" In the commotion of her feelings a sudden deep red followed the paleness. Dora was all fancy, changeableness, fastidiousness, imagination, as was natural to her age. Why was she disappointed to know that her yearly presents coming out ofthe unseen, the fairy gifts that testified to some love unknown, came from so legitimate a source, from her mother's sister, her own nearest relation—the lady of the other day? I cannot tell how it was, nor could she, nor any one, but it was so; and she felt this visionary, absurd disappointment go to the bottom of her heart. "Oh," she repeated, growing blank again, with a sort of opaque shadow closing over the brightness of her eyes and clouding her face, "so that was where my boxes came from? And you helped to pack the toys? I ought to have known," said Dora, very sedately, feeling as if she had suddenly fallen from a great height.

"Yes," said Miss Bethune, "we ought to have thought of that at once. Who else could have followed with such a faithful imagination, Dora? Who could have remembered your age, and the kind of things you want, and how you would grow, but a kind woman like that, with all the feelings of a mother? Oh, we should have thought of it before."

Dora at first made no reply. Her face, generally so changeable and full of expression, settled down more and more into opaqueness and a blank rigidity. She was deeply disappointed, though why she could not have told—nor what dream of a fairy patroness, an exalted friend, entirely belonging to the realms of fancy, she had conceived in her childish imagination as the giver of these gifts. At all events, the fact was so. Mrs. Bristow, with her heavy crape veil, ready to fall at any moment over her face, with the worn lines of her countenance, the flush and heat of emotion, her tears and repetitions, was a disappointing image to come between her and the vision of a tender friend, too delicate, too ethereal a figure for any commonplace embodiment which had been a kind of tutelary genius in Dora's dreams all her life. Any one in actual flesh and blood would have been a shock after that long-cherished, visionary dream. And young Gordon's laughing talk of the preparation of the box, and of his own suggestions as to its contents, and the picture he conjured up of a mystery which was half mischievous, and in which there was not only a desire to please but to puzzle the distant recipient of all these treasures, both offended and shocked the girl in the fantastic delicacy of her thoughts.

Without being himself aware of it, the young man gave a glimpse into the distant Southern home, in which it would appear he had been brought up, which was in reality very touching and attractive, though it reduced Dora to a more and more strong state of revolt. On the other hand, Miss Bethune listened to him with a rapt air of happiness, which was more wonderful still— asking a hundred questions, never tiring of any detail. Dora bore it all as long as she could, feeling herself sink more and more from the position of a young princess, mysteriously loved and cherished by a distant friend, half angelic, half queenly, into that of a little girl, whom a fantastic kind relation wished to pet and to bewilder, half in love and half in fun, taking the boy into her confidence, who was still more to her and nearer to her than Dora. She could not understand how Miss Bethune could sit and listen with that rapt countenance; and she finally broke in, in the very midst of the narrative to which she had listened (had any one taken any notice) with growing impatience, to say suddenly, "In the meantime father is by himself, and I shall have to go to him," with a tone of something like injury in her voice.

"But Gilchrist is there if he wants anything, Dora."

"Gilchrist is very kind, but she is not quite the same as me," said Dora, holding her head high.

She made Mr. Gordon a little gesture, something between farewell and dismissal, in a very lofty way, impressing upon the young man a sense of having somehow offended, which he could not understand. He himself was very much interested in Dora. He had known of her existence for years. She had been a sort of secret between him and the wife of his guardian, who, he was well aware, never discussed with her husband or mentioned in his presence the child who was so mysteriously dear to her; but bestowed all her confidence on this subject on the boy who had grown up in her house and filled to her the place of a son. He had liked the confidence and the secret and the mystery, without much inquiring what they meant. They meant, he supposed, a family quarrel, such as that which had affected all his own life. Such things are a bore and a nuisance; but, after all, don't matter very much to any but those with whom they originate. And young Gordon was not disposed to trouble his mind with any sort of mystery now.

"Have I said anything I should not have said? Is she displeased?" he said.

"It matters very little if she is displeased or not, a fantastic little girl!" cried Miss Bethune. "Go on, go on with what you are saying. I take more interest in it than words can say."

But it was not perhaps exactly the same thing to continue that story in the absence of the heroine whose name was its centre all through. She was too young to count with serious effect in the life of a man; and yet it would be difficult to draw any arbitrary line in respect to age with a tall girl full of that high flush of youth which adopts every semblance in turn, and can put all the dignity of womanhood in the eyes of a child. Young Gordon's impulse slackened in spite of himself; he was pleased, and still more amused, by the interest he excited in this lady, who had suddenly taken him into her intimacy with no reason that he knew of, and was so anxious to know all his story. It was droll to see her listening in that rapt way,—droll, yet touching too. She had said that he reminded her of somebody she knew—perhaps it was some one who was dead, a young brother, a friend of earlier years. He laughed a little to himself, though he was also affected by this curious unexpected interest in him. But he certainly had not the same freedom and eloquence in talking of the old South American home, now broken up, and the visionary little maiden, who, all unknown herself, had lent it a charm, when Dora was gone. Neither, perhaps, did Miss Bethune concentrate her interest on that part that related to Dora. When he began to flag she asked him questions of a different kind.

"Those guardians of yours must have been very good to you—as good as parents?" she said.

"Very good, but not perhaps like parents; for I remember my father very well, and I still have a mother, you know."

"Your father," she said, turning away her head a little, "was devoted to you, I suppose?"

"Devoted to me?" he said, with a little surprise, and then laughed. "He was kind enough. We got on very well together. Do men and their sons do more than that?"

"I know very little about men and their sons," she said hastily; "about men and women I maybe know a little, and not much to their advantage. Oh, you are there, Gilchrist! This is the gentleman I was speaking to you about. Do you see the likeness?"

Gilchrist advanced a step into the room, with much embarrassment in her honest face. She uttered a broken laugh, which was like a giggle, and began as usual to fold hems in her apron.

"I cannot say, mem, that I see a resemblance to any person," she said.

"You are just a stupid creature!" said her mistress,—"good for nothing but to make an invalid's beef tea. Just go away, go away and do that." She turned suddenly to young Gordon, as Gilchrist went out of the room. "That stupid woman's face doesn't bring anything to your mind?" she said hastily.

"Bring anything to my mind?" he cried, with great surprise. "What should she bring to my mind?"

"It was just a fancy that came into mine. Do you remember the scene in *Guy Mannering*, where Bertram first sees Dominie Sampson? Eh, I hope your education has not been neglected in that great particular?"

"I remember the scene," he said, with a smile.

"It was perhaps a little of what you young folk call melodramatic: but Harry Bertram's imagination gets a kind of shock, and he remembers. And so you are a reader of Sir Walter, and mind that scene?"

"I remember it very well," said the young man, bewildered. "But about the maid? You said——"

"Oh, nothing about the maid; she's my faithful maid, but a stupid woman as ever existed. Never you mind what I said. I say things that are very silly from time to time. But I would like to know how you ever heard your mother was living, when you have never seen her, nor know anything about her? I suppose not even her name?"

"My father told me so when he was dying: he told Mr. Bristow so, but he gave us no further information. I gathered that my mother—— It is painful to betray such an impression."

She looked at him with a deep red rising over her cheeks, and a half-defiant look. "I am old enough to be your mother, you need not hesitate to speak before me," she said.

"It is not that; it is that I can't associate that name with anything—anything—to be ashamed of."

"I would hope not, indeed!" she cried, standing up, towering over him as if she had added a foot to her height. She gave forth a long fiery breath, and then asked, "Did he dare to say that?" with a heaving breast.

"He did not say it: but my guardian thought——"

"Oh, your guardian thought! That was what your guardian would naturally think. A man—that is always of an evil mind where women are concerned! And what did she think?—her, his wife, the other guardian, the woman I have seen?"

"She is not like any one else," said young Gordon; "she will never believe in any harm. You have given me one scene, I will give you another. She said what Desdemona said, 'I do not believe there was ever any such woman'."

"Bless her! But oh, there are—there are!" cried Miss Bethune, tears filling her eyes, "in life as well as in men's ill imaginations. But not possible to her or to me!"

CHAPTER XI.

Young Gordon had gone, and silence had fallen over Miss Bethune's room. It was a commonplace room enough, well-sized, for the house was old and solid, with three tall windows swathed in red rep curtains, partially softened but not extinguished by the white muslin ones which had been put up over them. Neither Miss Bethune nor her maid belonged to the decorative age. They had no principles as to furniture, but accepted what they had, with rather a preference than otherwise for heavy articles in mahogany, and things that were likely to last. They thought Mr. Mannering's dainty furniture and his faded silken curtains were rather of the nature of trumpery. People could think so in these days, and in the locality of Bloomsbury, without being entirely abandoned in character, or given up to every vicious sentiment. Therefore, I cannot say, as I should be obliged to say now-a-days, in order to preserve any sympathy for Miss Bethune in the reader's mind, that the room was pretty, and contained an indication of its mistress's character in every carefully arranged corner. It was a room furnished by Mrs. Simcox, the landlady. It had been embellished, perhaps, by a warm hearthrug—not Persian, however, by any means—and made comfortable by a few easy chairs. There were a number of books about, and there was one glass full of wallflowers on the table, very sweet in sober colours—a flower that rather corresponds with the mahogany, and the old-fashioned indifference to ornament and love of use. You would have thought, had you looked into this room, which was full of spring sunshine, bringing out the golden tints in the wallflower, and reflected in the big mirror above the fireplace, that it was empty after young Gordon had gone. But it was not empty. It was occupied instead by a human heart, so overbursting with passionate hope, love, suspense, and anxiety, that it was a wonder the silence did not tinge, and the quiet atmosphere betray that strain and stress of feeling. Miss Bethune sat in the shadowed corner between the fireplace and the farther window, with the whiteness of the curtains blowing softly in her face as the air came in. That flutter dazzled the beholder, and made Gilchrist think when she entered that there was nobody there. The maid looked round, and then clasped her hands and said to herself softly: "She'll be gane into her bedroom to greet there".

"And why should I greet, you foolish woman?" cried Miss Bethune from her corner, with a thrill in her voice which betrayed the commotion in her mind.

Gilchrist started so violently that the bundle of clean "things," fresh and fragrant from the country cart which had brought home the washing, fell from her arms. "Oh, mem, if I had kent you were there."

"My bonnie clean things!" cried Miss Bethune, "with the scent of the grass upon them—and now they're all spoiled with the dust of Bloomsbury! Gather them up and carry them away, and then you can come back here." She remained for a moment as quiet as before, after Gilchrist had hurried away; but any touch would have been sufficient to move her in her agitation, and presently she rose and began to pace about the room. "Gone to my room to greet there, is that what she thinks? Like Mary going to the grave to weep there. No, no, that's not the truth. It's the other way. I might be going to laugh, and to clap my hands, as they say in the Psalms. But laughing is not the first expression of joy. I would maybe be more like greeting, as she says. A person laughs in idleness, for fun, not for joy. Joy has nothing, nothing but the old way of tears, which is just a contradiction. And maybe, after all, she was right. I'll go to my room and weep for thankfulness, and lightheartedness, and joy."

"Oh, mem," cried Gilchrist, coming in, "gang softly, gang softly! You're more sure than any mortal person has a right to be."

"Ye old unbeliever," cried Miss Bethune, pausing in the midst of her sob. "What has mortality to do with evidence? It would be just as true if I were to die to-morrow, for that matter."

"Eh, mem," cried Gilchrist again, "ye're awfu' easy to please in the way of evidence. What do you call evidence? A likeness ye think ye see, but I canna; and there's naething in a likeness. Miss Dora is no more like her papaw than me, there is nothing to be lippened to in the like of that. And then the age—that would maybe be about the same, I grant ye that, so much as it comes to; and a name that is no' the right name, but a kind of an approach to it."

"You are a bonnie person," cried Miss Bethune, "to take authority upon you about names, and never to think of the commonest old Scotch custom, that the son drops or turns the other way the name the father has taken to his own. I hope I know better! If nothing had ever happened, if the lad had been bred and trained at home, he would be Gordon, just as sure as he is Gordon now."

"I'm no' a person of quality, mem," said Gilchrist, holding her ground. "I have never set up for being wan of the gentry: it would ill become me, being just John Gilchrist the smith's daughter, and your servant-woman, that has served you this five and twenty years. But there are as many Gordons in Aberdeen as there are kirk steeples in this weary London town."

Miss Bethune made an impatient gesture. "You're a sagacious person, Gilchrist, altogether, and might be a ruling elder if you were but a man: but I think perhaps I know what's in it as well as you do, and if I'm satisfied that a thing is, I will not yield my faith, as you might know by this time, neither to the Lord President himself, nor even to you."

"Eh, bless me, mem, but I ken that weel!" cried Gilchrist; "and if I had thought you were taking it on that high line, never word would have come out of my mouth."

"I am taking it on no high line—but I see what is for it as well as what is against it. I have kept my head clear," said Miss

Bethune. "On other occasions, I grant you, I may have let myself go: but in all this I have been like a judge, and refused to listen to the voice in my own heart. But it was there all the time, though I crushed it down. How can the like of you understand? You've never felt a baby's cry go into the very marrow of your bones. I've set the evidence all out, and pled the cause before my own judgment, never listening one word to the voice in my heart." Miss Bethune spoke with greater and greater vehemence, but here paused to calm herself. "The boy that was carried off would have been twenty-five on the eighteenth of next month (as well you know), and this boy is just on five and twenty, he told me with his own lips; and his father told him with his dying breath that he had a mother living. He had the grace to do that! Maybe," said Miss Bethune, dropping her voice, which had again risen in excitement, "he was a true penitent when it came to that. I wish no other thing. Much harm and misery, God forgive him, has he wrought; but I wish no other thing. It would have done my heart good to think that his was touched and softened at the last, to his Maker at least, if no more."

"Oh, mem, the one would go with the other, if what you think is true."

"No," said Miss Bethune, shutting her lips tight, "no, there's no necessity. If it had been so what would have hindered him to give the boy chapter and verse? Her name is So-and-so, you will hear of her at such a place. But never that—never that, though it would have been so easy! Only that he had a mother living, a mother that the guardian man and the lad himself divined must have been a —— Do you not call that evidence?" cried Miss Bethune, with a harsh triumph. "Do you not divine our man in that? Oh, but I see him as clear as if he had signed his name."

"Dear mem," cried Gilchrist, with a "tchick, tchick," of troubled sympathy and spectatorship, "you canna wish he had been a true penitent and yet think of him like that."

"And who are you to lay down the law and say what I can do?" cried the lady. She added, with a wave of her hand and her head: "We'll not argue that question: but if there ever was an action more like the man!—just to give the hint and clear his conscience, but leave the woman's name to be torn to pieces by any dozen in the place! If that is not evidence, I don't know what evidence is."

Gilchrist could say nothing in reply. She shook her head, though whether in agreement or in dissidence it would have been difficult to tell, and folded hem upon hem on her apron, with her eyes fixed upon that, as if it had been the most important of work. "I was wanting to speak," she said, "when you had a moment to listen to me, about two young folk."

"What two young folk?" Miss Bethune's eyes lighted up with a gleam of soft light, her face grew tender in every line. "But Dora is too young, she is far too young for anything of the kind," she said.

"Eh, mem," cried Gilchrist, with a mingling of astonishment, admiration, and pity, "can ye think of nothing but yon strange young man?"

"I am thinking of nothing but the bairn, the boy that was stolen away before he knew his right hand from his left, and now is come home."

"Aweel, aweel," said Gilchrist, "we will just have to put up with it, as we have put up with it before. And sooner or later her mind will come back to what's reasonable and true. I was speaking not of the young gentleman, or of any like him, but of the two who were up in the attics that you were wanting to save, if save them ye can. They are just handless creatures, the one and the other; but the woman's no' an ill person, poor thing, and would do well if she knew the way. And a baby coming, and the man just a weirdless, feckless, ill man."

"He cannot help it if he is ill, Gilchrist."

"Maybe no'," said Gilchrist cautiously. "I'm never just so sure of that; but, anyway, he's a delicate creature, feared for everything, and for a Christian eye upon him, which is the worst of all; and wherefore we should take them upon our shoulders, folk that we have nothing to do with, a husband and wife, and the family that's coming——"

"Oh, woman," said her mistress, "if they have got just a step out of the safe way in the beginning, is that not reason the more for helping them back? And how can I ever know what straits *he* might have been put to, and his mother ignorant, and not able to help him?"

"Eh, but I'm thankful to hear you say that again!" Gilchrist cried.

"Not that I can ever have that fear now, for a finer young man, or a more sweet ingenuous look! But no credit to any of us, Gilchrist. I'm thankful to those kind people that have brought him up; but it will always be a pain in my heart that I have had nothing to do with the training of him, and will never be half so much to him as that—that lady, who is in herself a poor, weakly woman, if I may say such a word."

"It is just a very strange thing," said Gilchrist, "that yon lady is as much taken up about our Miss Dora as you are, mem, about the young lad."

"Ah!" said Miss Bethune, with a nod of her head, "but in a different way. Her mother's sister—very kind and very natural, but oh, how different! I am to contrive to take Dora to see her, for I fear she is not long for this world, Gilchrist. The young lad, as you call him, will soon have nobody to look to but——"

"Mem!" cried Gilchrist, drawing herself up, and looking her mistress sternly in the face.

Miss Bethune confronted her angrily for a moment, then coloured high, and flung down, as it were, her arms. "No, no!" she cried—"no, you are unjust to me, as you have been many times before. I am not glad of her illness, poor thing. God forbid it! I am not exulting, as you think, that she will be out of my way. Oh, Gilchrist, do you think so little of me—a woman you have known this long, long lifetime—as to believe that?"

"Eh, mem," said Gilchrist, "when you and me begin to think ill of each other, the world will come to an end. We ken each ither far too well for that. Ye may scold me whiles when I little deserve it, and I put a thing upon you for a minnit that is nae blame of yours; but na, na, there is nae misjudging possible between you and me."

It will be seen that Gilchrist was very cautious in the confession of faith just extorted. She was no flatterer. She knew of what her mistress was capable better than that mistress herself did, and had all her weaknesses on the tips of her fingers. But she had no intention of discouraging that faulty but well-beloved woman. She went on in indulgent, semi-maternal tones: "You've had a great deal to excite you and trouble you, and in my opinion it would do ye a great deal of good, and help ye to get back to your ordinary, if you would just put everything else away, and consider with me what was to be done for thae two feckless young folk. If the man is not put to do anything, he will be in more trouble than ever, or I'm no judge."

"And it might have been him!" said Miss Bethune to herself—the habitual utterance which had inspired so many acts of charity. "I think you are maybe right, Gilchrist," she added; "it will steady me, and do me good. Run downstairs and see if the doctor is in. He knows more about him than we do, and we'll just have a good consultation and see what is the best to be done."

The doctor was in, and came directly, and there was a very anxious consultation about the two young people, to whose apparently simple, commonplace mode of life there had come so sudden an interruption. Dr. Roland had done more harm than good by his action in the matter. He confessed that had he left things alone, and not terrified the young coward on the verge of crime, the catastrophe might perhaps, by more judicious ministrations, have been staved off. Terror of being found out is not always a preservative, it sometimes hurries on the act which it ought to prevent; and the young man who had been risking his soul in petty peculations which he might have made up for, fell over the precipice into a great one in sheer cowardice, when the doctor's keen eye read him, and made him tremble. Dr. Roland took blame to himself. He argued that it was of no use trying to find Hesketh another situation. "He has no character, and no one will take him without a character: or if some Quixote did, on your word, Miss Bethune, or mine, who are very little to be trusted in such a case, the unfortunate wretch would do the same again. It's not his fault, he cannot help himself. His grandfather, or perhaps a more distant relation——"

"Do not speak nonsense to me, doctor, for I will not listen to it," said Miss Bethune. "When there's a poor young wife in the case, and a baby coming, how dare you talk about the fool's grandfather?"

"Mem and sir," said Gilchrist, "if you would maybe listen for a moment to me. My mistress, she has little confidence in my sense, but I have seen mony a thing happen in my day, and twenty years' meddlin' and mellin' with poor folk under her, that is always too ready with her siller, makes ye learn if ye were ever sae silly. Now, here is what I would propose. He's maybe more feckless than anything worse. He will get no situation without a character, and it will not do for you—neither her nor you, sir, asking your pardon—to make yourselves caution for a silly gowk like yon. But set him up some place in a little shop of his ain. He'll no cheat himsel', and the wife she can keep an eye on him. If it's in him to do weel, he'll do weel, or at least we'll see if he tries; and if no', in that case ye'll ken just what you will lose. That is what I would advise, if you would lippen to me, though I am not saying I am anything but a stupid person, and often told so," Gilchrist said.

"It is not a bad idea, however," said Dr. Roland.

"Neither it is. But the hussy, to revenge herself on me like that!" her mistress cried.

CHAPTER XII.

Young Gordon left the house in Bloomsbury after he had delivered the message which was the object of his visit, but which he had forgotten in the amusement of seeing Dora, and the interest of these new scenes which had so suddenly opened up in his life. His object had been to beg that Miss Bethune would visit the lady for whom it had been his previous object to obtain an entrance into the house in which Dora was. Mrs. Bristow was ill, and could not go again, and she wanted to see Dora's friend, who could bring Dora herself, accepting the new acquaintance for the sake of the child on whom her heart was set, but whom for some occult reason she would not call to her in the more natural way. Gordon did not believe in occult reasons. He had no mind for mysteries; and was fully convinced that whatever quarrel there might have been, no man would be so ridiculously vindictive as to keep his child apart from a relation, her mother's sister, who was so anxious to see her.

But he was the kindest-hearted youth in the world, and though he smiled at these mysteries he yet respected them in the woman who had been everything to him in his early life, his guardian's wife, whom he also called aunt in the absence of any other suitable title. She liked that sort of thing—to make mountains of molehills, and to get over them with great expenditure of strategy and sentiment, when he was persuaded she might have marched straight forward and found no difficulty. But it was her way, and it had always been his business to see that she had her way and was crossed by nobody. He was so accustomed to her in all her weaknesses that he accepted them simply as the course of nature. Even her illness did not alarm or trouble him. She had been delicate since ever he could remember. From the time when he entered upon those duties of son or nephew which dated so far back in his life, he had always been used to make excuses to her visitors on account of her delicacy, her broken health, her inability to bear the effects of the hot climate. This was her habit, as it was the habit of some women to ride and of some to drive; and as it was the habit of her household to accept whatever she did as the only things for her to do, he had been brought up frankly in that faith.

His own life, too, had always appeared very simple and natural to Harry, though perhaps it scarcely seemed so to the spectator. His childhood had been passed with his father, who was more or less of an adventurer, and who had accustomed his son to ups and downs which he was too young to heed, having always his wants attended to, and somebody to play with, whatever happened. Then he had been transferred to the house of his guardian on a footing which he was too young to inquire into, which was indeed the simple footing of a son, receiving everything from his new parents, as he had received everything from his old. To find on his guardian's death that he had nothing, that no provision was made for him, was something of a shock; as had been the discovery on his twenty-first birthday that his guardian was simply his benefactor, and had no trust in respect to him. It came over Harry like a cloud on both occasions that he had no profession, no way of making his own living; and that a state of dependence like that in which he had been brought up could not continue. But the worst time in the world to break the link which had subsisted so long, or to take from his aunt, as he called her, the companion upon whom she leant for everything, was at the moment when her husband was gone, and there was nobody else except a maid to take care of her helplessness. He could not do this; he was as much bound to her, to provide for all her wants, and see that she missed nothing of her wonted comforts; nay, almost more than if he had been really her son. If it had not been for his easy nature, the light heart which goes with perfect health, great simplicity of mind, and a thoroughly generous disposition, young Gordon had enough of uncertainty in his life to have made him very serious, if not unhappy. But, as a matter of fact, he was neither. He took the days as they came, as only those can do who are to that manner born. When he thought on the subject, he said to himself that should the worst come to the worst, a young fellow of his age, with the use of his hands and a head on his shoulders, could surely find something to do, and that he would not mind what it was.

This was very easy to say, and Gordon was not at all aware what the real difficulties are in finding something to do. But had he known better, it would have done him no good; and his ignorance, combined as it was with constant occupations of one kind or another, was a kind of bliss. There was a hope, too, in his mind, that merely being in England would mend matters. It must open some mode of independence for him. Mrs. Bristow would settle somewhere, buy a "place," an estate, as it had always been the dream of her husband to do, and so give him occupation. Something would come of it that would settle the question for him; the mere certainty in his mind of this cleared away all clouds, and made the natural brightness of his temperature more assured than ever.

This young man had no education to speak of. He had read innumerable books, which do not count for very much in that way. He had, however, been brought up in what was supposed "the best" of society, and he had the advantage of that, which is no small advantage. He was at his ease in consequence, wherever he went, not supposing that any one looked down on him, or that he could be refused admittance anywhere. As he walked back with his heart at ease—full of an amused pleasure in the thought of Dora, whom he had known for years, and who had been, though he had never till to-day seen her, a sort of little playfellow in his life—walking westward from the seriousness of Bloomsbury, through the long line of Oxford Street, and across Hyde Park to the great hotel in which Mrs. Bristow had established herself, the young man, though he had not a penny, and was a mere colonial, to say the best of him, felt himself returning to a more congenial atmosphere, the region of ease and leisure, and beautiful surroundings, to which he had been born. He had not any feature of the man of fashion, yet he belonged instinctively to the *jeunesse dorée* wherever he went. He went along, swinging his cane, with a relief in his mind to be delivered from the narrow and noisy streets. He had been accustomed all his life to luxury, though of a different kind from that of London, and he smiled at the primness and respectability of Bloomsbury by instinct, though he had no right to do so. He recognised the difference of the traffic in Piccadilly, and distinguished between that great thoroughfare and the other with purely intuitive discrimination. Belgravia was narrow and formal to the Southerner, but yet it was different. All these intuitions were in him, he could not tell how.

He went back to his aunt with the pleasure of having something to say which he knew would please her. Dora, as has been said, had been their secret between them for many years. He had helped to think of toys and pretty trifles to send her, and the boxes had been the subject of many a consultation, calling forth tears from Mrs. Bristow, but pure fun to the young man, who thought of the unknown recipient as of a little sister whom he had never seen. He meant to please the kind woman who had been a mother to him, by telling her about Dora, how pretty she was, how tall, how full of character, delightful and amusing to behold, how she was half angry with him for knowing so much of her, half pleased, how she flashed from fun to seriousness, from kindness to quick indignation, and on the whole disapproved of him, but only in a way that was amusing, that he was not afraid of. Thus he went in cheerful, and intent upon making the invalid cheerful too.

A hotel is a hotel all the world over, a place essentially vulgar, commonplace, venal, the travesty of a human home. This one, however, was as stately as it could be, with a certain size about the building, big stairs, big rooms, at the end of one of which he found his patroness lying, in an elaborate dressing-gown, on a large sofa, with the vague figure of a maid floating about in the semi-darkness. The London sun in April is not generally violent; but all the blinds were down, the curtains half drawn over the windows, and the room so deeply shadowed that even young Gordon's sharp eyes coming out of the keen daylight did not preserve him from knocking against one piece of furniture after another as he made his way to the patient's side.

"Well, Harry dear, is she coming?" a faint voice said.

"I hope so, aunt. She was sorry to know you were ill. I told her you were quite used to being ill, and always patient over it. Are things going any better to-day?"

"They will never be better, Harry."

"Don't say that. They have been worse a great many times, and then things have always come round a little."

"He doesn't believe me, Miller. That is what comes of health like mine; nobody will believe that I am worse now than I have ever been before." Gordon patted the thin hand that lay on the bed. He had heard these words *many* times, and he was not alarmed by them.

"This lady is rather a character," he said; "she will amuse you. She is Scotch, and she is rather strong-minded, and——"

"I never could bear strong-minded women," cried the patient with some energy. "But what do I care whether she is Scotch or Spanish, or what she is? Besides that, she has helped me already, and all I want is Dora. Oh, Harry, did you see Dora?—my Dora, my little girl! And so tall, and so well grown, and so sweet! And to think that I cannot have her, cannot see her, now that I am going to die!"

"Why shouldn't you have her?" he said in his calm voice. "Her father is better; and no man, however unreasonable, would prevent her coming to see her own relation. You don't understand, dear aunt. You won't believe that people are all very like each other, not so cruel and hard-hearted as you suppose. You would not be unkind to a sick person, why should he?"

"Oh, it's different—very different!" the sick woman said.

"Why should it be different? A quarrel that is a dozen years old could never be so bitter as that."

"It is you who don't understand. I did him harm—oh, such harm! Never, never could he forgive me! I never want him to hear my name. And to ask Dora from him—oh no, no! Don't do it, Harry—not if I was at my last breath!"

"If you ever did him harm as you say—though I don't believe you ever did any one harm—that is why you cannot forgive him. Aunt, you may be sure he has forgiven you."

"I—I—forgive? Oh, never, never had I anything to forgive—never! I—oh if you only knew!"

"I wouldn't say anything to excite her, Mr. Harry," said the maid. "She isn't so well, really; she's very bad, as true as can be. I've sent for the doctor."

"Yes, tell him!" cried the poor lady eagerly; "tell him that you have never seen me so ill. Tell him, Miller, that I'm very bad, and going to die!"

"We'll wait and hear what the doctor says, ma'am," said the maid cautiously.

"But Dora, Harry—oh, bring her, bring her! How am I to die without my Dora? Oh, bring her! Ask this lady—I don't mind her being strong-minded or anything, if she will bring my child. Harry, you must steal her away, if he will not let her come. I have a right to her. It is—it is her duty to come to me when I am going to die!"

"Don't excite her, sir, for goodness' sake; promise anything," whispered the maid.

"I will, aunt. I'll run away with her. I'll have a carriage with a couple of ruffians to wait round the corner, and I'll throw something over her head to stifle her cries, and then we'll carry her away."

"It isn't any laughing matter," she said, recovering her composure a little. "If you only knew, Harry! But I couldn't, I couldn't tell you—or any one. Oh, Harry, my poor boy, you'll find out a great many things afterwards, and perhaps you'll blame me. I know you'll blame me. But remember I was always fond of you, and always kind to you all the same. You won't forget that, however badly you may think of me. Oh, Harry, my dear, my dear!"

"Dear aunt, as if there could ever be any question of blame from me to you!" he said, kissing her hand.

"But there will be a question. Everybody will blame me, and you will be obliged to do it too, though it goes against your kind heart. I seem to see everything, and feel what's wrong, and yet not be able to help it. I've always been like that," she said, sobbing. "Whatever I did, I've always known it would come to harm; but I've never been able to stop it, to do different. I've done so many, many things! Oh, if I could go back and begin different from the very first! But I shouldn't. I am just as helpless now as then. And I know just how you will look, Harry, and try not to believe, and try not to say anything against me——"

"If you don't keep quiet, ma'am, I'll have to go and leave you! and a nurse is what you will get—a nurse out of the hospital, as will stand no nonsense."

"Oh, Miller, just one word! Harry, promise me you'll think of what I said, and that you will not blame——"

"Never," he said, rising from her side. "I acquit you from this moment, aunt. You can never do anything that will be evil in my eyes. But is not the room too dark, and don't you mean to have any lunch? A little light and a little cutlet, don't you think, Miller? No? Well, I suppose you know best, but you'll see that is what the doctor will order. I'm going to get mine, anyhow, for I'm as hungry as a hunter. Blame you? Is it likely?" he said, stooping to kiss her.

Notwithstanding his affectionate fidelity, he was glad to be free of the darkened room and oppressive atmosphere and troubled colloquy. To return to ordinary daylight and life was a relief to him. But he had no very serious thoughts, either about the appeal she had made to him or her condition. He had known her as ill and as hysterical before. When she was ill she was often emotional, miserable, fond of referring to mysterious errors in her past. Harry thought he knew very well what these errors were. He knew her like the palm of his hand, as the French say. He knew the sort of things she would be likely to do, foolish things, inconsiderate, done in a hurry—done, very likely, as she said, with a full knowledge that they ought not to be done, yet that she could not help it. Poor little aunt! he could well believe in any sort of silly thing, heedless, and yet not altogether heedless either, disapproved of in her mind even while she did it. Our children know us better than any other spectators know us. They know the very moods in which we are likely to do wrong. What a good thing it is that with that they love us all the same, more or less, as the case may be! And that their eyes, though so terribly clear-sighted, are indulgent too; or, if not indulgent, yet are ruled by the use and wont, the habit of us, and of accepting us, whatever we may be. Young Gordon knew exactly, or thought he knew, what sort of foolish things she might have done, or even yet might be going to do. Her conscience was evidently very keen about this Mr. Mannering, this sister's husband, as he appeared to be; perhaps she had made mischief, not meaning it and yet half meaning it, between him and his wife, and could not forgive herself, or hope to be forgiven. Her own husband had been a grave man, very loving to her, yet very serious with her, and he knew that there had never been mention of Dora between these two. Once, he remembered, his guardian had seen the box ready to be despatched, and had asked no questions, but looked for a moment as if he would have pushed it out of the way with his foot. Perhaps he had disapproved of these feeble attempts to make up to the sister's child for harm done to her mother. Perhaps he had felt that the wrong was unforgiveable, whatever it was. He had taken it for granted that after his death his wife would go home; and Harry remembered a wistful strange look which he cast upon her when he was dying. But the young man gave himself a little shake to throw off these indications of a secret which he did not know. His nature, as had been said, was averse to secrets; he refused to have anything to do with a mystery. Everything in which he was concerned was honest and open as the day. He did not dwell on the fact that he had a mystery connected with himself, and was in the curious circumstance of having a mother whom he did not know. It was very odd, he admitted, when he thought of it; but as he spent his life by the side of a woman who was in all respects exactly like his mother to him, perhaps it is not so wonderful that his mind strayed seldom to that thought. He shook everything off as he went downstairs, and sat down to luncheon with the most hearty and healthy appetite in the world.

CHAPTER XIII.

"Dora," said Mr. Mannering, half raising his head from the large folio which had come from the old book dealer during his illness, and which, in these days of his slow convalescence, had occupied much of his time. After he had spoken that word he remained silent for some time, his head slightly raised, his shoulders bent over the big book. Then he repeated "Dora" again. "Do you think," he said, "you could carry one of these volumes as far as Fiddler's, and ask if he would take it back?"

"Take it back!" Dora cried in surprise.

"You can tell him that I do not find it as interesting as I expected—but no; for that might do it harm, and it is very interesting. You might say our shelves are all filled up with big books, and that I have really no room for it at present, which," he added, looking anxiously up into her face, "is quite true; for, you remember, when I was so foolish as to order it, we asked ourselves how it would be possible to find a place for it? But no, no," he said, "these are inventions, and I see your surprise in your face that I should send you with a message that is not genuine. It is true enough, you know, that I am much slackened in the work I wanted this book for. I am slackened in everything. I doubt if I can take up any piece of work again to do any good. I'm old, you see, to have such a long illness," he said, looking at her almost apologetically; "and, unless it had been with an idea of work, I never could have had any justification in ordering such an expensive book as this."

"You never used to think of that, father," Dora said.

"No, I never used to think of that; but I ought to have done so. I'm afraid I've been very extravagant. I could always have got it, and consulted it as much as I pleased at the Museum. It is a ridiculous craze I have had for having the books in my own possession. Many men cannot understand it. Williamson, for instance. He says: 'In your place I would never buy a book. Why, you have the finest library in the world at your disposal.' And it's quite true. There could not be a more ridiculous extravagance on my part, and pride, I suppose to be able to say I had it."

"I don't think that's the case at all," cried Dora. "What do you care for, father, except your library? You never go anywhere, you have no amusements like other people. You don't go into society, or go abroad, or—anything that the other people do."

"That is true enough," he said, with a little gleam of pleasure. Then, suddenly taking her hand as she stood beside him: "My poor child, you say that quite simply, without thinking what a terrible accusation it would be if it went on,—a sacrifice of your young life to my old one, and forgetfulness of all a girl's tastes and wishes. We'll try to put that right at least, Dora," he said, with a slight quiver in his lip, "in the future—if there is any future for me."

"Father!" she said indignantly, "as if I didn't like the books, and was not more proud of your work that you are doing——"

"And which never comes to anything," he interjected, sadly shaking his head.

"—— than of anything else in the world! I am very happy as I am. I have no tastes or pleasures but what are yours. I never have wanted anything that you did not get for me. You should see," cried Dora, with a laugh, "what Janie and Molly think downstairs. They think me a princess at the least, with nothing to do, and all my fine clothes!"

"Janie and Molly!" he said,—"Janie and Molly! And these are all that my girl has to compare herself with—the landlady's orphan granddaughters! You children make your arrows very sharp without knowing it. But it shall be so no more. Dora, more than ever I want you to go to Fiddler's; but you shall tell him what is the simple truth—that I have had a long illness, which has been very expensive, and that I cannot afford any more expensive books. He might even, indeed, be disposed to buy back some that we have. That is one thing," he added, with more animation, "all the books are really worth their price. I have always thought they would be something for you, whether you sold them or kept them, when I am gone. Do you think you could carry one of them as far as Fiddler's, Dora? They are in such excellent condition, and it would show him no harm had come to them. One may carry a book anywhere, even a young lady may. And it is not so very heavy."

"It is no weight at all," cried Dora, who never did anything by halves. "A little too big for my pocket, father; but I could carry it anywhere. As if I minded carrying a book, or even a parcel! I like it—it looks as if one had really something to do."

She went out a few minutes after, lightly with great energy and animation, carrying under one arm the big book as if it had been a feather-weight. It was a fine afternoon, and the big trees in the Square were full of the rustle and breath of life—life as vigorous as if their foliage waved in the heart of the country and not in Bloomsbury. There had been showers in the morning; but now the sun shone warm, and as it edged towards the west sent long rays down the cross streets, making them into openings of pure light, and dazzling the eyes of the passers-by. Dora was caught in this illumination at every street corner, and turned her face to it as she crossed the opening, not afraid, for either eyes or complexion, of that glow "angry and brave". The great folio, with its worn corners and its tarnished gilding, rather added to the effect of her tall, slim, young figure, strong as health and youth could make it, with limbs a little too long, and joints a little too pronounced, as belonged to her age. She carried her head lightly as a flower, her step was free and light; she looked, as she said, "as if she had something to do," and was wholly capable of doing it, which is a grace the more added, not unusually in these days, to the other graces of early life in the feminine subject. But it is not an easy thing to carry a large folio under your arm. After even a limited stretch of road, the lamb is apt to become a sheep: and to shift such a cumbrous volume from one arm to another is not an easy matter either, especially while walking along the streets. Dora held on her way as long as she could, till her wrist was like to break, and her shoulder to come out of its socket. Neither she nor her father had in the least realised what the burden was. Then she turned it over with difficulty in both arms, and transferred it to the other side, speedily reducing the second arm to a similar condition, while the first had as yet barely recovered.

It is not a very long way from the corner of the Square to those delightful old passages full of old book-shops, which had been the favourite pasturage of Mr. Mannering, and where Dora had so often accompanied her father. On ordinary occasions she thought the distance to Fiddler's no more than a few steps, but to-day it seemed miles long. And she was too proud to give in, or to go into a shop to rest, while it did not seem safe to trust a precious book, and one that she was going to give back to the dealer, to a passing boy. She toiled on accordingly, making but slow progress, and very much subdued by her task, her cheeks flushed, and the tears in her eyes only kept back by pride, when she suddenly met walking quickly along, skimming the pavement with his light tread, the young man who had so wounded and paralysed her in Miss Bethune's room, whom she had seen then only for the first time, but who had claimed her so cheerfully by her Christian name as an old friend.

She saw him before he saw her, and her first thought was the quick involuntary one, that here was succour coming towards her; but the second was not so cheerful. The second was, that this stranger would think it his duty to help her; that he would conceive criticisms, even if he did not utter them, as to the mistake of entrusting her with a burden she was not equal to; that he would assume more and more familiarity, perhaps treat her altogether as a little girl—talk again of the toys he had helped to choose, and all those injurious revolting particulars which had filled her with so much indignation on their previous meeting. The sudden rush and encounter of these thoughts distracting her

116

mind when her body had need of all its support, made Dora's limbs so tremble, and the light so go out of her eyes, that she found herself all at once unable to carry on her straight course, and awoke to the humiliating fact that she had stumbled to the support of the nearest area railing, that the book had slipped from under her tired arm, and that she was standing there, very near crying, holding it up between the rail and her knee.

"Why, Miss Dora!" cried that young man. He would have passed, had it not been for that deplorable exhibition of weakness. But when his eye caught the half-ridiculous, wholly overwhelming misery of the slipping book, the knee put forth to save it, the slim figure bending over it, he was beside her in a moment. "Give it to me," he cried, suiting the action to the word, and taking it from her as if it had been a feather. Well, she had herself said it was a feather at first.

Dora, relieved, shook her tired arms, straightened her figure, and raised her head; with all her pride coming back.

"Oh, please never mind. I had only got it out of balance. I am quite, quite able to carry it," she cried.

"Are you going far? And will you let me walk with you? It was indeed to see you I was going—not without a commission."

"To see me?"

The drooping head was thrown back with a pride that was haughty and almost scornful. A princess could not have treated a rash intruder more completely *de haut en bas*. "To me! what could you have to say to me?" the girl seemed to say, in the tremendous superiority of her sixteen years.

The young man laughed a little—one is not very wise at five and twenty on the subject of girls, yet he had experience enough to be amused by these remnants of the child in this half-developed maiden. "You are going this way?" he said, turning in the direction in which she had been going. "Then let me tell you while we walk. Miss Dora, you must remember this is not all presumption or intrusion on my side. I come from a lady who has a right to send you a message."

"I did not say you were intrusive," cried Dora, blushing for shame.

"You only looked it," said young Gordon; "but you know that lady is my aunt too—at least, I have always called her aunt, for many, many years."

"Ought I to call her aunt?" Dora said. "I suppose so indeed, if she is my mother's sister."

"Certainly you should, and you have a right; but I only because she allows me, because they wished it, to make me feel no stranger in the house. My poor dear aunt is very ill—worse, they say, than she has ever been before."

"Ill?" Dora seemed to find no words except these interjections that she could say.

"I hope perhaps they may be deceived. The doctors don't know her constitution. I think I have seen her just as bad and come quite round again. But even Miller is frightened: she may be worse than I think, and she has the greatest, the most anxious desire to see you, as she says, before she dies."

"Dies?" cried Dora. "But how can she die when she has only just come home?"

"That is what I feel, too," cried the young man, with eagerness. "But perhaps," he added, "it is no real reason; for doesn't it often happen that people break down just at the moment when they come in sight of what they have wished for for years and years?"

"I don't know," said Dora, recovering her courage. "I have not heard of things so dreadful as that. I can't imagine that it could be permitted to be; for things don't happen just by chance, do they? They are," she added quite inconclusively, "as father says, all in the day's work."

"I don't know either," said young Gordon; "but very cruel things do happen. However, there is nothing in the world she wishes for so much as you. Will you come to her? I am sure that you have never been out of her mind for years. She used to talk to me about you. It was our secret between us two. I think that was the chief thing that made her take to me as she did, that she might have some one to speak to about Dora. I used to wonder what you were at first,—an idol, or a prodigy, or a princess."

"You must have been rather disgusted when you found I was only a girl," Dora cried, in spite of herself.

He looked at her with a discriminative gaze, not uncritical, yet full of warm light that seemed to linger and brighten somehow upon her, and which, though Dora was looking straight before her, without a glance to the right or left, or any possibility of catching his eye, she perceived, though without knowing how.

"No," he said, with a little embarrassed laugh, "quite the reverse, and always hoping that one day we might be friends."

Dora made no reply. For one thing they had now come (somehow the walk went much faster, much more easily, when there was no big book to carry) to the passage leading to Holborn, a narrow lane paved with big flags, and with dull shops, principally book-shops, on either side, where Fiddler, the eminent old bookseller and collector, lived. Her mind had begun to be occupied by the question how to shake this young man off and discharge her commission, which was not an easy one. She hardly heard what he last said. She said to him hastily, "Please give me back the book, this is where I am going," holding out her hands for it. She added, "Thank you very much," with formality, but yet not without warmth.

"Mayn't I carry it in?" He saw by her face that this request was distasteful, and hastened to add, "I'll wait for you outside; there are quantities of books to look at in the windows," giving it back to her without a word.

Dora was scarcely old enough to appreciate the courtesy and good taste of his action altogether, but she was pleased and relieved, though she hardly knew why. She went into the shop, very glad to deposit it upon the counter, but rather troubled in mind as to how she was to accomplish her mission, as she waited till Mr. Fiddler was brought to her from the depths of the cavern of books. He began to turn over the book with mechanical interest, thinking it something brought to him to sell, then woke up, and said sharply: "Why, this is a book I sent to Mr. Mannering of the Museum a month ago".

"Yes," said Dora, breathless, "and I am Mr. Mannering's daughter. He has been very ill, and he wishes me to ask if you would be so good as to take it back. It is not likely to be of so much use to him as he thought. It is not quite what he expected it to be."

"Not what he expected it to be? It is an extremely fine copy, in perfect condition, and I've been on the outlook for it to him for the past year."

"Yes, indeed," said Dora, speaking like a bookman's daughter, "even I can see it is a fine example, and my father would like to keep it. But—but—he has had a long illness, and it has been very expensive, and he might not be able to pay for it for a long time. He would be glad if you would be so very obliging as to take it back."

Then Mr. Fiddler began to look blank. He told Dora that two or three people had been after the book, knowing what a chance it was to get a specimen of that edition in such a perfect state, and how he had shut his ears to all fascinations, and kept it for Mr. Mannering. Mr. Mannering had indeed ordered the book. It was not a book that could be picked up from any ordinary collection. It was one, as a matter of fact, which he himself would not have thought of buying on speculation, had it not been for a customer like Mr. Mannering. Probably it might lie for years on his hands, before he should have another opportunity of disposing of it. These arguments much intimidated Dora, who saw, but had not the courage to call his attention to, the discrepancy between the two or three people who had wanted it, and the unlikelihood of any one wanting it again.

The conclusion was, however, that Mr. Fiddler politely, but firmly, declined to take the book back. He had every confidence in Mr. Mannering of the Museum. He had not the slightest doubt of being paid. The smile, with which he assured her of this, compensated the girl, who was so little more than a child, for the refusal of her request. Of course Mr. Mannering of the Museum would pay, of course everybody had confidence in him. After her father's own depressed looks and anxiety, it comforted Dora's heart to make sure in this way that nobody outside shared these fears. She put out her arms, disappointed, yet relieved, to take back the big book again.

"Have you left it behind you?" cried young Gordon, who, lingering at the window outside, without the slightest sense of honour, had listened eagerly and heard a portion of the colloquy within.

"Mr. Fiddler will not take it back. He says papa will pay him sooner or later. He is going to send it. It is no matter," Dora said, with a little wave of her hand.

"Oh, let me carry it back," cried the young man, with a sudden dive into his pocket, and evident intention in some rude colonial way of solving the question of the payment there and then.

Dora drew herself up to the height of seven feet at least in her shoes. She waved him back from Mr. Fiddler's door with a large gesture.

"You may have known me for a long time," she said, "and you called me Dora, though I think it is a liberty; but I don't know you, not even your name."

"My name is Harry Gordon," he said, with something between amusement and deference, yet a twinkle in his eye.

Dora looked at him very gravely from head to foot, making as it were a *résumé* of him and the situation. Then she gave forth her judgment reflectively, as of a thing which she had much studied. "It is not an ugly name," she said, with a partially approving nod of her head.

CHAPTER XIV.

"No, Mannering," said Dr. Roland, "I can't say that you may go back to the Museum in a week. I don't know when you will be up to going. I should think you had a good right to a long holiday after working there for so many years."

"Not so many years," said Mr. Mannering, "since the long break which you know of, Roland."

"In the interest of science," cried the doctor.

The patient shook his head with a melancholy smile. "Not in my own at least," he said.

"Well, it is unnecessary to discuss that question. Back you cannot go, my good fellow, till you have recovered your strength to a very different point from that you are at now. You can't go till after you've had a change. At present you're nothing but a bundle of tendencies ready to develop into anything bad that's going. That must be stopped in the first place, and you must have sea air, or mountain air, or country air, whichever you fancy. I won't be dogmatic about the kind, but the thing you must have."

"Impossible, impossible, impossible!" Mannering had begun to cry out while the other was speaking. "Why, man, you're raving," he said. "I—so accustomed to the air of Bloomsbury, and that especially fine sort which is to be had at the Museum, that I couldn't breathe any other—I to have mountain air or sea air or country air! Nonsense! Any of them would stifle me in a couple of days."

"You will have your say, of course. And you are a great scientific gent, I'm aware; but you know as little about your own health and what it wants as this child with her message. Well, Janie, what is it, you constant bother? Mr. Mannering? Take it to Miss Bethune, or wait till Miss Dora comes back."

"Please, sir, the gentleman is waiting, and he says he won't go till he's pyed."

"You little ass!" said the doctor. "What do you mean by coming with your ridiculous stories here?"

Mannering stretched out his thin hand and took the paper. "You see," he said, with a faint laugh, "how right I was when I said I would have nothing to do with your changes of air. It is all that my pay will do to settle my bills, and no overplus for such vanities."

"Nonsense, Mannering! The money will be forthcoming when it is known to be necessary."

"From what quarter, I should be glad to hear? Do you think the Museum will grant me a premium for staying away, for being of no use? Not very likely! I shall not be left in the lurch; they will grant me three months' holiday, or even six months' holiday, and my salary as usual. But we shall have to reduce our expenses, Dora and I, and to live as quietly as possible, instead of going off like millionaires to revel upon fresh tipples of fancy air. No, no, nothing of the kind. And, besides, I don't believe in them. I have made myself, as the French say, to the air of Bloomsbury, and in that I shall live or die."

"You don't speak at all, my dear fellow, like the man of sense you are," said the doctor. "Fortunately, I can carry things with a high hand. When I open my mouth let no patient venture to contradict. You are going away to the country now. If you don't conform to my rules, I am not at all sure I may not go further, and ordain that there is to be no work for six months, a winter on the Riviera, and so forth. I have got all these pains and penalties in my hand."

"Better and better," said Mannering, "a palace to live in, and a *chef* to cook for us, and our dinner off gold plate every day."

"There is no telling what I may do if you put me to it," Dr. Roland said, with a laugh. "But seriously, if it were my last word, you must get out of London. Nothing that you can do or say will save you from that."

"We shall see," said Mr. Mannering. "The sovereign power of an empty purse does great wonders. But here is Dora back, and without the big book, I am glad to see. What did Fiddler say?"

"I will tell you afterwards, father," said Dora, developing suddenly a little proper pride.

"Nonsense! You can tell me now—that he had two or three people in his pocket who would have bought it willingly if he had not reserved it for me, and that it was a book that nobody wanted, and would be a drug on his hands."

"Oh, father, how clever you are! That was exactly what he said: and I did not point out that he was contradicting himself, for fear it should make him angry. But he did not mind me. He said he could trust Mr. Mannering of the Museum; he was quite sure he should get paid; and he is sending it back by one of the young men, because it was too heavy for me."

"My poor little girl! I ought to have known it would be too heavy for you."

"Oh, never mind," said Dora. "I only carried it half the way. It was getting very heavy indeed, I will not deny, when I met Mr. Gordon, and he carried it for me to Fiddler's shop."

"Who is Mr. Gordon?" said Mr. Mannering, raising his head.

"He is a friend of Miss Bethune's," said Dora, with something of hesitation in her voice which struck her father's ear.

Dr. Roland looked very straight before him, taking care to make no comment, and not to meet Dora's eye. There was a tacit understanding between them now on several subjects, which the invalid felt vaguely, but could not explain to himself. Fortunately, however, it had not even occurred to him that there was anything more remarkable in the fact of a young man, met at hazard, carrying Dora's book for her, than if the civility had been shown to himself.

"You see," he said, "it is painful to have to make you aware of all my indiscretions, Roland. What has a man to do with rare editions, who has a small income and an only child like mine? The only thing is," he added, with a short laugh, "they should bring their price when they come to the hammer,—that has always been my consolation."

"They are not coming to the hammer just yet," said the doctor. He possessed himself furtively, but carelessly, of the piece of paper on the table—the bill which, as Janie said, was wanted by a gentleman waiting downstairs. "You just manage to get over this thing, Mannering," he said, in an ingratiating tone, "and I'll promise you a long bill of health and plenty of time to make up all your lost way. You don't live in the same house with a doctor for nothing. I have been waiting for this for a long time. I could have told Vereker exactly what course it would take if he hadn't been an ass, as all these successful men are. He did take a hint or two in spite of himself; for a profession is too much for a man, it gives a certain fictitious sense in some cases, even when he is an ass. Well, Mannering, of course I couldn't prophesy what the end would be. You might have succumbed. With your habits, I thought it not unlikely."

"You cold-blooded practitioner! And what do you mean by my habits? I'm not a toper or a reveller by night."

"You are almost worse. You are a man of the Museum, drinking in bad air night and day, and never moving from your books when you can help it. It was ten to one against you; but some of you smoke-dried, gas-scented fellows have the devil's own constitution, and you've pulled through."

"Yes," said Mannering, holding up his thin hand to the light, and thrusting forth a long spindle-shank of a leg, "I've pulled through—as much as is left of me. It isn't a great deal to brag of."

"Having done that, with proper care I don't see why you shouldn't have a long spell of health before you—as much health as a man can expect who despises all the laws of nature—and attain a very respectable age before you die."

"Here's promises!" said Mannering. He paused and laughed, and then added in a lower tone: "Do you think that's so very desirable, after all?"

"Most men like it," said the doctor; "or, at least, think they do.

And for you, who have Dora to think of——"

"Yes, there's Dora," the patient said as if to himself.

"That being the case, you are not your own property, don't you see? You have got to take care of yourself, whether you will or not. You have got to make life livable, now that it's handed back to you. It's a responsibility, like another. Having had it handed back to you, as I say, and being comparatively a young man— what are you, fifty?"

"Thereabout; not what you would call the flower of youth."

"But a very practical, not disagreeable age—good for a great deal yet, if you treat it fairly; but, mind you, capable of giving you a great deal of annoyance, a great deal of trouble, if you don't."

"No more before the child," said Mannering hastily. "We must cut our coat according to our cloth, but she need not be in all our secrets. What! turtle-soup again? Am I to be made an alderman of in spite of myself? No more of this, Hal, if you love me," he said, shaking his gaunt head at the doctor, who was already disappearing downstairs.

Dr. Roland turned back to nod encouragingly to Dora, and to say: "All right, my dear; keep it up!" But his countenance changed as he turned away again, and when he had knocked and been admitted at Miss Bethune's door, it was with a melancholy face, and a look of the greatest despondency, that he flung himself into the nearest chair.

"It will be all of no use," he cried,—"of no use, if we can't manage means and possibilities to pack them off somewhere. He will not hear of it! Wants to go back to the Museum next week— in July!—and to go on in Bloomsbury all the year, as if he had not been within a straw's breadth of his life."

"I was afraid of that," said Miss Bethune, shaking her head.

"He ought to go to the country now," said the doctor, "then to the sea, and before the coming on of winter go abroad. That's the only programme for him. He ought to be a year away. Then he might come back to the Museum like a giant refreshed, and probably write some book, or make some discovery, or do some scientific business, that would crown him with glory, and cover all the expenses; but the obstinate beast will not see it. Upon my word!" cried Dr. Roland, "I wish there could be made a decree that only women should have the big illnesses; they have such faith in a doctor's word, and such a scorn of possibilities: it always does them good to order them something that can't be done, and then do it in face of everything—that's what I should like for the good of the race."

"I can't say much for the good of the race," said Miss Bethune; "but you'd easily find some poor wretch of a woman that would do it for the sake of some ungrateful brute of a man."

"Ah, we haven't come to that yet," said the doctor regretfully; "the vicarious principle has not gone so far. If it had I daresay there would be plenty of poor wretches ready to bear their neighbours' woes for a consideration. The simple rules of supply and demand would be enough to provide us proxies without any stronger sentiment: but philosophising won't do us any good; it won't coin money, or if it could, would not drop it into his pocket, which after all is the chief difficulty. He is not to be taken in any longer by your fictions about friendly offerings and cheap purchases. Here is a bill which that little anæmic nuisance Janie brought in, with word that a gentleman was 'wyaiting' for the payment."

"We'll send for the gentleman, and settle it," said Miss Bethune quietly, "and then it can't come up to shame us again."

The gentleman sent for turned up slowly, and came in with reluctance, keeping his face as much as possible averted. He was, however, too easily recognisable to make this contrivance available.

"Why, Hesketh, have you taken service with Fortnum and Mason?" the doctor cried.

"I'm in a trade protection office, sir," said Hesketh. "I collect bills for parties." He spoke with his eyes fixed on a distant corner, avoiding as much as possible every glance.

"In a trade protection office? And you mean to tell me that

Fortnum and Mason, before even the season is over, collect their bills in this way?"

"They don't have not to say so many customers in Bloomsbury, sir," said the young man, with that quickly-conceived impudence which is so powerful a weapon, and so congenial to his race.

"Confound their insolence! I have a good mind to go myself and give them a bit of my mind," cried Dr. Roland. "Bloomsbury has more sense, it seems, than I gave it credit for, and your pampered tradesman more impudence."

"I would just do that," said Miss Bethune. "And will it be long since you took to this trade protection, young man?—for Gilchrist brought me word you were ill in your bed not a week ago."

"A man can't stay in bed, when 'e has a wife to support, and with no 'ealth to speak of," Hesketh replied, with a little bravado; but he was very pale, and wiped the unwholesome dews from his forehead.

"Anæmia, body and soul," said the doctor to the lady, in an undertone.

"You'll come to his grandfather again in a moment," said the lady to the doctor. "Now, my lad, you shall just listen to me. Put down this moment your trade protections, and all your devices. Did you not hear, by Gilchrist, that we were meaning to give you a new chance? Not for your sake, but for your wife's, though she probably is just tarred with the same stick. We were meaning to set you up in a little shop in a quiet suburb."

Here the young fellow made a grimace, but recollected himself, and said no word.

"Eh!" cried Miss Bethune, "that wouldn't serve your purposes, my fine gentleman?"

"I never said so," said the young man. "It's awfully kind of you. Still, as I've got a place on my own hook, as it were—not that we mightn't combine the two, my wife and I. She ain't a bad saleswoman," he added, with condescension. "We was in the same house of business before we was married—not that beastly old shop where they do nothing but take away the young gentlemen's and young ladies' characters. It's as true as life what I say. Ask any one that has ever been there."

"Anæmia," said Miss Bethune, to the doctor, aside, "would not be proof enough, if there were facts on the other hand."

"I always mistrust facts," the doctor replied.

"Here is your money," she resumed. "Write me out the receipt, or rather, put your name to it. Now mind this, I will help you if you're meaning to do well; but if I find out anything wrong in this, or hear that you're in bed again to-morrow, and not fit to lift your head——"

"No man can answer for his health," said young Hesketh solemnly. "I may be bad, I may be dead to-morrow, for anything I can tell."

"That is true."

"And my poor wife a widder, and the poor baby not born."

"In these circumstances," said Dr. Roland, "we'll forgive her for what wasn't her fault, and look after her. But that's not likely, unless you are fool enough to let yourself be run over, or something of that sort, going out from here."

"Which I won't, sir, if I can help it."

"And no great loss, either," the doctor said in his undertone. He watched the payment grimly, and noticed that the young man's hand shook in signing the receipt. What was the meaning of it? He sat for a moment in silence, while Hesketh's steps, quickening as he went farther off, were heard going downstairs and towards the door. "I wish I were as sure that money would find its way to the pockets of Fortnum and Mason, as I am that yonder down-looking hound had a criminal grandfather," he said.

"Well, there is the receipt, anyhow. Will you go and inquire?"

"To what good? There would be a great fuss, and the young fool would get into prison probably; whereas we may still hope that it is all right, and that he has turned over a new leaf."

"I should not be content without being at the bottom of it," said Miss Bethune; and then, after a pause: "There is another thing. The lady from South America that was here has been taken ill, Dr. Roland."

"Ah, so!" cried the doctor. "I should like to go and see her."

"You are not wanted to go and see her. It is I—which you will be surprised at—that is wanted, or, rather, Dora with me. I have had an anxious pleader here, imploring me by all that I hold dear. You will say that is not much, doctor."

"I will say nothing of the kind. But I have little confidence in that lady from South America, or her young man."

"The young man is just as fine a young fellow! Doubt as you like, there is no deceit about him; a countenance like the day, and eyes that meet you fair, look at him as you please. Doctor," said Miss Bethune, faltering a little, "I have taken a great notion into my head that he may turn out to be a near relation of my own."

"A relation of yours?" cried Dr. Roland, suppressing a whistle of astonishment. "My thoughts were going a very different way."

"I know, and your thoughts are justified. The lady did not conceal that she was Mrs. Mannering's sister: but the one thing does not hinder the other."

"It would be a very curious coincidence—stranger, even, than usual."

"Everything that's strange is usual," cried Miss Bethune vehemently. "It is we that have no eyes to see."

"Perhaps," said the doctor, who loved a paradox. "I tell you what," he added briskly, "let me go and see this lady. I am very suspicious about her. I should like to make her out a little before risking it for Dora, even with you."

"You think, perhaps, you would make it out better than I should," said Miss Bethune, with some scorn. "Well, there is no saying. You would, no doubt, make out what is the matter with her, which is always the first thing that interests you."

"It explains most things, when you know how to read it," the doctor said; but in this point his opponent did not give in to him, it is hardly necessary to say. She was very much interested about Dora, but she was still more interested in the question which moved her own heart so deeply. The lady from South America might be in command of many facts on that point; and prudence seemed to argue that it was best to see and understand a little more about her first, before taking Dora, without her father's knowledge, to a stranger who made such a claim upon her.

"Though if it is her mother's sister, I don't know who could have a stronger claim upon her," said Miss Bethune.

"Provided her mother had a sister," the doctor said.

CHAPTER XV.

Miss Bethune set out accordingly, without saying anything further, to see the invalid. She took nobody into her confidence, not even Gilchrist, who had much offended her mistress by her scepticism. Much as she was interested in every unusual chain of circumstances, and much more still in anything happening to Dora Mannering, there was a still stronger impulse of personal feeling in her present expedition. It had gone to her head like wine; her eyes shone, and there was a nervous energy in every line of her tall figure in its middle-aged boniness and hardness. She walked quickly, pushing her way forward when there was any crowd with an unconscious movement, as of a strong swimmer dividing the waves. Her mind was tracing out every line of the supposed process of events known to herself alone. It was her own story, and such a strange one as occurs seldom in the almost endless variety of strange stories that are about the world—a story of secret marriage, secret birth, and sudden overwhelming calamity. She had as a young woman given herself foolishly and hastily to an adventurer: for she was an heiress, if she continued to please an old uncle who had her fate in his hands. The news of the unexpected approach of this old man brought the sudden crisis. The husband, who had been near her in the profound quiet of the country, fled, taking with him the child, and after that no more. The marriage was altogether unknown, except to Gilchrist, and a couple of old servants in the small secluded country-house where the strange little tragedy had taken place; and the young wife, who had never borne her husband's name, came to life again after a long illness, to find every trace of her piteous story, and of the fate of the man for whom she had risked so much, and the child whom she had scarcely seen, obliterated.

The agony through which she had lived in that first period of dismay and despair, the wild secret inquiries set on foot with so little knowledge of how to do anything of the kind, chiefly by means of the good and devoted Gilchrist, who, however, knew still less even than her mistress the way to do it—the long, monotonous years of living with the old uncle to whom that forlorn young woman in her secret anguish had to be nurse and companion; the dreadful freedom afterwards, when the fortune was hers, and the liberty so long desired—but still no clue, no knowledge whether the child on whom she had set her passionate heart existed or not. The hero, the husband, existed no longer in her imagination. That first year of furtive fatal intercourse had revealed him in his true colours as an adventurer, whose aim had been her fortune. But why had he not revealed himself when that fortune was secure? Why had he not brought back the child who would have secured his hold over her whatever had happened? These questions had been discussed between Miss Bethune and her maid, till there was no longer any contingency, any combination of things or theories possible, which had not been torn to pieces between them, with reasonings sometimes as acute as mother's wit could make them, sometimes as foolish as ignorance and inexperience suggested.

They had roamed all over the world in an anxious quest after the fugitives who had disappeared so completely into the darkness. What wind drifted them to Bloomsbury it would be too long to inquire. The wife of one furtive and troubled year, the mother of one anxious but heavenly week, had long, long ago settled into the angular, middle-aged unmarried lady of Mrs. Simcox's first floor. She had dropped all her former friends, all the people who knew about her. And those people who once knew her by her Christian name, and as they thought every incident in her life, in reality knew nothing, not a syllable of the brief romance and tragedy which formed its centre. She had developed, they all thought, into one of those eccentrics who are so often to be found in the loneliness of solitary life, odd as were all the Bethunes, with something added that was especially her own. By intervals an old friend would appear to visit her, marvelling much at the London lodging in which the mistress of more than one old comfortable house had chosen to bury herself. But the Bethunes were all queer, these visitors said; there was a bee in their bonnet, there was a screw loose somewhere. It is astonishing the number of Scotch families of whom this is said to account for everything their descendants may think or do.

This was the woman who marched along the hot July streets with the same vibration of impulse and energy which had on several occasions led her half over the world. She had been disappointed a thousand times, but never given up hope; and each new will-o'-the-wisp which had led her astray had been welcomed with the same strong confidence, the same ever-living hope. Few of them, she acknowledged to herself now, had possessed half the likelihood of this; and every new point of certitude grew and expanded within her as she proceeded on her way. The same age, the same name (more or less), a likeness which Gilchrist, fool that she was, would not see; and then the story, proving everything of the mother who was alive but unknown.

Could anything be more certain? Miss Bethune's progress through the streets was more like that of a bird on the wing, with that floating movement which is so full at once of strength and of repose, and wings ever ready for a swift *coup* to increase the impulse and clear the way, than of a pedestrian walking along a hot pavement. A strange coincidence! Yes, it would be a very strange coincidence if her own very unusual story and that of the poor Mannerings should thus be twined together. But why should it not be so? Truth is stranger than fiction. The most marvellous combinations happen every day. The stranger things are, the more likely they are to happen. This was what she kept saying to herself as she hurried upon her way.

She was received in the darkened room, in the hot atmosphere perfumed and damped by the spray of some essence, where at first Miss Bethune felt she could scarcely breathe. When she was brought in, in the gleam of light made by the opened door, there was a little scream of eagerness from the bed at the other end of the long room, and then a cry: "But Dora? Where is Dora? It is Dora, Dora, I want!" in a voice of disappointment and irritation close to tears.

"You must not be vexed that I came first by myself," Miss Bethune said. "To bring Dora without her father's knowledge is a strong step."

"But I have a right—I have a right!" cried the sick woman. "Nobody—not even he—could deny me a sight of her. I've hungered for years for a sight of her, and now that I am free I am going to die."

"No, no! don't say that," said Miss Bethune, with the natural instinct of denying that conclusion. "You must not let your heart go down, for that is the worst of all."

"It is perhaps the best, too," said the patient. "What could I have done? Always longing for her, never able to have her except by stealth, frightened always that she would find out, or that he should find out. Oh, no, it's better as it is. Now I can provide for my dear, and nobody to say a word. Now I can show her how I love her. And she will not judge me. A child like that doesn't judge. She will learn to pity her poor, poor —— Oh, why didn't you bring me my Dora? I may not live another day."

In the darkness, to which her eyes gradually became accustomed, Miss Bethune consulted silently with a look the attendant by the bed; and receiving from her the slight, scarcely distinguishable, answer of a shake of the head, took the sufferer's hand, and pressed it in her own.

"I will bring her," she said, "to-night, if you wish it, or to-morrow. I give you my word. If you think of yourself like that, whether you are right or not, I am not the one to disappoint you. To-night, if you wish it."

"Oh, to-night, to-night! I'll surely live till to-night," the poor woman cried.

"And many nights more, if you will only keep quite quiet,

ma'am. It depends upon yourself," said the maid.

"They always tell you," said Mrs. Bristow, "to keep quiet, as if that was the easiest thing to do. I might get up and walk all the long way to see my child; but to be quiet without her—that is what is impossible—and knowing that perhaps I may never see her again!"

"You shall—you shall," said Miss Bethune soothingly. "But you have a child, and a good child—a son, or as like a son as possible."

"I a son? Oh, no, no—none but Dora! No one I love but Dora." The poor lady paused then with a sob, and said in a changed voice: "You mean Harry Gordon? Oh, it is easy to see you are not a mother. He is very good—oh, very good. He was adopted by Mr. Bristow. Oh," she cried, with a long crying breath, "Mr. Bristow ought to have done something for Harry. He ought to—I always said so. I did not want to have everything left to me."

She wrung her thin hands, and a convulsive sob came out of the darkness.

"Ma'am," said the maid, "I must send this lady away, and put a stop to everything, if you get agitated like this."

"I'll be quite calm, Miller—quite calm," the patient cried, putting out her hand and clutching Miss Bethune's dress.

"To keep her calm I will talk to her of this other subject," said Miss Bethune, with an injured tone in her voice. She held her head high, elevating her spare figure, as if in disdain. "Let us forget Dora for the moment," she said, "and speak of this young man that has only been a son to you for the most of his life, only given you his affection and his services and everything a child could do—but is nothing, of course, in comparison with a little girl you know nothing about, who is your niece in blood."

"Oh, my niece, my niece!" the poor lady murmured under her breath.

"Tell me something about this Harry Gordon; it will let your mind down from the more exciting subject," said Miss Bethune, still with great dignity, as if of an offended person. "He has lived with you for years. He has shared your secrets."

"I have talked to him about Dora," she faltered.

"But yet," said the stern questioner, more and more severely, "it does not seem you have cared anything about him all these years?"

"Oh, don't say that! I have always been fond of him, always—always! He will never say I have not been kind to him," the invalid cried.

"Kind?" cried Miss Bethune, with an indignation and scorn which nothing could exceed. Then she added more gently, but with still the injured tone in her voice: "Will you tell me something about him? It will calm you down. I take an interest in the young man. He is like somebody I once knew, and his name recalls——"

"Perhaps you knew his father?" said Mrs. Bristow.

"Perhaps. I would like to hear more particulars. He tells me his mother is living."

"The father was very foolish to tell him. Mr. Bristow always said so. It was on his deathbed. I suppose," cried the poor lady, with a deep sigh, "that on your deathbed you feel that you must tell everything. Oh, I've been silent, silent, so long! I feel that too. She is not a mother that it would ever be good for him to find. Mr. Bristow wished him never to come back to England, only for that. He said better be ignorant—better know nothing."

"And why was the poor mother so easily condemned?"

"You would be shocked—you an unmarried lady—if I told you the story. She left him just after the boy was born. She fell from one degradation to another. He sent her money as long as he could keep any trace of her. Poor, poor man!"

"And his friends took everything for gospel that this man said?"

"He was an honest man. Why should he tell Mr. Bristow a lie? I said it was to be kept from poor Harry. It would only make him miserable. But there was no doubt about the truth of it—oh, none."

"I tell you," cried Miss Bethune, "that there is every doubt of it. His mother was a poor deceived girl, that was abandoned, deserted, left to bear her misery as she could."

"Did you know his mother?" said the patient, showing out of the darkness the gleam of eyes widened by astonishment.

"It does not matter," cried Miss Bethune. "I know this, that the marriage was in secret, and the boy was born in secret; and while she was ill and weak there came the news of some one coming that might leave her penniless; and for the sake of the money, the wretched money, this man took the child up in his arms out of her very bed, and carried it away."

The sick woman clutched the arm of the other, who sat by her side, tragic and passionate, the words coming from her lips like sobs. "Oh, my poor lady," she said, "if that is your story! But it was not that. My husband, Mr. Bristow, knew. He knew all about Gordon from the beginning. It was no secret to him. He did not take the child away till the mother had gone, till he had tried every way to find her, even to bring her back. He was a merciful man. I knew him too. Oh, poor woman, poor woman, my heart breaks for that other you knew. She is like me, she is worse off than me: but the one you know was not Harry's mother—oh, no, no—Harry's mother! If she is living it is—it is—in misery, and worse than misery."

"He said," uttered a hoarse voice, breathless, out of the dimness, which nobody could have recognised for Miss Bethune's, "that you said there was no such woman."

"I did—to comfort him, to make him believe that it was not true."

"By a lie! And such a lie—a shameful lie, when you knew so different! And how should any one believe now a word you say?"

"Oh, don't let her say such things to me, Miller, Miller!" cried the patient, with the cry of a sick child.

"Madam," said the maid, "she's very bad, as you see, and you're making her every minute worse. You can see it yourself. It's my duty to ask you to go away."

Miss Bethune rose from the side of the bed like a ghost, tall and stern, and towering over the agitated, weeping woman who lay back on the white pillows, holding out supplicating hands and panting for breath. She stood for a moment looking as if she would have taken her by the throat. Then she gave herself a little shake, and turned away.

Once more the invalid clutched at her dress and drew her back. "Oh," she cried, "have mercy upon me! Don't go away—don't go away! I will bear anything. Say what you like, but bring me Dora—bring me Dora—before I die."

"Why should I bring you Dora? Me to whom nobody brings—— What is it to me if you live or if you die?"

"Oh, bring me Dora—bring me Dora!" the poor woman wailed, holding fast by her visitor's dress. She flung herself half out of the bed, drawing towards her with all her little force the unwilling, resisting figure. "Oh, for the sake of all you wish for yourself, bring me Dora—Dora—before I die!"

"What have you left me to wish for?" cried the other woman; and she drew her skirts out of the patient's grasp.

No more different being from her who had entered an hour before by the long passages and staircases of the great hotel could have been than she who now repassed through them, looking neither to the right nor to the left—a woman like a straight line of motion and energy, as strong and stiff as iron, with expression banished from her face, and elasticity from her figure. She went back by the same streets she had come by, making her way straight through the crowd, which seemed to yield before the strength of passion and pain that was in her. There was a singing in her ears, and a buzzing in her head, and her heart was in her breast as if it had been turned to stone. Oh, she was not at her first shock of disappointment and despair. She had experienced it before; but never, she thought, in such terrible sort as now. She had so wrapped herself in this dream, which had been suggested to her by nothing but her own heart, what she thought her instinct, a sudden flash of divination, the voice of nature. She had felt sure of it the first glimpse she had of him, before he had even told her his name. She had been sure that this time it was the voice of nature, that intuition of a mother which could not be deceived. So many likenesses seemed to meet in Harry Gordon's face, so many circumstances to combine in establishing the likelihood, at least, that this was he. South America, the very ideal place for an adventurer, and the strange fact that he had a mother living whom he did not know. A mother living! These words made a thrill of passion, of opposition, of unmoved and immovable conviction, rush through all her veins. A mother living! Who could that be but she? What would such a man care—a man who had abandoned his wife at the moment of a woman's greatest weakness, and taken her child from her when she was helpless to resist him—for the ruin of her reputation after, for fixing upon her, among those who knew her not, the character of a profligate? He who had done the first, why should he hesitate to say the last? The one thing cost him trouble, the other none. It was easier to believe that than to give up what she concluded with certainty was her last hope.

Gilchrist, who had seen her coming, rushed downstairs to open the door for her. But Gilchrist, at this moment, was an enemy, the last person in the world in whom her mistress would confide; Gilchrist, who had never believed in it, had refused to see the likeness, or to encourage any delusion. She was blind to the woman's imploring looks, her breathless "Oh, mem!" which was more than any question, and brushed past her with the same iron rigidity of pose, which had taken all softness from her natural angularity. She walked straight into her bedroom, where she took off her bonnet before the glass, without awaiting Gilchrist's ministrations, nay, putting them aside with a quick impatient gesture. Then she went to her sitting-room, and drew her chair into her favourite position near the window, and took up the paper and began to read it with every appearance of intense interest. She had read it through every word, as is the practice of lonely ladies, before she went out: and she was profoundly conscious now of Gilchrist following her about, hovering behind her, and more anxious than words can say. Miss Bethune was an hour or more occupied about that newspaper, of which she did not see a single word, and then she rose suddenly to her feet.

"I cannot do it—I cannot do it!" she cried. "The woman has no claim on me. Most likely she's nothing but a fool, that has spoilt everything for herself, and more. Maybe it will not be good for Dora. But I cannot do it—I cannot do it. It's too strong for me. Whatever comes of it, she must see her child—she must see her child before she passes away and is no more seen. And oh, I wish—I wish that it was not her, but me!"

CHAPTER XVI.

Dora passed the long evening of that day in her father's room. It was one of those days in which the sun seems to refuse to set, the daylight to depart. It rolled out in afternoon sunshine, prolonged as it seemed for half a year's time, showing no inclination to wane. When the sun at last went down, there ensued a long interval of day without it, and slowly, slowly, the shades of twilight came on. Mr. Mannering had been very quiet all the afternoon. He had sat brooding, unwilling to speak. The big book came back with Mr. Fiddler's compliments, and was replaced upon his table, where he sat sometimes turning over the pages, not reading, doing nothing. There are few things more terrible to a looker-on than this silence, this self-absorption, taking no notice of anything outside of him, of a convalescent. The attitude of despondency, the bowed head, the curved shoulders, are bad enough in themselves: but nothing is so dreadful as the silence, the preoccupation with nothing, the eyes fixed on a page which is not read, or a horizon in which nothing is visible. Dora sat by him with a book, too, in which she was interested, which is perhaps the easiest way of bearing this; but the book ended before the afternoon did, and then she had nothing to do but to watch him and wonder what he was thinking of—whether his mind was roving over lands unknown to her, whether it was about the Museum he was thinking, or the doctor's orders, or the bills, two or three of which had by misadventure fallen into his hands. What was it? He remained in the same attitude, quite still and steady, not moving a finger. Sometimes she hoped he might have fallen asleep; sometimes she addressed to him a faltering question, to which he answered Yes or No. He was not impatient when she spoke to him. He replied to her in monosyllables, which are almost worse than silence. And Dora durst not protest, could not upbraid him with that dreadful silence, as an older person might have done. "Oh, father, talk to me a little!" she once cried in her despair; but he said gently that he had nothing to talk about, and silenced the girl. He had taken the various meals and refreshments that were ordered for him, when they came, with something that was half a smile and half a look of disgust; and this was the final exasperation to Dora.

"Oh, father! when you know that you must take it—that it is the only way of getting well again."

"I am taking it," he said, with that twist of the lip at every spoonful which betrayed how distasteful it was.

This is hard to bear for the most experienced of nurses, and what should it be for a girl of sixteen? She clasped her hands together in her impatience to keep herself down. And then there came a knock at the door, and Gilchrist appeared, begging that Miss Dora would put on her hat and go out for a walk with Miss Bethune.

"I'll come and sit with my work in a corner, and be there if he wants anything."

Mr. Mannering did not seem to take any notice, but he heard the whisper at the door.

"There is no occasion for any one sitting with me. I am quite able to ring if I want anything."

"But, father, I don't want to go out," said Dora.

"I want you to go out," he said peremptorily. "It is not proper that you should be shut up here all day."

"Let me light the candles, then, father?"

"I don't want any candles. I am not doing anything. There is plenty of light for what I want."

Oh, what despair it was to have to do with a man who would not be shaken, who would take his own way and no other! If he would but have read a novel, as Dora did—if he would but return to the study of his big book, which was the custom of his life. Dora felt that it was almost wicked to leave him: but what could she do, while he sat there absorbed in his thoughts, which she could not even divine what they were about?

To go out into the cool evening was a relief to her poor little exasperated temper and troubled mind. The air was sweet and fresh, even in Bloomsbury; the trees waved and rustled softly against the blue sky; there was a young moon somewhere, a white speck in the blue, though the light of day was not yet gone; the voices were softened and almost musical in the evening air, and it was so good to be out of doors, to be removed from the close controlling atmosphere of unaccustomed trouble. "Out of sight, out of mind," people say. It was very far from being that; on the contrary, it was but the natural impatience, the mere contrariety, that had made the girl ready to cry with a sense of the intolerable which now was softened and subdued, allowing love and pity to come back. She could talk of nothing but her father as she went along the street.

"Do you think he looks any better, Miss Bethune? Do you think he will soon be able to get out? Do you think the doctor will let him return soon to the Museum? He loves the Museum better than anything. He would have more chance to get well if he might go back."

"All that must be decided by time, Dora—time and the doctor, who, though we scoff at him sometimes, knows better, after all, than you or me. But I want you to think a little of the poor lady you are going to see."

"What am I going to see? Oh, that lady? I don't know if father will wish me to see her. Oh, I did not know what it was you wanted of me. I cannot go against father, Miss Bethune, when he is ill and does not know."

"You will just trust to another than your father for once in your life, Dora. If you think I am not a friend to your father, and one that would consider him in all things——"

The girl walked on silently, reluctantly, for some time without speaking, with sometimes a half pause, as if she would have turned back. Then she answered in a low voice, still not very willingly: "I know you are a friend".

"You do not put much heart in it," said Miss Bethune, with a laugh. The most magnanimous person, when conscious of having been very helpful and a truly good friend at his or her personal expense to another, may be pardoned a sense of humour, partially bitter, in the grudging acknowledgment of ignorance. Then she added more gravely: "When your father knows—and he shall know in time—where I am taking you, he will approve; whatever his feelings may be, he will tell you it was right and your duty: of that I am as sure as that I am living, Dora."

"Because she is my aunt? An aunt is not such a very tender relation, Miss Bethune. In books they are often very cold comforters, not kind to girls that are poor. I suppose," said Dora, after a little pause, "that I would be called poor?"

"You are just nothing, you foolish little thing! You have no character of your own; you are your father's daughter, and no more."

"I don't wish to be anything more," cried Dora, with her foolish young head held high.

"And this poor woman," said Miss Bethune, exasperated, "will not live long enough to be a friend to any one—so you need not be afraid either of her being too tender or unkind. She has come back, poor thing, after long years spent out of her own country, to die."

"To die?" the girl echoed in a horrified tone.

"Just that, and nothing less or more."

Dora walked on by Miss Bethune's side for some time in silence. There was a long, very long walk through the streets before they reached the coolness and freshness of the Park. She said nothing for a long time, until they had arrived at the Serpentine, which— veiled in shadows and mists of night, with the stars reflected in it, and the big buildings in the distance standing up solemnly, half seen, yet with gleams of lamps and light all over them, beyond, and apparently among the trees—has a sort of splendour and reality, like a great natural river flowing between its banks. She paused there for a moment, and asked, with a quick drawing of her breath: "Is it some one—who is dying—that you are taking me to see?"

"Yes, Dora; and next to your father, your nearest relation in the world."

"I thought at one time that he was going to die, Miss Bethune."

"So did we all, Dora."

"And I was very much afraid—oh, not only heartbroken, but afraid. I thought he would suffer so, in himself," she said very low, "and to leave me."

"They do not," said Miss Bethune with great solemnity, as if not of any individual, but of a mysterious class of people. "They are delivered; anxious though they may have been, they are anxious no more; though their hearts would have broken to part with you a little while before, it is no longer so; they are delivered. It's a very solemn thing," she went on, with something like a sob in her voice; "but it's comforting, at least to the like of me. Their spirits are changed, they are separated; there are other things before them greater than what they leave behind."

"Oh," cried the girl, "I should not like to think of that: if father had ceased to think of me even before——"

"It is comforting to me," said Miss Bethune, "because I am of those that are going, and you, Dora, are of those that are staying. I'm glad to think that the silver chain will be loosed and the golden bowl broken—all the links that bind us to the earth, and all the cares about what is to happen after."

"Have you cares about what is to happen after?" cried Dora, "Father has, for he has me; but you, Miss Bethune?"

Dora never forgot, or thought she would never forget, the look that was cast upon her. "And I," said Miss Bethune, "have not even you, have nobody belonging to me. Well," she said, going on with a heavy long-drawn breath, "it looks as if it were true."

This was the girl's first discovery of what youth is generally so long in finding out, that in her heedlessness and unconscious conviction that what related to herself was the most important in the world, and what befel an elderly neighbour of so much less consequence, she had done, or at least said, a cruel thing. But she did not know how to mend matters, and so went on by her friend's side dumb, confusedly trying to enter into, now that it was too late, the sombre complications of another's thought. Nothing morewas said till they were close to the great hotel, which shone out with its many windows luminous upon the soft background of the night. Then Miss Bethune put her hand almost harshly upon Dora's arm.

"You will remember, Dora," she said, "that the person we are going to see is a dying person, and in all the world it is agreed that where a dying person is he or she is the chief person, and to be considered above all. It is, maybe, a superstition, but it is so allowed. Their wants and their wishes go before all; and the queen herself, if she were coming into that chamber, would bow to it like all the rest: and so must you. It is, perhaps, not quite sincere, for why should a woman be more thought of because she is going to die? That is not a quality, you will say: but yet it's a superstition, and approved of by all the civilised world."

"Oh, Miss Bethune," cried Dora, "I know that I deserve that you should say this to me: but yet——"

Her companion made no reply, but led the way up the great stairs.

The room was not so dark as before, though it was night; a number of candles were shining in the farther corner near the bed, and the pale face on the pillow, the nostrils dark and widely opened with the panting breath, was in full light, turned towards the door. A nurse in her white apron and cap was near the bed, beside a maid whose anxious face was strangely contrasted with the calm of the professional person. These accessories Dora's quick glance took in at once, while yet her attention was absorbed in the central figure, which she needed no further explanation to perceive had at once become the first object, the chief interest, to all near her. Dying! It was more than mere reigning, more than being great. To think that where she lay there she was going fast away into the most august presence, to the deepest wonders! Dora held her breath with awe. She never, save when her father was swimming for his life, and her thoughts were concentrated on the struggle with all the force of personal passion, as if it were she herself who was fighting against death, had seen any such sight before.

"Is it Dora?" cried the patient. "Dora! Oh, my child, my child, have you come at last?"

And then Dora found arms round her clutching her close, and felt with a strange awe, not unmingled with terror, the wild beating of a feverish heart, and the panting of a laborious breath. The wan face was pressed against hers. She felt herself held for a moment with extraordinary force, and kisses, tears, and always the beat of that troubled breathing, upon her cheek. Then the grasp relaxed reluctantly, because the sufferer could do no more.

"Oh, gently, gently; do not wear yourself out. She is not going away. She has come to stay with you," a soothing voice said.

"That's all I want—all I want in this world—what I came for," gave forth the panting lips.

Dora's impulse was to cry, "No, no!" to rise up from her knees, upon which she had fallen unconsciously by the sick bed, to withdraw from it, and if possible get away altogether, terrified of that close vicinity: but partly what Miss Bethune had said, and partly natural feeling, the instinct of humanity, kept her in spite of herself where she was. The poor lady lay with her face intent upon Dora, stroking her hair and her forehead with those hot thin hands, beaming upon her with that ineffable smile which is the prerogative of the dying.

"Oh, my little girl," she said,—"my only one, my only one! Twelve years it is—twelve long years—and all the time thinking of this! When I've been ill,—and I've been very ill, Miller will tell you,—I've kept up, I've forced myself to be better for this—for this!"

"You will wear yourself out, ma'am," said the nurse. "You must not talk, you must be quiet, or I shall have to send the young lady away."

"No, no!" cried the dying woman, again clutching Dora with fevered arms. "For what must I be quiet?—to live a little longer? I only want to live while she's here. I only want it as long as I can see her—Dora, you'll stay with me, you'll stay with your poor—poor ——"

"She shall stay as long as you want her: but for God's sake think of something else, woman—think of where you're going!" cried Miss Bethune harshly over Dora's head.

They disposed of her at their ease, talking over her head, bandying her about—she who was mistress of her own actions, who had never been made to stay where she did not wish to stay, or to go where she did not care to go. But Dora was silent even in the rebellion of her spirit. There was a something more strong than herself, which kept her there on her knees in the middle of the circle—all, as Miss Bethune had said, attending on the one who was dying, the one who was of the first interest, to whom even the queen would bow and defer if she were to come in here. Dora did not know what to say to a person in such a position. She approved, yet was angry that Miss Bethune should bid the poor lady think where she was going. She was frightened and excited, not knowing what dreadful change might take place, what alteration, before her very eyes. Her heart began to beat wildly against her breast; pity was in it, but fear too, which is masterful and obliterates other emotions: yet even that was kept in check by the overwhelming influence, the fascination of the chamber of death.

Then there was a pause; and Dora, still on her knees by the side of the bed, met as best she could the light which dazzled her, which enveloped her in a kind of pale flame, from the eyes preternaturally bright that were fixed upon her face, and listened, as to a kind of strange lullaby, to the broken words of fondness, a murmur of fond names, of half sentences, and monosyllables, in the silence of the hushed room. This seemed to last for a long time. She was conscious of people passing with hushed steps behind her, looking over her head, a man's low voice, the whisper of the nurses, a movement of the lights; but always that transfigured face, all made of whiteness, luminous, the hot breath coming and going, the hands about her face, the murmur of words. The girl was cramped with her attitude for a time, and then the cramp went away, and her body became numb, keeping its position like a mechanical thing, while her mind too was lulled into a curious sense of torpor, yet spectatorship. This lasted she did not know how long. She ceased to be aware of what was being said to her. Her own name, "Dora," over and over again repeated, and strange words, that came back to her afterwards, went on in a faltering stream. Hours might have passed for anything she knew, when at last she was raised, scarcely capable of feeling anything, and put into a chair by the bedside. She became dimly conscious that the brilliant eyes that had been gazing at her so long were being veiled as with sleep, but they opened again suddenly as she was removed, and were fixed upon her with an anguish of entreaty. "Dora, my child,—my child! Don't take her away!"

"She is going to sit by you here," said a voice, which could only be a doctor's voice, "here by your bedside. It is easier for her. She is not going away."

Then the ineffable smile came back. The two thin hands enveloped Dora's wrist, holding her hand close between them; and again there came a wonderful interval—the dark room, the little stars of lights, the soft movements of the attendants gradually fixing themselves like a picture on Dora's mind. Miss Bethune was behind in the dark, sitting bolt upright against the wall, and never moving. Shadowed by the curtains at the foot of the bed was some one with a white and anxious face, whom Dora had only seen in the cheerful light, and could scarcely identify as Harry Gordon. A doctor and the white-capped nurse were in front, the maid crying behind. It seemed to go on again and last for hours this strange scene—until there suddenly arose a little commotion and movement about the bed, Dora could not tell why. Her hand was liberated; the other figures came between her and the wan face on the pillow, and she found herself suddenly, swiftly swept away. She neither made any resistance nor yet moved of her own will, and scarcely knew what was happening until she felt the fresh night air on her face, and found herself in a carriage, with Harry Gordon's face, very grave and white, at the window.

"You will come to me in the morning and let me know the arrangements," Miss Bethune said, in a low voice.

"Yes, I will come; and thank you, thank you a thousand times for bringing her," he said.

They all talked of Dora as if she were a thing, as if she had nothing to do with herself. Her mind was roused by the motion, by the air blowing in her face. "What has happened? What has happened?" she asked as they drove away.

"Will she be up yonder already, beyond that shining sky? Will she know as she is known? Will she be satisfied with His likeness, and be like Him, seeing Him as He is?" said Miss Bethune, looking up at the stars, with her eyes full of big tears.

"Oh, tell me," cried Dora, "what has happened?" with a sob of excitement; for whether she was sorry, or only awe-stricken, she did not know.

"Just everything has happened that can happen to a woman here. She has got safe away out of it all; and there are few, few at my time of life, that would not be thankful to be like her—out of it all: though it may be a great thought to go."

"Do you mean that the lady is dead?" Dora asked in a voice of awe.

"She is dead, as we say; and content, having had her heart's desire."

"Was that me?" cried Dora, humbled by a great wonder. "Me? Why should she have wanted me so much as that, and not to let me go?"

"Oh, child, I know no more than you, and yet I know well, well! Because she was your mother, and you were all she had in the world."

"My mother's sister," said Dora, with childish sternness; "and," she added after a moment, "not my father's friend."

"Oh, hard life and hard judgment!" cried Miss Bethune. "Your mother's own self, a poor martyr: except that at the last she has had, what not every woman has, for a little moment, her heart's desire!"

CHAPTER XVII.

Young Gordon went into Miss Bethune's sitting-room next morning so early that she was still at breakfast, lingering over her second cup of tea. His eyes had the look of eyes which had not slept, and that air of mingled fatigue and excitement which shows that a great crisis which had just come was about his whole person. His energetic young limbs were languid with it. He threw himself into a chair, as if even that support and repose were comfortable, and an ease to his whole being.

"She rallied for a moment after you were gone," he said in a low voice, not looking at his companion, "but not enough to notice anything. The doctor said there was no pain or suffering—if he knows anything about it."

"Ay, if he knows," Miss Bethune said.

"And so she is gone," said the young man with a deep sigh. He struggled for a moment with his voice, which went from him in the sudden access of sorrow. After a minute he resumed: "She's gone, and my occupation, all my reasons for living, seem to be gone too. I know no more what is going to happen. I was her son yesterday, and did everything for her; now I don't know what I am. I am nobody, with scarcely the right even to be there."

"What do you mean? Everybody must know what you have been to her, and her to you, all your life."

The young man was leaning forward in his chair bent almost double, with his eyes fixed on the floor. "Yes," he said, "I never understood it before: but I know now what it is to have no rightful place, to have been only a dependent on their kindness. When my guardian died I did not feel it, because she was still there to think of me, and I was her representative in everything; but now the solicitor has taken the command, and makes me see

153

I am nobody. It is not for the money," the young man said, with a wave of his hand. "Let that go however she wished. God knows I would never complain. But I might have been allowed to do something for her, to manage things for her as I have done—oh, almost ever since I can remember." He looked up with a pale and troubled smile, wistful for sympathy. "I feel as if I had been cut adrift," he said.

"My poor boy! But she must have provided for you, fulfilled the expectations——"

"Don't say that!" he cried quickly. "There were no expectations. I can truly say I never thought upon the subject—never!—until we came here to London. Then it was forced upon me that I was good for nothing, did not know how to make my living. It was almost amusing at first, I was so unused to it; but not now I am afraid I am quite useless," he added, with again a piteous smile. "I am in the state of the poor fellow in the Bible. 'I can't dig, and to beg I am ashamed.' I don't know," he cried, "why I should trouble you with all this. But you said I was to come to you in the morning, and I feel I can speak to you. That's about all the explanation there is."

"It's the voice of nature," cried Miss Bethune quickly, an eager flush covering her face. "Don't you know, don't you feel, that there is nobody but me you could come to?—that you are sure of me whoever fails you—that there's a sympathy, and more than a sympathy? Oh, my boy, I will be to you all, and more than all!"

She was so overcome with her own emotion that she could not get out another word.

A flush came also upon Harry Gordon's pale face, a look abashed and full of wonder. He felt that this lady, whom he liked and respected, went so much too far, so much farther than there was any justification for doing. He was troubled instinctively for her, that she should be so impulsive, so strangely affected. He shook his head. "Don't think me ungrateful," he cried. "Indeed, I don't know if you mean all that your words seem to mean—as how should you indeed, and I only a stranger to you? But, dear

Miss Bethune, that can never be again. It is bad enough, as I find out, to have had no real tie to her, my dear lady that's gone—and to feel that everybody must think my grief for my poor aunt is partly disappointment because she has not provided for me. But no such link could be forged again. I was a child when that was made. It was natural; they settled things for me as they pleased, and I knew nothing but that I was very happy there, and loved them, and they me. But now I am a man, and must stand for myself. Don't think me ungracious. It's impossible but that a man with full use of his limbs must be able to earn his bread. It's only going back to South America, if the worst comes to the worst, where everybody knows me," he said.

Miss Bethune's countenance had been like a drama while young Gordon made this long speech, most of which was uttered with little breaks and pauses, without looking at her, in the same attitude, with his eyes on the ground. Yet he looked up once or twice with that flitting sad smile, and an air of begging pardon for anything he said which might wound her. Trouble, and almost shame, and swift contradiction, and anger, and sympathy, and tender pity, and a kind of admiration, all went over her face in waves. She was wounded by what he said, and disappointed, and yet approved. Could there be all these things in the hard lines of a middle-aged face? And yet there were all, and more. She recovered herself quickly as he came to an end, and with her usual voice replied:—

"We must not be so hasty to begin with. It is more than likely that the poor lady has made the position clear in her will. We must not jump to the conclusion that things are not explained in that and set right; it would be a slur upon her memory even to think that it would not be so."

"There must be no slur on her memory," said young Gordon quickly; "but I am almost sure that it will not be so. She told me repeatedly that I was not to blame her—as if it were likely I should blame her!"

"She would deserve blame," cried Miss Bethune quickly, "if

after all that has passed she should leave you with no provision, no acknowledgment——"

He put up his hand to stop her.

"Not a word of that! What I wanted was to keep my place until after—until all was done for her. I am a mere baby," he cried, dashing away the tears from his eyes. "It was that solicitor coming in to take charge of everything, to lock up everything, to give all the orders, that was more than I could bear."

She did not trust herself to say anything, but laid her hand upon his arm. And the poor young fellow was at the end of his forces, worn out bodily with anxiety and want of sleep, and mentally by grief and the conflict of emotions. He bent down his face upon her hand, kissing it with a kind of passion, and burst out, leaning his head upon her arm, into a storm of tears, that broke from him against his will. Miss Bethune put her other hand upon his bowed head; her face quivered with the yearning of her whole life. "Oh, God, is he my bairn?—Oh, God, that he were my bairn!" she cried.

But nobody would have guessed what this crisis had been who saw them a little after, as Dora saw them, who came into the room pale too with the unusual vigil of the previous night, but full of an indignant something which she had to say. "Miss Bethune," she cried, almost before she had closed the door, "do you know what Gilchrist told father about last night?—that I was tired when I came in, and had a headache, and she had put me to bed! And now I have to tell lies too, to say I am better, and to agree when he thanks Gilchrist for her care, and says it was the best thing for me. Oh, what a horrible thing it is to tell lies! To hide things from him, and invent excuses, and cheat him—cheat him with stories that are not true!"

Her hair waved behind her, half curling, crisp, inspired by indignation: her slim figure seemed to expand and grow, her eyes shone. Miss Bethune had certainly not gained anything by the deceptions, which were very innocent ones after all, practised upon Mr. Mannering: but she had to bear the brunt of this shock with what composure she might. She laughed a little, half glad to shake off the fumes of deeper emotion in this new incident. "As soon as he is stronger you shall explain everything to him, Dora," she said. "When the body is weak the mind should not be vexed more than is possible with perplexing things or petty cares. But as soon as he is better——"

"And now," cried Dora, flinging back her hair, all crisped, and almost scintillating, with anger and distress, her eyes filled with tears, "here comes the doctor now—far, far worse than any bills or any perplexities, and tells him straight out that he must ask for a year's holiday and go away, first for the rest of the summer, and then for the winter, as father says, to one of those places where all the fools go!—father, whose life is in the Museum, who cares for nothing else, who can't bear to go away! Oh!" cried Dora, stamping her foot, "to think I should be made to lie, to keep little, little things from him—contemptible things! and that then the doctor should come straight upstairs and without any preface, without any apology, blurt out that!"

"The doctor must have thought, Dora, it was better for him to know. He says all will go well, he will get quite strong, and be able to work in the Museum to his heart's content, if only he will do this now."

"If only he will do this! If only he will invent a lot of money, father says, which we haven't got. And how is the money to be invented? It is like telling poor Mrs. Hesketh not to walk, but to go out in a carriage every day. Perhaps that would make her quite well, poor thing. It would make the beggar at the corner quite well if he had turtle soup and champagne like father. And we must stop even the turtle soup and the champagne. He will not have them; they make him angry now that he has come to himself. Cannot you see, Miss Bethune," cried Dora with youthful superiority, as if such a thought could never have occurred to her friend, "that we can only do things which we can do—that there are some things that are impossible? Oh!" she said suddenly, perceiving for the first time young Gordon with a start of annoyance and surprise. "I did not know," cried Dora, "that I was discussing our affairs before a gentleman who can't take any interest in them."

"Dora, is that all you have to say to one that shared our watch last night—that has just come, as it were, from her that is gone? Have you no thought of that poor lady, and what took place so lately? Oh, my dear, have a softer heart."

"Miss Bethune," said Dora with dignity, "I am very sorry for the poor lady of last night. I was a little angry because I was made to deceive father, but my heart was not hard. I was very sorry. But how can I go on thinking about her when I have father to think of? I could not be fond of her, could I? I did not know her—I never saw her but once before. If she was my mother's sister, she was—she confessed it herself—father's enemy. I must—I must be on father's side," cried Dora. "I have had no one else all my life."

Miss Bethune and her visitor looked at each other,—he with a strange painful smile, she with tears in her eyes. "It is just the common way," she said,—"just the common way! You look over the one that loves you, and you heap love upon the one that loves you not."

"It cannot be the common way," said Gordon, "for the circumstances are not common. It is because of strange things, and relations that are not natural. I had no right to that love you speak of, and Dora had. But I have got all the advantages of it for many a year. There is no injustice if she who has the natural right to it gets it now."

"Oh, my poor boy," cried Miss Bethune, "you argue well, but you know better in your heart."

"I have not a grudge in my heart," he exclaimed, "not one, nor a complaint. Oh, believe me!—except to be put away as if I were nobody, just at this moment when there was still something to do for her," he said, after a pause.

Dora looked from one to the other, half wondering, half impatient. "You are talking of Mr. Gordon's business now," she said; "and I have nothing to do with that, any more than he has to do with mine. I had better go back to father, Miss Bethune, if you will tell Dr. Roland that he is cruel—that he ought to have waited till father was stronger—that it was wicked—wicked— to go and pour out all that upon him without any preparation, when even I was out of the way."

"Indeed, I think there is reason in what you say, Dora," said Miss Bethune, as the girl went away.

"It will not matter," said Gordon, after the door was closed. "That is one thing to be glad of, there will be no more want of money. Now," he said, rising, "I must go back again. It has been a relief to come and tell you everything, but now it seems as if I had a hunger to go back: and yet it is strange to go back. It is strange to walk about the streets and to know that I have nobody to go home to, that she is far away, and unmoved by anything that can happen to me." He paused a moment, and added, with that low laugh which is the alternative of tears: "Not to say that there is no home to go back to, nothing but a room in a hotel which I must get out of as soon as possible, and nobody belonging to me, or that I belong to. It is so difficult to get accustomed to the idea."

Miss Bethune gave a low cry. It was inarticulate, but she could not restrain it. She put out both her hands, then drew them back again; and after he had gone away, she went on pacing up and down the room, making this involuntary movement, murmuring that outcry, which was not even a word, to herself. She put out her hands, sometimes her arms, then brought them back and pressed them to the heart which seemed to be bursting from her breast. "Oh, if it might still be that he were mine! Oh, if I might believe it (as I do—I do!) and take him to me whether or no!" Her thoughts shaped themselves as their self-repression gave way to that uncontrollable tide. "Oh, well might he say that it was not the common way! the woman that had been a mother to him, thinking no more of him the moment her own comes in! And might I be like that? If I took him to my heart, that I think must be mine, and then the other, the true one—that would know nothing of me! And he, what does he know of me?—what does he think of me?—an old fool that puts out my arms to him without rhyme or reason. But then it's to me he comes when he's in trouble; he comes to me, he leans his head on me, just by instinct, by nature. And nature cries out in me here." She put her hands once more with unconscious dramatic action to her heart. "Nature cries out—nature cries out!"

Unconsciously she said these words aloud, and herself startled by the sound of her own voice, looked up suddenly, to see Gilchrist, who had just come into the room, standing gazing at her with an expression of pity and condemnation which drove her mistress frantic. Miss Bethune coloured high. She stopped in a moment her agitated walk, and placed herself in a chair with an air of hauteur and loftiness difficult to describe. "Well," she said, "were you wanting anything?" as if the excellent and respectable person standing before her had been, as Gilchrist herself said afterwards, "the scum of the earth".

"No' much, mem," said Gilchrist; "only to know if you were"— poor Gilchrist was so frightened by her mistress's aspect that she invented reasons which had no sound of truth in them—"going out this morning, or wanting your seam or the stocking you were knitting."

"Did you think I had all at once become doited, and did not know what I wanted?" asked Miss Bethune sternly.

Gilchrist made no reply, but dropped her guilty head.

"To think," cried the lady, "that I cannot have a visitor in the morning—a common visitor like those that come and go about every idle person,—nor take a thought into my mind, nor say a word even to myself, but in comes an intrusive serving-woman to worm out of me, with her frightened looks and her peety and her compassion, what it's all about! Lord! if it were any other than a woman that's been about me twenty years, and had just got herself in to be a habit and a custom, that would dare to come with her soft looks peetying me!"

Having come to a climax, voice and feeling together, in those words, Miss Bethune suddenly burst into the tempest of tears which all this time had been gathering and growing beyond any power of hers to restrain them.

"Oh, my dear leddy, my dear leddy!" Gilchrist said; then, gradually drawing nearer, took her mistress's head upon her ample bosom till the fit was over.

When Miss Bethune had calmed herself again, she pushed the maid away.

"I'll have no communication with you," she said. "You're a good enough servant, you're not an ill woman; but as for real sympathy or support in what is most dear, it's no' you that will give them to any person. I'm neither wanting to go out nor to take my seam. I will maybe read a book to quiet myself down, but I'm not meaning to hold any communication with you."

"Oh, mem!" said Gilchrist, in appeal: but she was not deeply cast down. "If it was about the young gentleman," she added, after a moment, "I just think he is as nice a young gentleman as the world contains."

"Did I not tell you so?" cried the mistress in triumph. "And like the gracious blood he's come of," she said, rising to her feet again, as if she were waving a flag of victory. Then she sat down abruptly, and opened upside down the book she had taken from the table. "But I'll hold no communication with you on that subject," she said.

CHAPTER XVIII.

Mr. Mannering had got into his sitting-room the next day, as the first change for which he was able in his convalescent state. The doctor's decree, that he must give up work for a year, and spend the winter abroad, had been fulminated forth upon him in the manner described by Dora, as a means of rousing him from the lethargy into which he was falling. After Dr. Roland had refused to permit of his speedy return to the Museum, he had become indifferent to everything except the expenses, concerning which he was now on the most jealous watch, declining to taste the dainties that were brought to him. "I cannot afford it," was his constant cry. He had ceased to desire to get up, to dress, to read, which, in preparation, as he hoped, for going out again, he had been at first so eager to do. Then the doctor had delivered his full broadside. "You may think what you like of me, Mannering; of course, it's in your power to defy me and die. You can if you like, and nobody can stop you: but if you care for anything in this world,—for that child who has no protector but you,"—here the doctor made a pause full of force, and fixed the patient with his eyes,—"you will dismiss all other considerations, and make up your mind to do what will make you well again, without any more nonsense. You must do it, and nothing less will do."

"Tell the beggar round the corner to go to Italy for the winter," said the invalid; "he'll manage it better than I. A man can beg anywhere, he carries his profession about with him. That's, I suppose, what you mean me to do."

"I don't care what you do," cried Dr. Roland, "as long as you do what I say."

Mr. Mannering was so indignant, so angry, so roused and excited, that he walked into his sitting-room that afternoon breathing fire and flame. "I shall return to the Museum next week," he said. "Let them do what they please, Dora. Italy! And what better is Italy than England, I should like to know? A blazing hot, deadly cold, impudently beautiful country. No repose in it, always in extremes like a scene in a theatre, or else like chill desolation, misery, and death. I'll not hear a word of Italy. The South of France is worse; all the exaggerations of the other, and a volcano underneath. He may rave till he burst, I will not go. The Museum is the place for me—or the grave, which might be better still."

"Would you take me there with you, father?" said Dora.

"Child!" He said this word in such a tone that no capitals in the world could give any idea of it; and then that brought him to a pause, and increased the force of the hot stimulant that already was working in his veins. "But we have no money," he cried,—"no money—no money. Do you understand that? I have been a fool. I have been going on spending everything I had. I never expected a long illness, doctors and nurses, and all those idiotic luxuries. I can eat a chop—do you hear, Dora?—a chop, the cheapest you can get. I can live on dry bread. But get into debt I will not—not for you and all your doctors. There's that Fiddler and his odious book—three pounds ten—what for? For a piece of vanity, to say I had the 1490 edition: not even to say it, for who cares except some of the men at the Museum? What does Roland understand about the 1490 edition? He probably thinks the latest edition is always the best. And I—a confounded fool—throwing away my money—your money, my poor child!—for I can't take you with me, Dora, as you say. God forbid—God forbid!"

"Well, father," said Dora, who had gone through many questions with herself since the conversation in Miss Bethune's room, "suppose we were to try and think how it is to be done. No doubt, as he is the doctor, however we rebel, he will make us do it at the last."

"How can he make us do it? He cannot put money in my pocket, he cannot coin money, however much he would like it;

and if he could, I suppose he would keep it for himself."

"I am not so sure of that, father."

"I am sure of this, that he ought to, if he is not a fool. Every man ought to who has a spark of sense in him. I have not done it, and you see what happens. Roland may be a great idiot, but not so great an idiot as I."

"Oh, father, what is the use of talking like this? Let us try and think how we are to do it," Dora cried.

His renewed outcry that he could not do it, that it was not a thing to be thought of for a moment, was stopped by a knock at the door, at which, when Dora, after vainly bidding the unknown applicant come in, opened it, there appeared an old gentleman, utterly unknown to both, and whose appearance was extremely disturbing to the invalid newly issued from his sick room, and the girl who still felt herself his nurse and protector.

"I hope I do not come at a bad moment," the stranger said. "I took the opportunity of an open door to come straight up without having myself announced. I trust I may be pardoned for the liberty. Mr. Mannering, you do not recollect me, but I have seen you before. I am Mr. Templar, of Gray's Inn. I have something of importance to say to you, which will, I trust, excuse my intrusion."

"Oh," cried Dora. "I am sure you cannot know that my father has been very ill. He is out of his room for the first time to-day."

The old gentleman said that he was very sorry, and then that he was very glad. "That means in a fair way of recovery," he said. "I don't know," he added, addressing Mannering, who was pondering over him with a somewhat sombre countenance, "whether I may speak to you about my business, Mr. Mannering, at such an early date: but I am almost forced to do so by my orders: and whether you would rather hear my commission in presence of this young lady or not."

"Where is it we have met?" Mannering said, with a more and more gloomy look.

"I will tell you afterwards, if you will hear me in the first place. I come to announce to you, Mr. Mannering, the death of a client of mine, who has left a very considerable fortune to your daughter, Dora Mannering—this young lady, I presume: and with it a prayer that the young lady, to whom she leaves everything, may be permitted to—may, with your consent——"

"Oh," cried Dora, "I know! It is the poor lady from South America!" And then she became silent and grew red. "Father, I have hid something from you," she said, faltering. "I have seen a lady, forgive me, who was your enemy. She said you would never forgive her. Oh, how one's sins find one out! It was not my fault that I went, and I thought you would never know. She was mamma's sister, father."

"She was—who?" Mr. Mannering rose from his chair. He had been pale before, he became now livid, yellow, his thin cheek-bones standing out, his hollow eyes with a glow in them, his mouth drawn in. He towered over the two people beside him—Dora frightened and protesting, the visitor very calm and observant—looking twice his height in his extreme leanness and gauntness. "Who—who was it? Who?" His whole face asked the question. He stood a moment tottering, then dropped back in complete exhaustion into his chair.

"Father," cried Dora, "I did not know who she was. She was very ill and wanted me. It was she who used to send me those things. Miss Bethune took me, it was only once, and I—I was there when she died." The recollection choked her voice, and made her tremble. "Father, she said you would not forgive her, that you were never to be told; but I could not believe," cried Dora, "that there was any one, ill or sorry, and very, very weak, and in trouble, whom you would not forgive."

Mr. Mannering sat gazing at his child, with his eyes burning in their sockets. At these words he covered his face with his hands. And there was silence, save for a sob of excitement from Dora, excitement so long repressed that it burst forth now with all the greater force. The visitor, for some time, did not say a word. Then suddenly he put forth his hand and touched the elbow which rested like a sharp point on the table. He said softly: "It was the lady you imagine. She is dead. She has led a life of suffering and trouble. She has neither been well nor happy. Her one wish was to see her child before she died. When she was left free, as happened by death some time ago, she came to England for that purpose. I can't tell you how much or how little the friends knew, who helped her. They thought it, I believe, a family quarrel."

Mr. Mannering uncovered his ghastly countenance. "It is better they should continue to think so."

"That is as you please. For my own part, I think the child at least should know. The request, the prayer that was made on her deathbed in all humility, was that Dora should follow her remains to the grave."

"To what good?" he cried, "to what good?"

"To no good. Have you forgotten her, that you ask that? I told her, if she had asked to see you, to get your forgiveness——"

"Silence!" cried Mr. Mannering, lifting his thin hand as if with a threat.

"But she had not courage. She wanted only, she said, her own flesh and blood to stand by her grave."

Mannering made again a gesture with his hand, but no reply.

"She has left everything of which she died possessed—a considerable, I may say a large fortune—to her only child."

"I refuse her fortune!" cried Mannering, bringing down his clenched hand on the table with a feverish force that made the room ring.

"You will not be so pitiless," said the visitor; "you will not pursue an unfortunate woman, who never in her unhappy life meant any harm."

"In her unhappy life!—in her pursuit of a happy life at any cost, that is what you mean."

"I will not argue. She is dead. Say she was thoughtless, fickle. I can't tell. She did only what she was justified in doing. She meant no harm."

"I will allow no one," cried Mr. Mannering, "to discuss the

question with me. Your client, I understand, is dead,—it was proper, perhaps, that I should know,—and has left a fortune to my daughter. Well, I refuse it. There is no occasion for further parley. I refuse it. Dora, show this gentleman downstairs."

"There is only one thing to be said," said the visitor, rising, "you have not the power to refuse it. It is vested in trustees, of whom I am one. The young lady herself may take any foolish step—if you will allow me to say so—when she comes of age. But you have not the power to do this. The allowance to be made to her during her minority and all other particulars will be settled as soon as the arrangements are sufficiently advanced."

"I tell you that I refuse it," repeated Mr. Mannering.

"And I repeat that you have no power to do so. I leave her the directions in respect to the other event, in which you have full power. I implore you to use it mercifully," the visitor said.

He went away without any further farewell—Mannering, not moving, sitting at the table with his eyes fixed on the empty air. Dora, who had followed the conversation with astonished uncomprehension, but with an acute sense of the incivility with which the stranger had been treated, hurried to open the door for him, to offer him her hand, to make what apologies were possible.

"Father has been very ill," she said. "He nearly died. This is the first time he has been out of his room. I don't understand what it all means, but please do not think he is uncivil. He is excited, and still ill and weak. I never in my life saw him rude to any one before."

"Never mind," said the old gentleman, pausing outside the door; "I can make allowances. You and I may have a great deal to do with each other, Miss Dora. I hope you will have confidence in me?"

"I don't know what it all means," Dora said.

"No, but some day you will; and in the meantime remember that some one, who has the best right to do so, has left you a great deal of money, and that whenever you want anything, or even wish for anything, you must come to me."

"A great deal of money?" Dora said. She had heard him speak of a fortune—a considerable fortune, but the words had not struck her as these did. A great deal of money? And money was all that was wanted to make everything smooth, and open out vistas of peace and pleasure, where all had been trouble and care. The sudden lighting up of her countenance was as if the sun had come out all at once from among the clouds. The old gentleman, who, like so many old gentlemen, entertained cynical views, chuckled to see that even at this youthful age, and in Mannering's daughter, who had refused it so fiercely, the name of a great deal of money should light up a girl's face. "They are all alike," he said to himself as he went downstairs.

When Dora returned to the room, she found her father as she had left him, staring straight before him, seeing nothing, his head supported on his hands, his hollow eyes fixed. He did not notice her return, as he had not noticed her absence. What was she to do? One of those crises had arrived which are so petty, yet so important, when the wisest of women are reduced to semi-imbecility by an emergency not contemplated in any moral code. It was time for him to take his beef tea. The doctor had commanded that under no circumstances was this duty to be omitted or postponed; but who could have foreseen such circumstances as these, in which evidently matters of life and death were going through his mind? After such an agitating interview he wanted it more and more, the nourishment upon which his recovery depended. But how suggest it to a man whose mind was gone away into troubled roamings through the past, or still more troubled questions about the future? It could have been no small matters that had been brought back to Mr. Mannering's mind by that strange visit. Dora, who was not weak-minded, trembled to approach him with any prosaic, petty suggestion. And yet how did she dare to pass it by? Dora went about the room very quietly, longing to rouse yet unwilling to disturb him. How was she to speak of such a small matter as his beef tea?

168

And yet it was not a small matter. She heard Gilchrist go into the other room, bringing it all ready on the little tray, and hurried thither to inquire what that experienced woman would advise. "He has had some one to see him about business. He has been very much put out, dreadfully disturbed. I don't know how to tell you how much. His mind is full of some dreadful thing I don't understand. How can I ask him to take his beef tea? And yet he must want it. He is looking so ill. He is so worn out. Oh, Gilchrist, what am I to do?"

"It is just a very hard question, Miss Dora. He should not have seen any person on business. He's no' in a fit state to see anybody the first day he is out of his bedroom: though, for my part, I think he might have been out of his bedroom three or four days ago," Gilchrist said.

"As if that was the question now! The question is about the beef tea. Can I go and say, 'Father, never mind whatever has happened, there is nothing so important as your beef tea'? Can I tell him that everything else may come and go, but that beef tea runs on for ever? Oh, Gilchrist, you are no good at all! Tell me what to do."

Dora could not help being light-hearted, though it was in the present circumstances so inappropriate, when she thought of that "great deal of money"—money that would sweep all bills away, that would make almost everything possible. That consciousness lightened more and more upon her, as she saw the little bundle of bills carefully labelled and tied up, which she had intended to remove surreptitiously from her father's room while he was out of it. With what comfort and satisfaction could she remove them now!

"Just put it down on the table by his side, Miss Dora," said Gilchrist. "Say no word, just put it there within reach of his hand. Maybe he will fly out at you, and ask if you think there's nothing in the world so important as your confounded—— But no, he will not say that; he's no' a man that gets relief in that way. But, on the other hand, he will maybe just be conscious that there's a good smell, and he will feel he's wanting something, and he will drink it off without more ado. But do not, Miss Dora, whatever you do, let more folk on business bother your poor papaw, for I could not answer for what might come of it. You had better let me sit here on the watch, and see that nobody comes near the door."

"I will do what you say, and you can do what you like," said Dora. She could almost have danced along the passage. Poor lady from America, who was dead! Dora had been very sorry. She had been much troubled by the interview about her which she did not understand: but even if father were pitiless, which was so incredible, it could do that poor woman no harm now: and the money—money which would be deliverance, which would pay all the bills, and leave the quarter's money free to go to the country with, to go abroad with! Dora had to tone her countenance down, not to look too guiltily glad when she went in to where her father was sitting in the same abstraction and gloom. But this time he observed her entrance, looking up as if he had been waiting for her. She had barely time to follow Gilchrist's directions when he stretched out his hand and took hers, drawing her near to him. He was very grave and pale, but no longer so terrible as before.

"Dora," he said, "how often have you seen this lady of whom I have heard to-day?"

"Twice, father; once in Miss Bethune's room, where she had come. I don't know how."

"In this house?" he said with a strong quiver, which Dora felt, as if it had been communicated to herself.

"And the night before last, when Miss Bethune took me to where she was living, a long way off, by Hyde Park. I knelt at the bed a long time, and then they put me in a chair. She said many things I did not understand—but chiefly," Dora said, her eyes filling with tears—the scene seemed to come before her more touchingly in recollection than when, to her wonder and dismay, it took place, "chiefly that she loved me, that she had wanted me all my life, and that she wished for me above everything before she died."

"And then?" he said, with a catch in his breath.

"I don't know, father; I was so confused and dizzy with being there so long. All of a sudden they took me away, and the others all came round the bed. And then there was nothing more. Miss Bethune brought me home. I understood that the lady—that my poor—my poor aunt—if that is what she was—was dead. Oh, father, whatever she did, forgive her now!"

Dora for the moment had forgotten everything but the pity and the wonder, which she only now began to realise for the first time, of that strange scene. She saw, as if for the first time, the dark room, the twinkling lights, the ineffable smile upon the dying face: and her big tears fell fast upon her father's hand, which held hers in a trembling grasp. The quiver that was in him ran through and through her, so that she trembled too.

"Dora," he said, "perhaps you ought to know, as that man said. The lady was not your aunt: she was your mother—my"—there seemed a convulsion in his throat, as though he could not pronounce the word—"my wife. And yet she was not to blame, as the world judges. I went on a long expedition after you were born, leaving her very young still, and poor. I did not mean her to be poor. I did not mean to be long away. But I went to Africa, which is terrible enough now, but was far more terrible in those days. I fell ill again and again. I was left behind for dead. I was lost in those dreadful wilds. It was more than three years before I came to the light of day at all, and it seemed a hundred. I had been given up by everybody. The money had failed her, her people were poor, the Museum gave her a small allowance as to the widow of a man killed in its service. And there was another man who loved her. They meant no harm, it is true. She did nothing that was wrong. She married him, thinking I was dead."

"Father!" Dora cried, clasping his arm with both her hands: his other arm supported his head.

"It was a pity that I was not dead—that was the pity. If I had known, I should never have come back to put everything wrong.

171

But I never heard a word till I came back. And she would not face me—never. She fled as if she had been guilty. She was not guilty, you know. She had only married again, which the best of women do. She fled by herself at first, leaving you to me. She said it was all she could do, but that she never, never could look me in the face again. It has not been that I could not forgive her, Dora. No, but we could not look each other in the face again."

"Is it she," said Dora, struggling to speak, "whose picture is in your cabinet, on its face? May I take it, father? I should like to have it."

He put his other arm round her and pressed her close. "And after this," he said, "my little girl, we will never say a word on this subject again."

CHAPTER XIX.

The little old gentleman had withdrawn from the apartment of the Mannerings very quietly, leaving all that excitement and commotion behind him; but he did not leave in this way the house in Bloomsbury. He went downstairs cautiously and quietly, though why he should have done so he could not himself have told, since, had he made all the noise in the world, it could have had no effect upon the matter in hand in either case. Then he knocked at Miss Bethune's door. When he was bidden to enter, he opened the door gently, with great precaution, and going in, closed it with equal care behind him.

"I am speaking, I think, to Mrs. Gordon Grant?" he said.

Miss Bethune was alone. She had many things to think of, and very likely the book which she seemed to be reading was not much more than a pretence to conceal her thoughts. It fell down upon her lap at these words, and she looked at her questioner with a gasp, unable to make any reply.

"Mrs. Gordon Grant, I believe?" he said again, then made a step farther into the room. "Pardon me for startling you, there is no one here. I am a solicitor, John Templar, of Gray's Inn. Precautions taken with other persons need not apply to me. You are Mrs. Gordon Grant, I know."

"I have never borne that name," she said, very pale. "Janet Bethune, that is my name."

"Not as signed to a document which is in my possession. You will pardon me, but this is no doing of mine. You witnessed Mrs. Bristow's will?"

She gave a slight nod with her head in acquiescence.

"And then, to my great surprise, I found this name, which I have been in search of for so long."

"You have been in search of it?"

"Yes, for many years. The skill with which you have concealed it is wonderful. I have advertised, even. I have sought the help of old friends who must see you often, who come to you here even, I know. But I never found the name I was in search of, never till the other day at the signing of Mrs. Bristow's will—which, by the way," he said, "that young fellow might have signed safely enough, for he has no share in it."

"Do you mean to say that she has left him nothing—nothing, Mr. Templar? The boy that was like her son!"

"Not a penny," said the old gentleman—"not a penny. Everything has gone the one way—perhaps it was not wonderful—to her own child."

"I could not have done that!" cried the lady. "Oh, I could not have done it! I would have felt it would bring a curse upon my own child."

"Perhaps, madam, you never had a child of your own, which would make all the difference," he said.

She looked at him again, silent, with her lips pressed very closely together, and a kind of defiance in her eyes.

"But this," he said again, softly, "is no answer to my question. You were a witness of Mrs. Bristow's will, and you signed a certain name to it. You cannot have done so hoping to vitiate the document by a feigned name. It would have been perfectly futile to begin with, and no woman could have thought of such a thing. That was, I presume, your lawful name?"

"It is a name I have never borne; that you will very easily ascertain."

"Still it is your name, or why should you have signed it—in inadvertence, I suppose?"

"Not certainly in inadvertence. Has anything ever made it familiar to me? If you will know, I had my reasons. I thought the sight of it might put things in a lawyer's hands, would maybe guide inquiries, would make easier an object of my own."

"That object," said Mr. Templar, "was to discover your

husband?"

She half rose to her feet, flushed and angry.

"Who said I had a husband, or that to find him or lose him was anything to me?" Then, with a strong effort, she reseated herself in her chair. "That was a bold guess," she said, "Mr. Templar, not to say a little insulting, don't you think, to a respectable single lady that has never had a finger lifted upon her? I am of a well-known race enough. I have never concealed myself. There are plenty of people in Scotland who will give you full details of me and all my ways. It is not like a lawyer—a cautious man, bound by his profession to be careful—to make such a strange attempt upon me."

"I make no attempt. I only ask a question, and one surely most justifiable. You did not sign a name to which you had no right, on so important a document as a will; therefore you are Mrs. Gordon Grant, and a person to whom for many years I have had a statement to make."

She looked at him again with a dumb rigidity of aspect, but said not a word.

"The communication I had to make to you," he said, "was of a death—not one, so far as I know, that could bring you any advantage, or harm either, I suppose. I may say that it took place years ago. I have no reason, either, to suppose that it would be the cause of any deep sorrow."

"Sorrow?" she said, but her lips were dry, and could articulate no more.

"I have nothing to do with your reasons for having kept your marriage so profound a secret," he said. "The result has naturally been the long delay of a piece of information which perhaps would have been welcome to you. Mrs. Grant, your husband, George Gordon Grant, died nearly twenty years ago."

"Twenty years ago!" she cried, with a start, "twenty years?" Then she raised her voice suddenly and cried, "Gilchrist!" She was very pale, and her excitement great, her eyes gleaming, her nerves quivering. She paid no attention to the little lawyer, who on his side observed her so closely. "Gilchrist," she said, when the maid came in hurriedly from the inner room in which she had been, "we have often wondered why there was no sign of him when I came into my fortune. The reason is he was dead before my uncle died."

"Dead?" said Gilchrist, and put up at once her apron to her eyes, "dead? Oh, mem, that bonnie young man!"

"Yes," said Miss Bethune. She rose up and began to move about the room in great excitement. "Yes, he would still be a bonnie young man then—oh, a bonnie young man, as his son is now. I wondered how it was he made no sign. Before, it was natural: but when my uncle was dead—when I had come into my fortune! That explains it—that explains it all. He was dead before the day he had reckoned on came."

"Oh, dinna say that, now!" cried Gilchrist. "How can we tell if it was the day he had reckoned on? Why might it no' be your comfort he was aye thinking of—that you might lose nothing, that your uncle might keep his faith in you, that your fortune might be safe?"

"Ay, that my fortune might be safe, that was the one thing. What did it matter about me? Only a woman that was so silly as to believe in him—and believed in him, God help me, long after he had proved what he was. Gilchrist, go down on your knees and thank God that he did not live to cheat us more, to come when you and me made sure he would come, and fleece us with his fair face and his fair ways, till he had got what he wanted,—the filthy money which was the end of all."

"Oh, mem," cried Gilchrist, again weeping, "dinna say that now. Even if it were true, which the Lord forbid, dinna say it now!"

But her mistress was not to be controlled. The stream of recollection, of pent-up feeling, the brooding of a lifetime, set free by this sudden discovery of her story, which was like the breaking down of a dyke to a river, rushed forth like that river in flood. "I have thought many a time," she cried,—"when my heart was sick of the silence, when I still trembled that he would come, and wished he would come for all that I knew, like a fool woman that I am, as all women are,—that maybe his not coming was a sign of grace, that he had maybe forgotten, maybe been untrue; but that it was not at least the money, the money and nothing more. To know that I had that accursed siller and not to come for it was a sign of grace. I was a kind of glad. But it was not that!" she cried, pacing to and fro like a wild creature,—"it was not that! He would have come, oh, and explained everything, made everything clear, and told me to my face it was for my sake!—if it had not been that death stepped in and disappointed him as he had disappointed me!"

Miss Bethune ended with a harsh laugh, and after a moment seated herself again in her chair. The tempest of personal feeling had carried her away, quenching even the other and yet stronger sentiment, which for so many years had been the passion of her life. She had been suddenly, strangely driven back to a period which even now, in her sober middle age, it was a kind of madness to think of—the years which she had lived through in awful silence, a wife yet no wife, a mother yet no mother, cut off from everything but the monotonous, prolonged, unending formula of a girlhood out of date, the life without individuality, without meaning, and without hope, of a large-minded and active woman, kept to the rôle of a child, in a house where there was not even affection to sweeten it. The recollection of those terrible, endless, changeless days, running into years as indistinguishable, the falsehood of every circumstance and appearance, the secret existence of love and sacrifice, of dread knowledge and disenchantment, of strained hope and failing illusion, and final and awful despair, of which Gilchrist alone knew anything,—Gilchrist, the faithful servant, the sole companion of her heart,—came back upon her with all that horrible sense of the intolerable which such a martyrdom brings. She had borne it in its day—how had she borne it? Was it possible that a woman could go through that and live? her heart torn from her bosom, her baby torn from her side, and no one, no one but Gilchrist, to keep a little life alive in her heart! And it had lasted for years—many, many, many years,—all the years of her life, except those first twenty which tell for so little. In that rush of passion she did not know how time passed, whether it was five minutes or an hour that she sat under the inspection of the old lawyer, whom this puzzle of humanity filled with a sort of professional interest, and who did not think it necessary to withdraw, or had any feeling of intrusion upon the sufferer. It was not really a long time, though it might have been a year, when she roused herself and took hold of her forces, and the dread panorama rolled away.

Gradually the familiar things around her came back. She remembered herself, no despairing girl, no soul in bondage, but a sober woman, disenchanted in many ways, but never yet cured of those hopes and that faith which hold the ardent spirit to life. Her countenance changed with her thoughts, her eyes ceased to be abstracted and visionary, her colour came back. She turned to the old gentleman with a look which for the first time disturbed and bewildered that old and hardened spectator of the vicissitudes of life. Her eyes filled with a curious liquid light, an expression wistful, flattering, entreating. She looked at him as a child looks who has a favour to ask, her head a little on one side, her lips quivering with a smile. There came into the old lawyer's mind, he could not tell how, a ridiculous sense of being a superior being, a kind of god, able to confer untold advantages and favours. What did the woman want of him? What—it did not matter what she wanted—could he do for her? Nothing that he was aware of: and a sense of the danger of being cajoled came into his mind, but along with that, which was ridiculous, though he could not help it, a sense of being really a superior being, able to grant favours, and benignant, as he had never quite known himself to be.

"Mr. Templar," she said, "now all is over there is not another word to say: and now the boy—my boy——"

"The boy?" he repeated, with a surprised air.

"My child that was taken from me as soon as he was born, my little helpless bairn that never knew his mother—my son, my son! Give me a right to him, give me my lawful title to him, and there can be no more doubt about it—that nobody may say he is not mine."

The old lawyer was more confused than words could say. The very sense she had managed to convey to his mind of being a superior being, full of graces and gifts to confer, made his downfall the more ludicrous to himself. He seemed to tumble down from an altitude quite visionary, yet very real, as if by some neglect or ill-will of his own. He felt himself humiliated, a culprit before her. "My dear lady," he said, "you are going too fast and too far for me. I did not even know there was any—— Stop! I think I begin to remember."

"Yes," she said, breathless,—"yes!" looking at him with supplicating eyes.

"Now it comes back to me," he said. "I—I—am afraid I gave it no importance. There was a baby—yes, a little thing a few weeks, or a few months old—that died."

She sprang up again once more to her feet, menacing, terrible. She was bigger, stronger, far more full of life, than he was. She towered over him, her face full of tragic passion. "It is not true—it is not true!" she cried.

"My dear lady, how can I know? What can I do? I can but tell you the instructions given to me; it had slipped out of my mind, it seemed of little importance in comparison. A baby that was too delicate to bear the separation from its mother—I remember it all now. I am very sorry, very sorry, if I have conveyed any false hopes to your mind. The baby died not long after it was taken away."

"It is not true," Miss Bethune said, with a hoarse and harsh voice. After the excitement and passion, she stood like a figure cut out of stone. This statement, so calm and steady, struck her like a blow. Her lips denied, but her heart received the cruel news. It may be necessary to explain good fortune, but misery

179

comes with its own guarantee. It struck her like a sword, like a scythe, shearing down her hopes. She rose into a brief blaze of fury, denying it. "Oh, you think I will believe that?" she cried,— "me that have followed him in my thoughts through every stage, have seen him grow and blossom, and come to be a man! Do you think there would have been no angel to stop me in my vain imaginations, no kind creature in heaven or earth that would have breathed into my heart and said, 'Go on no more, hope no more'? Oh no—oh no! Heaven is not like that, nor earth! Pain comes and trouble, but not cruel fate. No, I do not believe it—I will not believe it! It is not true."

"My dear lady," said the old gentleman, distressed.

"I am no dear lady to you. I am nothing to you. I am a poor, deserted, heartbroken woman, that have lived false, false, but never meant it: that have had no one to stand by me, to help me out of it. And now you sit there calm, and look me in the face, and take away my son. My baby first was taken from me, forced out of my arms, new-born: and now you take the boy I've followed with my heart these long, long years, the bonnie lad, the young man I've seen. I tell you I've seen him, then. How can a mother be deceived? We've seen him, both Gilchrist and me. Ask her, if you doubt my word. We have seen him, can any lie stand against that? And my heart has spoken, and his heart has spoken; we have sought each other in the dark, and taken hands. I know him by his bonnie eyes, and a trick in his mouth that is just my father over again: and he knows me by nature, and the touch of kindly blood."

"Oh, mem," Gilchrist cried, "I warned ye—I warned ye! What is a likeness to lippen to? And I never saw it," the woman said, with tears.

"And who asked ye to see it, or thought ye could see it, a serving-woman, not a drop's blood to him or to me? It would be a bonnie thing," said Miss Bethune, pausing, looking round, as if to appeal to an unseen audience, with an almost smile of scorn, "if my hired woman's word was to be taken instead of his mother's. Did she bear him in pain and anguish? Did she wait for him, lying dreaming, month after month, that he was to cure all? She got him in her arms when he was born, but he had been in mine for long before; he had grown a man in my heart before ever he saw the light of day. Oh, ask her, and there is many a fable she will tell ye. But me!"—she calmed down again, a smile came upon her face,—"I have seen my son. Now, as I have nobody but him, he has nobody but me: and I mean from this day to take him home and acknowledge him before all the world."

Mr. Templar had risen, and stood with his hand on the back of his chair. "I have nothing more to say," he said. "If I can be of any use to you in any way, command me, madam. It is no wish of mine to take any comfort from you, or even to dispel any pleasing illusion."

"As if you could!" she said, rising again, proud and smiling. "As if any old lawyer's words, as dry as dust, could shake my conviction, or persuade me out of what is a certainty. It is a certainty. Seeing is believing, the very vulgar say. And I have seen him—do you think you could make me believe after that, that there is no one to see?"

He shook his head and turned away. "Good-morning to you, ma'am," he said. "I have told you the truth, but I cannot make you believe it, and why should I try? It may be happier for you the other way."

"Happier?" she said, with a laugh. "Ay, because it's true. Falsehood has been my fate too long—I am happy because it is true."

Miss Bethune sat down again, when her visitor closed the door behind him. The triumph and brightness gradually died out of her face. "What are you greetin' there for, you fool?" she said, "and me the happiest woman, and the proudest mother! Gilchrist," she said, suddenly turning round upon her maid, "the woman that is dead was a weak creature, bound hand and foot all her life. She meant no harm, poor thing, I will allow, but yet she broke one man's life in pieces, and it must have been a poor kind of happiness she gave the other, with her heart always straying after another man's bairn. And I've done nothing, nothing to injure any mortal. I was true till I could be true no longer, till he showed all he was; and true I have been in spite of that all my life, and endured and never said a word. Do you think it's possible, possible that yon woman should be rewarded with her child in her arms, and her soul satisfied?—and me left desolate, with my very imaginations torn from me, torn out of me, and my heart left bleeding, and all my thoughts turned into lies, like myself, that have been no better than a lie?—turned into lies?"

"Oh, mem!" cried Gilchrist—"oh, my dear leddy, that has been more to me than a' this world! Is it for me to say that it's no' justice we have to expect, for we deserve nothing; and that the Lord knows His ain reasons; and that the time will come when we'll get it all back—you, your bairn, the Lord bless him! and me to see ye as happy as the angels, which is all I ever wanted or thought to get either here or otherwhere!"

CHAPTER XX.

There was nothing more said to Mr. Mannering on the subject of Mr. Templar's mission, neither did he himself say anything, either to sanction or prevent his child from carrying out the strange desire of her mother—her mother! Dora did not accept the thought. She made a struggle within herself to keep up the fiction that it was her mother's sister—a relation, something near, yet ever inferior to the vision of a benignant, melancholy being, unknown, which a dead mother so often is to an imaginative girl.

It pleased her to find, as she said to herself, "no likeness" to the suffering and hysterical woman she had seen, in that calm, pensive portrait, which she instantly secured and took possession of—the little picture which had lain so long buried with its face downward in the secret drawer. She gazed at it for an hour together, and found nothing—nothing, she declared to herself with indignant satisfaction, to remind her of the other face— flushed, weeping, middle-aged—which had so implored her affection. Had it been her mother, was it possible that it should have required an effort to give that affection? No! Dora at sixteen believed very fully in the voice of nature. It would have been impossible, her heart at once would have spoken, she would have known by some infallible instinct. She put the picture up in her own room, and filled her heart with the luxury, the melancholy, the sadness, and pleasure of this possession—her mother's portrait, more touching to the imagination than any other image could be. But then there began to steal a little shadow over Dora's thoughts. She would not give up her determined resistance to the idea that this face and the other face, living and dying, which she had seen, could be one; but when she raised her eyes suddenly, to her mother's picture, a consciousness would steal over her, an involuntary glance of recognition. What more likely than that there should be a resemblance, faint and far away, between sister and sister? And then there came to be a gleam of reproach to Dora in those eyes, and the girl began to feel as if there was an irreverence, a want of feeling, in turning that long recluse and covered face to the light of day, and carrying on all the affairs of life under it, as if it were a common thing. Finally she arranged over it a little piece of drapery, a morsel of faded embroidered silk which was among her treasures, soft and faint in its colours—a veil which she could draw in her moments of thinking and quiet, those moments which it would not be irreverent any longer to call a dead mother or an angelic presence to hallow and to share.

But she said nothing when she was called to Miss Bethune's room, and clad in mourning, recognising with a thrill, half of horror, half of pride, the crape upon her dress which proved her right to that new exaltation among human creatures—that position of a mourner which is in its way a step in life. Dora did not ask where she was going when she followed Miss Bethune, also in black from head to foot, to the plain little brougham which had been ordered to do fit and solemn honour to the occasion; the great white wreath and basket of flowers, which filled up the space, called no observation from her. They drove in silence to the great cemetery, with all its gay flowers and elaborate aspect of cheerfulness. It was a fine but cloudy day, warm and soft, yet without sunshine; and Dora had a curious sense of importance, of meaning, as if she had attained an advanced stage of being. Already an experience had fallen to her share, more than one experience. She had knelt, troubled and awe-stricken, by a death-bed; she was now going to stand by a grave. Even where real sorrow exists, this curious sorrowful elation of sentiment is apt to come into the mind of the very young. Dora was deeply impressed by the circumstances and the position, but it was impossible that she could feel any real grief. Tears came to her eyes as she dropped the shower of flowers, white and lovely, into the darkness of that last abode. Her face was full of awe and pity, but her breast of that vague, inexplainable expansion and growth, as of a creature entered into the larger developments and knowledge of life. There were very few other mourners. Mr. Templar, the lawyer, with his keen but veiled observation of everything, serious and businesslike; the doctor, with professional gravity and indifference; Miss Bethune, with almost stern seriousness, standing like a statue in her black dress and with her pale face. Why should any of these spectators care? The woman was far the most moved, thinking of the likeness and difference of her own fate, of the failure of that life which was now over, and of her own, a deeper failure still, without any fault of hers. And Dora, wondering, developing, her eyes full of abstract tears, and her mind of awe.

Only one mourner stood pale with watching and thought beside the open grave, his heart aching with loneliness and a profound natural vacancy and pain. He knew that she had neglected him, almost wronged him at the last, cut him off, taking no thought of what was to become of him. He felt even that in so doing this woman was unfaithful to her trust, and had done what she ought not to have done. But all that mattered nothing in face of natural sorrow, natural love. She had been a mother to him, and she was gone. The ear always open to his boyish talk and confidence, always ready to listen, could hear him no more; and, almost more poignant, his care of her was over, there was nothing more to do for her, none of the hundred commissions that used to send him flying, the hundred things that had to be done. His occupation in life seemed to be over, his home, his natural place. It had not perhaps ever been a natural place, but he had not felt that. She had been his mother, though no drop of her blood ran in his veins; and now he was nobody's son, belonging to no family. The other people round looked like ghosts to Harry Gordon. They were part of the strange cutting off, the severance he already felt; none of them had anything to do with her, and yet it was he who was pushed out and put aside, as if he had nothing to do with her, the only mother he had ever known! The little sharp old lawyer was her representative now, not he who had been her son. He stood languid, in a moment of utter depression, collapse of soul and body, by the grave. When all was over, and the solemn voice which sounds as no other voice ever does, falling calm through the still air, bidding earth return to earth, and dust to dust, had ceased, he still stood as if unable to comprehend that all was over—no one to bid him come away, no other place to go to. His brain was not relieved by tears, or his mind set in activity by anything to do. He stood there half stupefied, left behind, in that condition when simply to remain as we are seems the only thing possible to us.

Miss Bethune had placed Dora in the little brougham, in rigorous fulfilment of her duty to the child. Mr. Templar and the doctor had both departed, the two other women, Mrs. Bristow's maid and the nurse who had accompanied her, had driven away: and still the young man stood, not paying any attention. Miss Bethune waited for a little by the carriage door. She did not answer the appeal of the coachman, asking if he was to drive away; she said nothing to Dora, whose eyes endeavoured in vain to read the changes in her friend's face; but, after standing there for a few minutes quite silent, she suddenly turned and went back to the cemetery. It was strange to her to hesitate in anything she did, and from the moment she left the carriage door all uncertainty was over. She went back with a quick step, treading her way among the graves, and put her hand upon young Gordon's arm.

"You are coming home with me," she said.

The new, keen voice, irregular and full of life, so unlike the measured tones to which he had been listening, struck the young man uneasily in the midst of his melancholy reverie, which was half trance, half exhaustion. He moved a step away, as if to shake off the interruption, scarcely conscious what, and not at all who it was.

"My dear young man, you must come home with me," she said again.

He looked at her, with consciousness re-awakening, and

attempted to smile, with his natural ready response to every kindness. "It is you," he said, and then, "I might have known it could only be you."

What did that mean? Nothing at all. Merely his sense that the one person who had spoken kindly to him, looked tenderly at him (though he had never known why, and had been both amused and embarrassed by the consciousness), was the most likely among all the strangers by whom he was surrounded to be kind to him now. But it produced an effect upon Miss Bethune which was far beyond any meaning it bore.

A great light seemed suddenly to blaze over her face; her eyes, which had been so veiled and stern, awoke; every line of a face which could be harsh and almost rigid in repose, began to melt and soften; her composure, which had been almost solemn, failed; her lip began to quiver, tears came dropping upon his arm, which she suddenly clasped with both her hands, clinging to it. "You say right," she cried, "my dear, my dear!—more right than all the reasons. It is you and nature that makes everything clear. You are just coming home with me."

"I don't seem," he said, "to know what the word means."

"But you will soon learn again. God bless the good woman that cherished you and loved you, my bonnie boy. I'll not say a word against her—oh, no, no! God's blessing upon her as she lies there. I will never grudge a good word you say of her, never a regret. But now"—she put her arm within his with a proud and tender movement, which so far penetrated his languor as to revive the bewilderment which he had felt before—"now you are coming home with me."

He did not resist; he allowed himself to be led to the little carriage and packed into it, which was not quite an easy thing to do. On another occasion he would have laughed and protested, but on this he submitted gravely to whatever was required of him, thankful, in the failure of all motive, to have some one to tell him what to do, to move him as if he were an automaton. He sat bundled up on the little front seat, with Dora's wondering countenance opposite to him, and that other inexplicable face, inspired and lighted up with tenderness. He had not strength enough to inquire why this stranger took possession of him so; neither could Dora tell, who sat opposite to him, her mind awakened, her thoughts busy. This was the almost son of the woman who they said was Dora's mother. What was he to Dora? Was he the nearer to her, or the farther from her, for that relationship? Did she like him better or worse for having done everything that it ought, they said, have been her part to do?

These questions were all confused in Dora's mind, but they were not favourable to this new interloper into her life—he who had known about her for years while she had never heard of him. She sat very upright, reluctant to make room for him, yet scrupulously doing so, and a little indignant that he should thus be brought in to interfere with her own claims to the first place. The drive to Bloomsbury seemed very long in these circumstances, and it was indeed a long drive. They all came back into the streets after the long suburban road with a sense almost of relief in the growing noise, the rattle of the causeway, and sound of the carts and carriages—which made it unnecessary, as it had been impossible for them, to say anything to each other, and brought back the affairs of common life to dispel the influences of the solemn moment that was past.

When they had reached Miss Bethune's rooms, and returned altogether to existence, and the sight of a table spread for a meal, it was a shock, but not an ungrateful one. Miss Bethune at once threw off the gravity which had wrapped her like a cloak, when she put away her black bonnet. She bade Gilchrist hurry to have the luncheon brought up. "These two young creatures have eaten nothing, I am sure, this day. Probably they think they cannot: but when food is set before them they will learn better. Haste ye, Gilchrist, to have it served up. No, Dora, you will stay with me too. Your father is a troubled man this day. You will not go in upon him with that cloud about you, not till you are refreshed and rested, and have got your colour and your natural look back.

And you, my bonnie man!" She could not refrain from touching, caressing his shoulder as she passed him; her eyes kept filling with tears as she looked at him. He for his part moved and took his place as she told him, still in a dream.

It was a curious meal, more daintily prepared and delicate than usual, and Miss Bethune was a woman who at all times was "very particular," and exercised all the gifts of the landlady, whose other lodgers demanded much less of her. And the mistress of the little feast was still less as usual. She scarcely sat down at her own table, but served her young guests with anxious care, carving choice morsels for them, watching their faces, their little movements of impatience, and the gradual development of natural appetite, which came as the previous spell gradually wore off. She talked all the time, her countenance a little flushed and full of emotion, her eyes moist and shining, with frequent sallies at Gilchrist, who hovered round the table waiting upon the young guests, and in her excitement making continual mistakes and stumblings, which soon roused Dora to laugh, and Harry to apologise.

"It is all right," he cried, when Miss Bethune at last made a dart at her attendant, and gave her, what is called in feminine language, "a shake," to bring her to herself.

"Are you out of your wits, woman?" Miss Bethune exclaimed. "Go away and leave me to look after the bairns, if ye cannot keep your head. Are you out of your wits?"

"Indeed, mem, and I have plenty of reason, Gilchrist said, weeping, and feeling for her apron, while the dish in her hand wavered wildly; and then it was that Harry Gordon, coming to himself, cried out that it was all right.

"And I am going to have some of that," he added, steadying the kind creature, whose instinct of service had more effect than either encouragement or reproof. And this little touch of reality settled him too. He began to respond a little, to rouse himself, even to see the humour of the situation, at which Dora had begun to laugh, but which brought a soft moisture, in which was ease and consolation, to his eyes.

It was not until about an hour later that Miss Bethune was left alone with the young man. He had begun by this time to speak about himself. "I am not so discouraged as you think," he said, "I don't seem to be afraid. After all, it doesn't matter much, does it, what happens to a young fellow all alone in the world? It's only me, anyhow. I have no wife," he said, with a faint laugh, "no sister to be involved—nothing but my own rather useless person, a thing of no account. It wasn't that that knocked me down. It was just the feeling of the end of everything, and that she was laid there that had been so good to me—so good—and nothing ever to be done for her any more."

"I can forgive you that," said Miss Bethune, with a sort of sob in her throat. "And yet she was ill to you, unjust at the last."

"No, not that. I have had everything, too much for a man capable of earning his living to accept—but then it seemed all so natural, it was the common course of life. I was scarcely waking up to see that it could not be."

"And a cruel rousing you have had at last, my poor boy."

"No," he said steadily, "I will never allow it was cruel; it has been sharp and effectual. It couldn't help being effectual, could it? since I have no alternative. The pity is I am good for so little. No education to speak of."

"You shall have education—as much as you can set your face to."

He looked up at her with a little air of surprise, and shook his head. "No," he said, "not now. I am too old. I must lose no more time. The thing is, that my work will be worth so much less, being guided by no skill. Skill is a beautiful thing. I envy the very scavengers," he said (who were working underneath the window), "for piling up their mud like that, straight. I should never get it straight." The poor young fellow was so near tears that he was glad from time to time to have a chance of a feeble laugh, which relieved him. "And that is humble enough! I think much the best thing for me will be to go back to South America.

There are people who know me, who would give me a little place where I could learn. Book-keeping can't be such a tremendous mystery. There's an old clerk or two of my guardians"—here he paused to swallow down the climbing sorrow—"who would give me a hint or two. And if the pay was very small at first, why, I'm not an extravagant fellow."

"Are you sure of that?" his confidante said.

He looked at her again, surprised, then glanced at himself and his dress, which was not economical, and reddened and laughed again. "I am afraid you are right," he said. "I haven't known much what economy was. I have lived like the other people; but I am not too old to learn, and I should not mind in the least what I looked like, or how I lived, for a time. Things would get better after a time."

They were standing together near the window, for he had begun to roam about the room as he talked, and she had risen from her chair with one of the sudden movements of excitement. "There will be no need," she said,—"there will be no need. Something will be found for you at home."

He shook his head. "You forget it is scarcely home to me. And what could I do here that would be worth paying me for? I must no more be dependent upon kindness. Oh, don't think I do not feel kindness. What should I have done this miserable day but for you, who have been so good to me—as good as—as a mother, though I had no claim?"

She gave a great cry, and seized him by both his hands. "Oh, lad, if you knew what you were saying! That word to me, that have died for it, and have no claim! Gilchrist, Gilchrist!" she cried, suddenly dropping his hands again, "come here and speak to me! Help me! have pity upon me! For if this is not him, all nature and God's against me. Come here before I speak or die!"

CHAPTER XXI.

It was young Gordon himself, alarmed but not excited as by any idea of a new discovery which could affect his fate, who brought Miss Bethune back to herself, far better than Gilchrist could do, who had no art but to weep and entreat, and then yield to her mistress whatever she might wish. *A quelque chose malheur est bon.* He had been in the habit of soothing and calming down an excitable, sometimes hysterical woman, whose *accès des nerfs* meant nothing, or were, at least, supposed to mean nothing, except indeed nerves, and the ups and downs which are characteristic of them. He was roused by the not dissimilar outburst of feeling or passion, wholly incomprehensible to him from any other point of view, to which his new friend had given way. He took it very quietly, with the composure of use and wont. The sight of her emotion and excitement brought him quite back to himself. He could imagine no reason whatever for it, except the sympathetic effect of all the troublous circumstances in which she had been, without any real reason, involved. It was her sympathy, her kindness for himself and for Dora, he had not the least doubt, which, by bringing her into those scenes of pain and trouble, and associating her so completely with the complicated and intricate story, had brought on this "attack." What he had known to be characteristic of the one woman with whom he had been in familiar intercourse for so long a period of his life seemed to Harry characteristic of all women. He was quite equal to the occasion. Dr. Roland himself, who would have been so full of professional curiosity, so anxious to make out what it was all about, as perhaps to lessen his promptitude in action, would scarcely have been of so much real use as Harry, who had no *arrière pensée*, but addressed himself to the immediate

192

emergency with all his might. He soothed the sufferer, so that she was soon relieved by copious floods of tears, which seemed to him the natural method of getting rid of all that emotion and excitement, but which surprised Gilchrist beyond description, and even Miss Bethune herself, whose complete breakdown was so unusual and unlike her. He left her quite at ease in his mind as to her condition, having persuaded her to lie down, and recommended Gilchrist to darken the room, and keep her mistress in perfect quiet.

"I will go and look after my things," he said, "and I'll come back when I have made all my arrangements, and tell you everything. Oh, don't speak now! You will be all right in the evening if you keep quite quiet now: and if you will give me your advice then, it will be very, very grateful to me." He made a little warning gesture, keeping her from replying, and then kissed her hand and went away. He had himself pulled down the blind to subdue a little of the garish July daylight, and placed her on a sofa in the corner—ministrations which both mistress and maid permitted with bewilderment, so strange to them was at once the care and the authority of such proceedings. They remained, Miss Bethune on the sofa, Gilchrist, open-mouthed, staring at her, until the door was heard to close upon the young man. Then Miss Bethune rose slowly, with a kind of awe in her face.

"As soon as you think he is out of sight," she said, "Gilchrist, we'll have up the blinds again, but not veesibly, to go against the boy."

"Eh, mem," cried Gilchrist, between laughing and crying, "to bid me darken the room, and you that canna abide the dark, night or day!"

"It was a sweet thought, Gilchrist—all the pure goodness of him and the kind heart."

"I am not saying, mem, but what the young gentleman has a very kind heart."

"You are not saying? And what can you know beyond what's veesible to every person that sees him? It is more than that.

Gilchrist, you and all the rest, what do I care what you say? If that is not the voice of nature, what is there to trust to in this whole world? Why should that young lad, bred up so different, knowing nothing of me or my ways, have taken to me? Look at Dora. What a difference! She has no instinct, nothing drawing her to her poor mother. That was a most misfortunate woman, but not an ill woman, Gilchrist. Look how she has done by mine! But Dora has no leaning towards her, no tender thought; whereas he, my bonnie boy——"

"Mem," said Gilchrist, "but if it was the voice of nature, it would be double strong in Miss Dora; for there is no doubt that it was her mother: and with this one—oh, my dear leddy, you ken yoursel'——"

Miss Bethune gave her faithful servant a look of flame, and going to the windows, drew up energetically the blinds, making the springs resound. Then she said in her most satirical tone: "And what is it I ken mysel'?"

"Oh, mem," said Gilchrist, "there's a' the evidence, first his ain story, and then the leddy's that convinced ye for a moment; and then, what is most o' a, the old gentleman, the writer, one of them that kens everything: of the father that died so many long years ago, and the baby before him."

Miss Bethune put up her hands to her ears, she stamped her foot upon the ground. "How dare ye—how dare ye?" she cried. "Either man or woman that repeats that fool story to me is no friend of mine. My child, that I've felt in my heart growing up, and seen him boy and man! What's that old man's word—a stranger that knows nothing, that had even forgotten what he was put up to say—in comparison with what is in my heart? Is there such a thing as nature, or no? Is a mother just like any other person, no better, rather worse? Oh, woman!—you that are a woman! with no call to be rigid about your evidence like a man—what's your evidence to me? I will just tell him when he comes back. 'My bonnie man,' I will say, 'you have been driven here and there in this world, and them that liked you best have failed you; but here is the place where you belong, and here is a love that will never fail!'"

"Oh, my dear leddy, my own mistress," cried Gilchrist, "think—think before you do that! He will ask ye for the evidence, if I am not to ask for it. He's a fine, independent-spirited young gentleman, and he will just shake his head, and say he'll lippen to nobody again. Oh, dinna deceive the young man! Ye might find out after——"

"What, Gilchrist? Do you think I would change my mind about my own son, and abandon him, like this woman, at the last?"

"I never knew you forsake one that trusted in ye, I'm not saying that; but there might come one after all that had a better claim. There might appear one that even the like of me would believe in—that would have real evidence in his favour, that was no more to be doubted than if he had never been taken away out of your arms."

Miss Bethune turned round quick as lightning upon her maid, her eyes shining, her face full of sudden colour and light. "God bless you, Gilchrist!" she cried, seizing the maid by her shoulders with a half embrace; "I see now you have never believed in that story—no more than me."

Poor Gilchrist could but gape with her mouth open at this unlooked-for turning of the tables. She had presented, without knowing it, the strongest argument of all.

After this, the patient, whom poor Harry had left to the happy influences of quiet and darkness, with all the blinds drawn up and the afternoon sunshine pouring in, went through an hour or two of restless occupation, her mind in the highest activity, her thoughts and her hands full. She promised finally to Gilchrist, not without a mental reservation in the case of special impulse or new light, not to disclose her conviction to Harry, but to wait for at least a day or two on events. But even this resolution did not suffice to reduce her to any condition of quiet, or make the rest which he had prescribed possible. She turned to a number of things which had been laid aside to be done one time or another; arrangement of new possessions and putting away of old, for which previously she had never found a fit occasion, and despatched them, scarcely allowing Gilchrist to help her, at lightning speed.

Finally, she took out an old and heavy jewel-box, which had stood untouched in her bedroom for years; for, save an old brooch or two and some habitual rings which never left her fingers, Miss Bethune wore no ornaments. She took them into her sitting-room as the time approached when Harry might be expected back. It would give her a countenance, she thought; it would keep her from fixing her eyes on him while he spoke, and thus being assailed through all the armour of the heart at the same time. She could not look him in the face and see that likeness which Gilchrist, unconvincible, would not see, and yet remain silent. Turning over the old-fashioned jewels, telling him about them, to whom they had belonged, and all the traditions regarding them, would help her in that severe task of self-repression. She put the box on the table before her, and pulled out the trays.

Nobody in Bloomsbury had seen these treasures before: the box had been kept carefully locked, disguised in an old brown cover, that no one might even guess how valuable it was. Miss Bethune was almost tempted to send for Dora to see the diamonds in their old-fashioned settings, and that pearl necklace which was still finer in its perfection of lustre and shape. To call Dora when there was anything to show was so natural, and it might make it easier for her to keep her own counsel; but she reflected that in Dora's presence the young man would not be more than half hers, and forbore.

Never in her life had those jewels given her so much pleasure. They had given her no pleasure, indeed. She had not been allowed to have them in that far-off stormy youth, which had been lightened by such a sweet, guilty gleam of happiness, and quenched in such misery of downfall. When they came to her by inheritance, like all the rest, these beautiful things had made her heart sick. What could she do with them—a woman whose life no longer contained any possible festival, who had nobody coming after her, no heir to make heirlooms sweet? She had locked the box, and almost thrown away the key, which, however, was a passionate suggestion repugnant to common sense, and resolved itself naturally into confiding the key to Gilchrist, in whose most secret repositories it had been kept, with an occasional furtive interval during which the maid had secretly visited and "polished up" the jewels, making sure that they were all right. Neither mistress nor maid was quite aware of their value, and both probably exaggerated it in their thoughts; but some of the diamonds were fine, though all were very old-fashioned in arrangement, and the pearls were noted. Miss Bethune pulled out the trays, and the gems flashed and sparkled in a thousand colours in the slant of sunshine which poured in its last level ray through one window, just before the sun set—and made a dazzling show upon the table, almost blinding Janie, who came up with a message, and could not restrain a little shriek of wonder and admiration. The letter was one of trouble and appeal from poor Mrs. Hesketh, who and her husband were becoming more and more a burden on the shoulders of their friends. It asked for money, as usual, just a little money to go on with, as the shop in which they had been set up was not as yet producing much. The letter had been written with evident reluctance, and was marked with blots of tears. Miss Bethune's mind was too much excited to consider calmly any such petition. Full herself of anticipation, of passionate hope, and visionary enthusiasm, which transported her above all common things, how was she to refuse a poor woman's appeal for the bare necessities of existence—a woman "near her trouble," with a useless husband, who was unworthy, yet whom the poor soul loved? She called Gilchrist, who generally carried the purse, to get something for the poor little pair.

"Is there anybody waiting?" she asked.

"Oh ay, mem," said Gilchrist, "there's somebody waiting,— just him himsel', the weirdless creature, that is good for nothing."

Gilchrist did not approve of all her mistress's liberalities. "I would not just be their milch cow to give them whatever they're wanting," she said. "It's awful bad for any person to just know where to run when they are in trouble."

"Hold your peace!" cried her mistress. "Am I one to shut up my heart when the blessing of God has come to me?"

"Oh, mem!" cried Gilchrist, remonstrating, holding up her hands.

But Miss Bethune stamped her foot, and the wiser woman yielded.

She found Hesketh standing at the door of the sitting-room, when she went out to give him, very unwillingly, the money for his wife. "The impident weirdless creature! He would have been in upon my leddy in another moment, pressing to her very presence with his impident ways!" cried Gilchrist, hot and indignant. The faithful woman paused at the door as she came back, and looked at her mistress turning over and rearranging these treasures. "And her sitting playing with her bonnie dies, in a rapture like a little bairn!" she said to herself, putting up her apron to her eyes. And then Gilchrist shook her head—shook it, growing quicker and quicker in the movement, as if she would have twisted it off.

But Miss Bethune was "very composed" when young Gordon came back. With an intense sense of the humour of the position, which mistress and maid communicated to each other with one glance of tacit co-operation, these two women comported themselves as if the behests of the young visitor who had taken the management of Miss Bethune's *accès des nerfs* upon himself, had been carried out. She assumed, almost unconsciously, notwithstanding the twinkle in her eye, the languid aspect of a woman who has been resting after unusual excitement. All women, they say (as they say so many foolish things), are actors; all women, at all events, let us allow, learn as the A B C of their training the art of taking up a rôle assigned to them, and fulfilling the necessities of a position. "You will see what I'm reduced to by what I'm doing," she said. "As if there was nothing of more importance in life, I am just playing myself with my toys, like Dora, or any other little thing."

"So much the best thing you could do," said young Harry; and he was eager and delighted to look through the contents of the box with her.

He was far better acquainted with their value than she was, and while she told him the family associations connected with each ornament, he discussed very learnedly what they were, and distinguished the old-fashioned rose diamonds which were amongst those of greater value, with a knowledge that seemed to her extraordinary. They spent, in fact, an hour easily and happily over that box, quite relieved from graver considerations by the interposition of a new thing, in which there were no deep secrets of the heart or commotions of being involved: and thus were brought down into the ordinary from the high and troublous level of feeling and excitement on which they had been. To Miss Bethune the little episode was one of child's play in the midst of the most serious questions of the world. Had she thought it possible beforehand that such an interval could have been, she would, in all likelihood, have scorned herself for the dereliction, and almost scorned the young man for being able to forget at once his sorrow and the gravity of his circumstances at sight of anything so trifling as a collection of trinkets. But in reality this interlude was balm to them both. It revealed to Miss Bethune a possibility of ordinary life and intercourse, made sweet by understanding and affection, which was a revelation to her repressed and passionate spirit; and it soothed the youth with that renewing of fresh interests, reviving and succeeding the old, which gives elasticity to the mind, and courage to face the world anew. They did not know how long they had been occupied over the jewels, when the hour of dinner came round again, and Gilchrist appeared with her preparations, still further increasing that sense of peaceful life renewed, and the order of common things begun again. It was only after this meal was over, the jewels being all restored to their places, and the box to its old brown cover in Miss Bethune's bedroom, that the discussion of the graver question was resumed.

"There is one thing," Miss Bethune said, "that, however proud you may be, you must let me say: and that is, that everything having turned out so different to your thoughts, and you left— you will not be offended?—astray, as it were, in this big unfriendly place——"

"I cannot call it unfriendly," said young Gordon. "If other people find it so, it is not my experience. I have found you." He looked up at her with a half laugh, with moisture in his eyes.

"Ay," she said, with emphasis, "you have found me—you say well—found me when you were not looking for me. I accept the word as a good omen. And after that?"

If only she would not have abashed him from time to time with those dark sayings, which seemed to mean something to which he had no clue! He felt himself brought suddenly to a standstill in his grateful effusion of feeling, and put up his hand to arrest her in what she was evidently going on to say.

"Apart from that," he said hurriedly, "I am not penniless. I have not been altogether dependent; at least, the form of my dependence has been the easiest one. I have had my allowance from my guardian ever since I came to man's estate. It was my own, though, of course, of his giving. And I am not an extravagant fellow. It was not as if I wanted money for to-morrow's living, for daily bread." He coloured as he spoke, with the half pride, half shame, of discussing such a subject. "I think," he said, throwing off that flush with a shake of his head, "that I have enough to take me back to South America, and there, I told you, I have friends. I don't think I can fail to find work there."

"But under such different circumstances! Have you considered? A poor clerk where you were one of the fine gentlemen of the place. Such a change of position is easier where you are not known."

He grew red again, with a more painful colour. "I don't think so," he said quickly. "I don't believe that my old friends would cast me off because, instead of being a useless fellow about town, I was a poor clerk."

"Maybe you are right," said Miss Bethune very gravely. "I am not one that thinks so ill of human nature. They would not cast you off. But you, working hard all day, wearied at night, with no house to entertain them in that entertained you, would it not be you that would cast off them?"

He looked at her, startled, for a moment. "Do you think," he cried, "that poverty makes a man mean like that?" And then he added slowly: "It is possible, perhaps, that it might be so." Then he brightened up again, and looked her full in the face. "But then there would be nobody to blame for that, it would be simply my own fault."

"God bless you, laddie!" cried Miss Bethune quite irrelevantly; and then she too paused. "If it should happen so that there was a place provided for you at home. No, no, not what you call dependence—far from it, hard work. I know one—a lady that has property in the North—property that has not been well managed—that has given her more trouble than it is worth. But there's much to be made of it, if she had a man who would give his mind to it as if—as if it were his own."

"But I," he said, "know nothing about the North. I would not know how to manage. I told you I had no education. And would this lady have me, trust me, put that in my hands, without knowing, without——"

"She would trust you," said Miss Bethune, clasping her hands together firmly, and looking him in the face, in a rigid position which showed how little steady she was—"she would trust you, for life and death, on my word."

His eyes fell before that unfathomable concentration of hers. "And you would trust me like that—knowing so little, so little? And how can you tell even that I am honest—even that I am true? That there's nothing behind, no weakness, no failure?"

"Don't speak to me," she said harshly. "I know."

CHAPTER XXII.

The evening passed, however, without any further revelations. Miss Bethune explained to the young man, with all the lucidity of a man of business, the situation and requirements of that "property in the North," which would give returns, she believed, of various kinds, not always calculated in balance sheets, if it was looked after by a man who would deal with it "as if it were his own." The return would be something in money and rents, but much more in human comfort and happiness. She had never had the courage to tackle that problem, she said, and the place had been terrible to her, full of associations which would be thought of no more if he were there. The result was, that young Gordon went away thoughtful, somewhat touched by the feeling with which Miss Bethune had spoken of her poor crofters, somewhat roused by the thought of "the North," that vague and unknown country which was the country of his fathers, the land of brown heath and shaggy wood, the country of Scott, which is, after all, distinction enough for any well-conditioned stranger. Should he try that strange new opening of life suddenly put before him? The unknown of itself has a charm—

> If the pass were dangerous known,
> The danger's self were lure alone.

He went back to his hotel with at least a new project fully occupying all his thoughts.

On the next evening, in the dusk of the summer night, Miss Bethune was in her bed-chamber alone. She had no light, though she was a lover of the light, and had drawn up the blinds as soon as the young physician who prescribed a darkened room had disappeared. She had a habit of watching out the last departing rays of daylight, and loved to sit in the gloaming, as she called it, reposing from all the cares of the day in that meditative moment. It was a bad sign of Miss Bethune's state of mind when she called early for her lamp. She was seated thus in the dark, when young Gordon came in audibly to the sitting-room, introduced by Gilchrist, who told him her mistress would be with him directly; but, knowing Miss Bethune would hear what she said, did not come to call her. The lamps were lighted in that room, and showed a little outline of light through the chinks of the door. She smiled to herself in the dark, with a beatitude that ought to have lighted it up, as she listened to the big movements of the young man in the lighted room next door. He had seated himself under Gilchrist's ministrations; but when she went away he got up and moved about, looking, as Miss Bethune divined, at the pictures on the walls and the books and little silver toys on the tables.

He made more noise, she thought to herself proudly, than a woman does: filled the space more, seemed to occupy and fill out everything. Her countenance and her heart expanded in the dark; she would have liked to peep at him through the crevice of light round the door, or even the keyhole, to see him when he did not know she was looking, to read the secrets of his heart in his face. There were none there, she said to herself with an effusion of happiness which brought the tears to her eyes, none there which a mother should be afraid to discover. The luxury of sitting there, holding her breath, hearing him move, knowing him so near, was so sweet and so great, that she sat, too blessed to move, taking all the good out of that happy moment before it should fleet away.

Suddenly, however, there came a dead silence. Had he sat down again? Had he gone out on the balcony? What had become of him? She sat breathless, wondering, listening for the next sound. Surely he had stepped outside the window to look out upon the Bloomsbury street, and the waving of the trees in the

203

Square, and the stars shining overhead. Not a sound—yet, yes, there was something. What was it? A faint, stealthy rustling, not to be called a sound at all, rather some stealthy movement to annihilate sound—the strangest contrast to the light firm step that had come into the room, and the free movements which she had felt to be bigger than a woman's.

Miss Bethune in the dark held her breath; fear seized possession of her, she knew not why; her heart sank, she knew not why. Oh, his father—his father was not a good man!

The rustling continued, very faint; it might have been a small animal rubbing against the door. She sat bolt upright in her chair, motionless, silent as a waxen image, listening. If perhaps, after all, it should be only one of the little girls, or even the cat rubbing against the wall idly on the way downstairs! A troubled smile came over her face, her heart gave a throb of relief. But then the sound changed, and Miss Bethune's face again grew rigid, her heart stood still.

Some one was trying very cautiously, without noise, to open the door; to turn the handle without making any sound required some time; it creaked a little, and then there was silence—guilty silence, the pause of stealth alarmed by the faintest noise; then it began again. Slowly, slowly the handle turned round, the door opened, a hair's breadth at a time. O Lord above! his father—his father was an ill man.

There was some one with her in the room—some one unseen, as she was, swallowed up in the darkness, veiled by the curtains at the windows, which showed faintly a pale streak of sky only, letting in no light. Unseen, but not inaudible; a hurried, fluttering breath betraying him, and that faint sound of cautious, uneasy movement, now and then instantly, guiltily silenced, and then resumed. She could feel the stealthy step thrill the flooring, making a jar, which was followed by one of those complete silences in which the intruder too held his breath, then another stealthy step.

A thousand thoughts, a very avalanche, precipitated

themselves through her mind. A man did not steal into a dark room like that if he were doing it for the first time. And his words last night, "How do you know even that I am honest?" And then his father—his father—oh, God help him, God forgive him!—that was an ill man! And his upbringing in a country where lies were common, with a guardian that did him no justice, and the woman that cut him off. And not to know that he had a creature belonging to him in the world to be made glad or sorry whatever happened! Oh, God forgive him, God help him! the unfortunate, the miserable boy! "Mine all the same—mine all the same!" her heart said, bleeding—oh, that was no metaphor! bleeding with the anguish, the awful, immeasurable blow.

If there was any light at all in the room, it was a faint greyness, just showing in the midst of the dark the vague form of a little table against the wall, and a box in a brown cover—a box—no, no, the shape of a box, but only something standing there, something, the accursed thing for which life and love were to be wrecked once more. Oh, his father—his father! But his father would not have done that. Yet it was honester to take the trinkets, the miserable stones that would bring in money, than to wring a woman's heart. And what did the boy know? He had never been taught, never had any example, God help him, God forgive him! and mine—mine all the time!

Then out of the complete darkness came into that faint grey where the box was, an arm, a hand. It touched, not calculating the distance, the solid substance with a faint jar, and retired like a ghost, while she sat rigid, looking on; then more cautiously, more slowly still, it stole forth again, and grasped the box. Miss Bethune had settled nothing what to do, she had thought of nothing but the misery of it, she had intended, so far as she had any intention, to watch while the tragedy was played out, the dreadful act accomplished. But she was a woman of sudden impulses, moved by flashes of resolution almost independent of her will.

Suddenly, more ghostlike still than the arm of the thief, she made a swift movement forward, and put her hand upon his. Her grasp seemed to crush through the quivering clammy fingers, and she felt under her own the leap of the pulses; but the criminal was prepared for every emergency, and uttered no cry. She felt the quick noiseless change of attitude, and then the free arm swing to strike her—heaven and earth! to strike her, a woman twice his age, to strike her, his friend, his—— She was a strong woman, in the fulness of health and courage. As quick as lightning, she seized the arm as it descended, and held him as in a grip of iron. Was it guilt that made him like a child in her hold? He had a stick in his hand, shortened, with a heavy head, ready to deal a blow. Oh, the coward, the wretched coward! She held him panting for a moment, unable to say a word; and then she called out with a voice that was no voice, but a kind of roar of misery, for "Gilchrist, Gilchrist!"

Gilchrist, who was never far off, who always had her ear open for her mistress, heard, and came flying from up or down stairs with her candle: and some one else heard it, who was standing pensive on the balcony, looking out, and wondering what fate had now in store for him, and mingling his thoughts with the waving of the trees and the nameless noises of the street. Which of them arrived first was never known, he from the other room throwing wide the door of communication, or she from the stairs with the impish, malicious light of that candle throwing in its sudden illumination as with a pleasure in the deed.

The spectators were startled beyond measure to see the lady in apparent conflict with a man, but they had no time to make any remarks. The moment the light flashed upon her, Miss Bethune gave a great cry. "It's you, ye vermin!" she cried, flinging the furtive creature in her grasp from her against the wall, which half stunned him for the moment. And then she stood for a moment, her head bent back, her face without a trace of colour, confronting the eager figure in the doorway, surrounded by the glow of the light, flying forward to help her.

"O God, forgive me!" she cried, "God, forgive me, for I am an ill woman: but I will never forgive myself!"

The man who lay against the wall, having dropped there on the floor with the vehemence of her action, perhaps exaggerating the force that had been used against him, to excite pity—for Gilchrist, no mean opponent, held one door, and that unexpected dreadful apparition of the young man out of the lighted room bearing down upon him, filled the other—was Alfred Hesketh, white, miserable, and cowardly, huddled up in a wretched heap, with furtive eyes gleaming, and the heavy-headed stick furtively grasped, still ready to deal an unexpected blow, had he the opportunity, though he was at the same time rubbing the wrist that held it, as if in pain.

Young Gordon had made a hurried step towards him, when Miss Bethune put out her hand. She had dropped into a chair, where she sat panting for breath.

"Wait," she said, "wait till I can speak."

"You brute!" cried Harry; "how dare you come in here? What have you done to frighten the lady?"

He was interrupted by a strange chuckle of a laugh from Miss Bethune's panting throat.

"It's rather me, I'm thinking, that's frightened him," she said. "Ye wretched vermin of a creature, how did ye know? What told ye in your meeserable mind that there was something here to steal? And ye would have struck me—me that am dealing out to ye your daily bread! No, my dear, you're not to touch him; don't lay a finger on him. The Lord be thanked—though God forgive me for thanking Him for the wickedness of any man!"

How enigmatical this all was to Harry Gordon, and how little he could imagine any clue to the mystery, it is needless to say. Gilchrist herself thought her mistress was temporarily out of her mind. She was quicker, however, to realise what had happened than the young man, who did not think of the jewels, nor remember anything about them. Gilchrist looked with anxiety at her lady's white face and gleaming eyes.

"Take her into the parlour, Master Harry," she said: "she's just done out. And I'll send for the police."

"You'll do nothing of the kind, Gilchrist," said Miss Bethune. "Get up, ye creature. You're not worth either man's or woman's while; you have no more fusion than a cat. Get up, and begone, ye poor, weak, wretched, cowardly vermin, for that's what ye are: and I thank the Lord with all my heart that it was only you! Gilchrist, stand away from the door, and let the creature go."

He rose, dragging himself up by degrees, with a furtive look at Gordon, who, indeed, looked a still less easy opponent than Miss Bethune.

"I take that gentleman to witness," he said, "as there's no evidence against me but just a lady's fancy: and I've been treated very bad, and my wrist broken, for aught I know, and bruised all over, and I——"

Miss Bethune stamped her foot on the floor. "Begone, ye born liar and robber!" she said. "Gilchrist will see ye off the premises; and mind, you never come within my sight again. Now, Mr. Harry, as she calls ye, I'll go into the parlour, as she says; and the Lord, that only knows the wickedness that has been in my mind, forgive me this night! and it would be a comfort to my heart, my bonnie man, if you would say Amen."

"Amen with all my heart," said the young man, with a smile, "but, so far as I can make out, your wickedness is to be far too good and forgiving. What did the fellow do? I confess I should not like to be called a vermin, as you called him freely—but if he came with intent to steal, he should have been handed over to the police, indeed he should."

"I am more worthy of the police than him, if ye but knew: but, heaven be praised, you'll never know. I mind now, he came with a message when I was playing with these wretched diamonds, like an old fool: and he must have seen or scented them with the creeminal instinct Dr. Roland speaks about."

She drew a long breath, for she had not yet recovered from the panting of excitement, and then told her story, the rustling without, the opening of the door, the hand extended to the box.

When she had told all this with much vividness, Miss Bethune suddenly stopped, drew another long breath, and dropped back upon the sofa where she was sitting. It was not her way; the lights had been dazzling and confusing her ever since they blazed upon her by the opening of the two doors, and the overwhelming horror, and blessed but tremendous revulsion of feeling, which had passed in succession over her, had been more than her strength, already undermined by excitement, could bear. Her breath, her consciousness, her life, seemed to ebb away in a moment, leaving only a pale shadow of her, fallen back upon the cushions.

Once more Harry was the master of the situation. He had seen a woman faint before, which was almost more than Gilchrist, with all her experience, had done, and he had the usual remedies at his fingers' ends. But this was not like the usual easy faints, over in a minute, to which young Gordon had been accustomed, and Dr. Roland had to be summoned from below, and a thrill of alarm had run through the house, Mrs. Simcox herself coming up from the kitchen, with strong salts and feathers to burn, before Miss Bethune came to herself. The house was frightened, and so at last was the experienced Harry; but Dr. Roland's interest and excitement may be said to have been pleasurable. "I have always thought this was what was likely. I've been prepared for it," he said to himself, as he hovered round the sofa. It would be wrong to suppose that he lengthened, or at least did nothing to shorten, this faint for his own base purposes, that he might the better make out certain signs which he thought he had recognised. But the fact was, that not only Dora had come from abovestairs, but even Mr. Mannering had dragged himself down, on the alarm that Miss Bethune was dead or dying; and that the whole household had gathered in her room, or on the landing outside; while she lay, in complicity (or not) with the doctor, in that long-continued swoon, which the spectators afterwards said lasted an hour, or two, or even three hours, according to their temperaments.

When she came to herself at last, the scene upon which she

opened her eyes was one which helped her recovery greatly, by filling her with wrath and indignation. She lay in the middle of her room, in a strong draught, the night air blowing from window to window across her, the lamp even under its shade, much more the candles on the mantelpiece, blown about, and throwing a wavering glare upon the agitated group, Gilchrist in the foreground with her apron at her eyes, and behind her Dora, red with restrained emotions, and Janie and Molly crying freely, while Mrs. Simcox brandished a bunch of fuming feathers, and Mr. Mannering peered over the landlady's head with his "pince-nez" insecurely balanced on his nose, and his legs trembling under him in a harmony of unsteadiness, but anxiety. Miss Bethune's wrist was in the grasp of the doctor; and Harry stood behind with a fan, which, in the strong wind blowing across her from window to window, struck the patient as ludicrously unnecessary. "What is all this fuss about?" she cried, trying to raise herself up.

"There's no fuss, my dear lady," said the doctor; "but you must keep perfectly quiet."

"Oh, you're there, Dr. Roland? Then there's one sane person. But, for goodness' sake, make Mr. Mannering sit down, and send all these idiots away. What's the matter with me, that I've to get my death of cold, and be murdered with that awful smell, and even Harry Gordon behaving like a fool, making an air with a fan, when there's a gale blowing? Go away, go away."

"You see that our friend has come to herself," said the doctor. "Shut that window, somebody, the other will be enough; and, my dear woman, for the sake of all that's good, take those horrid feathers away."

"I am murdered with the smell!" cried Miss Bethune, placing her hands over her face. "But make Mr. Mannering sit down, he's not fit to stand after his illness; and Harry, boy, sit down, too, and don't drive me out of my senses. Go away, go all of you away."

The last to be got rid of was Dr. Roland, who assured everybody that the patient was now quite well, but languid. "You want to get rid of me too, I know," he said, "and I'm going; but I should like to see you in bed first."

"You shall not see me in bed, nor no other man," said Miss Bethune. "I will go to bed when I am disposed, doctor. I'm not your patient, mind, at all events, now."

"You were half an hour since: but I'm not going to pretend to any authority," said the doctor. "I hope I know better. Don't agitate yourself any more, if you'll be guided by me. You have been screwing up that heart of yours far too tight."

"How do you know," she said, "that I have got a heart at all?"

"Probably not from the sentimental point of view," he replied, with a little fling of sarcasm: "but I know you couldn't live without the physical organ, and it's over-strained. Good-night, since I see you want to get rid of me. But I'll be handy downstairs, and mind you come for me, Gilchrist, on the moment if she should show any signs again."

This was said to Gilchrist in an undertone as the doctor went away.

Miss Bethune sat up on her sofa, still very pale, still with a singing in her ears, and the glitter of fever in her eyes. "You are not to go away, Harry," she said. "I have something to tell you before you go."

"Oh, mem," said Gilchrist, "for any sake, not to-night."

"Go away, and bide away till I send for you," cried the mistress. "And, Harry, sit you down here by me. I am going to tell you a story. This night has taught me many things. I might die, or I might be murdered for the sake of a few gewgaws that are nothing to me, and go down to my grave with a burden on my heart. I want to speak before I die."

"Not to-night," he cried. "You are in no danger. I'll sleep here on the sofa by way of guard, and to-morrow you will send them to your bankers. Don't tire yourself any more to-night."

"You are like all the rest, and understand nothing about it," she cried impatiently. "It is just precisely now that I will speak, and no other time. Harry, I am going to tell you a story. It is like

211

most women's stories—about a young creature that was beguiled and loved a man. He was a man that had a fine outside, and looked as good as he was bonnie, or at least this misfortunate thing thought so. He had nothing, and she had nothing. But she was the last of her family, and would come into a good fortune if she pleased her uncle that was the head of the name. But the uncle could not abide this man. Are you listening to me? Mind, it is a story, but not an idle story, and every word tells. Well, she was sent away to a lonely country place, an old house, with two old servants in it, to keep her free of the man. But the man followed; and in that solitude who was to hinder them seeing each other? They did for a while every day. And then the two married each other, as two can do in Scotland that make up their minds to risk it, and were living together in secret in the depths of the Highlands, as I told you, nobody knowing but the old servants that had been far fonder of her father than of the uncle that was head of the house, and were faithful to her in life and death. And then there came terrible news that the master was coming back. That poor young woman—oh, she was a fool, and I do not defend her!—had just been delivered in secret, in trouble and misery— for she dared not seek help or nursing but what she got at home— of a bonnie bairn,"—she put out her hand and grasped him by the arm,—"a boy, a darling, though she had him but for two or three days. Think if you can what that was. The master coming that had, so to speak, the power of life and death in his hands, and the young, subdued girl that he had put there to be in safety, the mother of a son——" Miss Bethune drew a long breath. She silenced the remonstrance on the lips of her hearer by a gesture, and went on:—

"It was the man, her husband, that she thought loved her, that brought the news. He said everything was lost if it should be known. He bid her to be brave and put a good face upon it, for his sake and the boy's. Keep her fortune and cling to her inheritance she must, whatever happened, for their sake. And while she was dazed in her weakness, and could not tell what to think, he took the baby out of her arms, and carried him away.

"Harry Gordon, that's five and twenty years ago, and man or bairn I have never seen since, though I did that for them. I dreed my weird for ten long years—ten years of mortal trouble—and never said a word, and nobody knew. Then my uncle died, and the money, the terrible money, bought with my life's blood, became mine. And I looked for him then to come back. But he never came back nor word nor sign of him. And my son—the father, I had discovered what he was, I wanted never to hear his name again—but my son—Harry Gordon, that's you! They may say what they will, but I know better. Who should know, if not the mother who bore you? My heart went out to you when I saw you first, and yours to me. You'll not tell me that your heart did not speak for your mother? It is you, my darling, it is you!"

He had staggered to his feet, pale, trembling, and awe-stricken. The sight of her emotion, the pity of her story, the revolt and resistance in his own heart were too much for him. "I!" he cried.

CHAPTER XXIII.

Harry Gordon passed the night upon the sofa in Miss Bethune's sitting-room. It was his opinion that her nerves were so shaken and her mind so agitated that the consciousness of having some one at hand within call, in case of anything happening, was of the utmost consequence. I don't know that any one else in the house entertained these sentiments, but it was an idea in which he could not be shaken, his experience all tending in that way.

As a matter of fact, his nerves were scarcely less shaken than he imagined hers to be. His mother! Was that his mother who called good-night to him from the next room? who held that amusing colloquy with the doctor through the closed door, defying all interference, and bidding Dr. Roland look after his patient upstairs, and leave her in peace with Gilchrist, who was better than any doctor? Was that his mother? His heart beat with a strange confusion, but made no answer. And his thoughts went over all the details with an involuntary scepticism. No, there was no voice of nature, as she had fondly hoped; nothing but the merest response to kind words and a kind look had drawn him towards this old Scotch maiden lady, who he had thought, with a smile, reminded him of something in Scott, and therefore had an attraction such as belongs to those whom we may have known in some previous state of being.

What a strange fate was his, to be drawn into one circle after another, one family after another, to which he had no right! And how was he to convince this lady, who was so determined in her own way of thinking, that he had no right, no title, to consider himself her son? But had he indeed no title? Was she likely to make such a statement without proof that it was true, without evidence? He thought of her with a kind of amused but by no means disrespectful admiration, as she had stood flinging from her the miserable would-be thief, the wretched, furtive creature who was no match for a resolute and dauntless woman. All the women Harry had ever known would have screamed or fled or fainted at sight of a live burglar in their very bed-chamber. She flung him off like a fly, like a reptile. That was not a weak woman, liable to be deceived by any fancy. She had the look in her eyes of a human creature afraid of nothing, ready to confront any danger. And could she then be so easily deceived? Or was it true, actually true? Was he the son—not of a woman whom it might be shame to discover, as he had always feared—but of a spotless mother, a person of note, with an established position and secure fortune? The land which he was to manage, which she had roused him almost to enthusiasm about, by her talk of crofters and cotters to be helped forward, and human service to be done—was that land his own, coming to him by right, his natural place and inheritance? Was he no waif and stray, no vague atom in the world drifting hither and thither, but a man with an assured position, a certain home, a place in society? How different from going back to South America, and at the best becoming a laborious clerk where he had been the young master! But he could not believe in it.

He lay there silent through the short summer night, moving with precaution upon the uneasy couch, which was too short and too small, but where the good fellow would have passed the night waking and dosing for anybody's comfort, even were it only an old woman's who had been kind to him. But was she his mother— his mother? He could not believe it—he could not, he could not! Her wonderful speeches and looks were all explained now, and went to his heart: but they did not convince him, or bring any enlightenment into his. Was she the victim of an illusion, poor lady, self-deceived altogether? Or was there something in it, or was there nothing in it? He thought of his father, and his heart revolted. His poor father, whom he remembered with the halo round him of childish affection, but whom he had learned to see

215

through other people's eyes, not a strong man, not good for very much, but yet not one to desert a woman who trusted in him. But of the young man's thoughts through that long uneasy night there was no end. He heard whisperings and movements in the next room, subdued for his sake as he subdued his inclination to turn and toss upon his sofa for hers, during half the night. And then when the daylight came bright into the room through the bars of the venetian blind there came silence, just when he had fully woke up to the consciousness that life had begun again in a new world. A little later, Gilchrist stole into his room, bringing him a cup of tea. "You must come upstairs now; there's a room where ye will get some sleep. She's sound now, and it's broad daylight, and no fear of any disturbance," she said.

"I want no more sleep. I'll go and get a bath, and be ready for whatever is wanted." He caught her apron as she was turning away, that apron on which so many hems had been folded. "Don't go away," he said. "Speak to me, tell me, Gilchrist, for heaven's sake, is this true?"

"The Lord knows!" cried Gilchrist, shaking her head and clasping her hands; "but oh, my young gentleman, dinna ask me!"

"Whom can I ask?" he said. "Surely, surely you, that have been always with her, can throw some light upon it. Is it true?"

"It is true—true as death," said the woman, "that all that happened to my dear leddy; but oh, if you are the bairn, the Lord knows; he was but two days old, and he would have been about your age. I can say not a word, but only the Lord knows. And there's nothing—nothing, though she thinks sae, that speaks in your heart?"

He shook his head, with a faint smile upon his face.

"Oh, dinna laugh, dinna laugh. I canna bear it, Mr. Harry; true or no' true, it's woven in with every fibre o' her heart. You have nae parents, my bonnie man. Oh, could you no' take it upon ye, true or no' true? There's naebody I can hear of that it would harm or wrong if you were to accept it. And there's naebody kens but me how good she is. Her exterior is maybe no' sae smooth as many; but her heart it is gold—oh, her heart it is gold! For God's sake, who is the Father of all of us, and full of mercy—such peety as a father hath unto his children dear—oh, my young man, let her believe it, take her at her word! You will make her a happy woman at the end of a' her trouble, and it will do ye nae harm."

"Not if it is a fiction all the time," he said, shaking his head.

"Who is to prove it's a fiction? He would have been your age. She thinks you have your grandfather's een. I'm no' sure now I look at you but she's right. She's far more likely to be right than me: and now I look at you well I think I can see it. Oh, Mr. Harry, what harm would it do you? A good home and a good inheritance, and to make her happy. Is that no' worth while, even if maybe it were not what you would think perfitly true?"

"It can't be half true, Gilchrist; it must be whole or nothing."

"Weel, then, it's whole true; and I'll gang to the stake for it. Is she not the one that should know? And if you were to cast her off the morn and break her heart, she would still believe it till her dying day. Turn round your head and let me look at you again. Oh, laddie, if I were to gang to the stake for it, you have—you have your grandfather's een!"

CHAPTER XXIV.

The house in Bloomsbury was profoundly agitated by all these discoveries. Curiously enough, and against all the previsions of his friends, Mr. Mannering had not been thrown back by the excitement. The sharp sting of these events which had brought back before him once more the tragic climax of his life—the time when he had come back as out of the grave and found his home desolate—when his wife had fled before his face, not daring to meet his eye, although she had not knowingly sinned against him, and when all the triumph of his return to life, and of his discoveries and the fruit of his dreadful labours, had become bitterness to him and misery—came back upon him, every incident standing out as if it had been yesterday. He had fallen into the dead calm of failure, he had dropped his tools from his hands, and all his ambition from his heart. He had retired—he who had reappeared in existence after all his sufferings, with the consciousness that now the ball was at his foot, and fame if not fortune secured—into the second desert, more impenetrable than any African forest, of these rooms in Bloomsbury, and vegetated there all these years, forgetting more or less all that had happened to him, and all that might have happened to him, and desiring only to linger out the last of his life unknowing and unknown. And now into his calm there had come back, clear as yesterday, all that terrible climax, every detail of his own tragedy.

It ought to have killed him: that would have seemed the most likely event in his weakness, after his long illness; and perhaps,—who could say?—the best thing that could have happened, in face of the new circumstances, which he could not accept and had no right to refuse. But no, it did not kill him. It acted upon him as great trouble acts on some minds, like a strong stimulant. It stung him back into life, it seemed to transfuse something, some new revivifying principle, into his veins. He had wanted, perhaps, something to disperse the mists of illness and physical dejection. He found it not in soothing influences or pleasure, but in pain. From the day when he stumbled downstairs to Miss Bethune's room on the dreadful report that she was dying, he began at once to resume his usual habits, and with almost more than his usual strength. Was it possible that Death, that healer of all wounds, that peacemaker in all tumults, had restored a rest that was wanting to the man's secret heart, never disclosed to any ear? She was dead, the woman who unwittingly, without meaning it, had made of his life the silent tragedy it had been. That she was guiltless, and that the catastrophe was all a terrible mistake, had made it worse instead of better. He had thought often that had she erred in passion, had she been carried away from him by some strong gale of personal feeling, it would have been more bearable: but the cruel fatality, the network of accident which had made his life desolate, and hers he knew not what—this was what was intolerable, a thing not to bear thinking of.

But now she was dead, all the misery over, nothing left but the silence. She had been nothing to him for years, torn out of his heart, flung out of his life, perhaps with too little pity, perhaps with little perception of the great sacrifice she had made in giving up to him without even a protest her only child: but her very existence had been a canker in his life; the thought that still the same circle of earth enclosed them—him and the woman who had once been everything to him, and then nothing, yet always something, something, a consciousness, a fever, a jarring note that set all life out of tune. And now she was dead. The strong pain of all this revival stung him back to strength. He went out in defiance of the doctor, back to his usual work, resuming the daily round. He had much to meet, to settle, to set right again, in his renewed existence. And she was dead. The other side of life was closed and sealed, and the stone rolled to the door of the sepulchre. Nothing could happen to bring that back, to renew any consciousness of it more. Strange and sad and disturbing as this event was, it seemed to settle and clear the turbid current of a spoiled life.

And perhaps the other excitement and climax of the life of his neighbour which had been going on under the same roof, helped Mr. Mannering in the renewal of his own history. When he heard Miss Bethune's story, the silent rebellion against his own, which had been ever in his mind, was silenced. It is hard, in the comparison of troubles, which people who have been more or less crushed in life are so fond of making, when brought into sufficiently intimate relation with each other, to have to acknowledge that perhaps a brother pilgrim, a sister, has had more to bear than oneself. Even in misery we love to be foremost, to have the bitter in our cup acknowledged as more bitter than that of others. But yet, when Mr. Mannering heard, as she could tell him, the story of the woman who had lived so near him for years with that unsuspected secret, he did not deny that her lot had been more terrible than his own. Miss Bethune was eager to communicate her own tale in those days of excitement and transition. She went to him of her own accord after the first day of his return to his work, while the doctor hovered about the stairs, up and down, and could not rest, in terror for the result. Dr. Roland could not believe that his patient would not break down. He could not go out, nor even sit quietly in his own room, less he should be wanted, and not ready at the first call. He could not refrain from a gibe at the lady he met on the stairs. "Yes, by all means," he said, "go and tell him all about your own business. Go and send him out to look after that wretched Hesketh, whom you are going to keep up, I hear, all the same."

"Not him, doctor. The poor unhappy young creature, his wife."

"Oh, yes; that is how these miserable villains get hold upon people of weak minds. His wife! I'd have sent him to gaol. His wife would have been far better without a low blackguard like that. But don't let me keep you. Go and give the *coup de grace* to Mannering. I shall be ready, whatever happens, downstairs."

But Miss Bethune did not give Mannering the *coup de grace*. On the contrary, she helped forward the cure which the climax of his own personal tragedy had begun. It gave both these people a kind of forlorn pleasure to think that there was a kind of resemblance in their fate, and that they had lived so long beside each other without knowing it, without suspecting how unlike other people their respective lives had been. The thought of the unhappy young woman, whose husband of a year and whose child of a day had been torn from her, who had learnt so sadly to know the unworthiness of the one, and whose heart and imagination had for five and twenty years dwelt upon the other, without any possible outlet, and with a hope which she had herself known to be fantastic and without hope, filled Mannering with a certain awe. He had suffered for little more than half that time, and he had not been deprived of his Dora. He began to think pitifully, even mercifully, of the woman who had left him that one alleviation in his life.

"I bow my head before her," Miss Bethune said. "She must have been a just woman. The bairn was yours, and she had no right to take her from you. She fled before your appearance, she could not look you in the face, but she left the little child that she adored to be your comfort. Mr. Mannering, you will come with me to that poor woman's grave, and you will forgive her. She gave you up what was most dear to her in life."

He shook his head. "She had others that were more dear to her."

"I could find it in my heart, if I were you, to hope that it was so; but I do not believe it. How could she look you in the face again, having sinned against you? But she left you what she loved most. 'Dora, Dora,' was all her cry: but she put Dora out of her arms for you. Think kindly of her, man! A woman loves nothing on this earth," cried Miss Bethune with passion, "like the little child that has come from her, and is of her, flesh of her flesh, bone of her bone: and she gave that over to you. She must have been a woman more just than most other women," Miss Bethune said.

Mr. Mannering made no reply. Perhaps he did not understand or believe in that definition of what a woman loves best; but he thought of the passion of the other woman before him, and of the long hunger of her heart, with nothing to solace her, nothing to divert her thoughts from that hopeless loss and vacancy, nothing to compensate her for the ruin of her life. She had been a spirit in prison, shut up as in an iron cage, and she had borne it and not uttered even a cry. All three, or rather all four, of these lives, equally shipwrecked, came before him. His own stricken low in what would have been the triumph of another man; his wife's, turned in a moment from such second possibilities of happiness as he could not yet bear to think of, and from the bliss of her child, into shame and guilt such as did not permit her to look her husband in the face, but drove her into exile and renunciation. And then this other pair. The woman with her secret romance, and long, long penitence and punishment. The man (whom she condemned yet more bitterly, perhaps with better cause than he had condemned his wife), a fugitive too, disappearing from country and home with the infant who died, or who did not die. What a round of dreadful mistake, misapprehension, rashness, failure! And who was he that he should count himself more badly treated than other men?

Miss Bethune thus gave him no *coup de grace*. She helped him after the prick of revival, to another more steadfast philosophy, in the comparison of his fate with that of others. He saw with very clear eyes her delusion—that Harry Gordon was no son of hers, and that she would be compelled to acknowledge this and go back to the dreariness and emptiness of her life, accepting the dead baby as all that ever was hers: and he was sorry for her to the bottom of his heart; while she, full of her illusions, went back to her own apartment full of pity for him, to whom Dora did not make up for everything as Harry, she felt triumphantly, did to herself.

Dr. Roland watched them both, more concerned for Mannering, who had been ill, than for Miss Bethune, who had all that curious elasticity which makes a woman generally so much more the servant of her emotions than a man, often, in fact, so much less affected by them. But there still remained in the case of the patient another fiery trial to go through, which still kept the doctor on the alert and anxiously watching the course of events. Mannering had said nothing of Dora's fortune, of the money which he had refused vehemently for her, but which he had no right to refuse, and upon which, as Dr. Roland was aware, she had already drawn. One ordeal had passed, and had done no harm, but this other was still to come.

It came a day or two after, when Dr. Roland sat by Mannering's side after his return from the Museum, holding his pulse, and investigating in every way the effect upon him of the day's confinement. It was evening, and the day had been hot and fatiguing. Mr. Mannering was a little tired of this medical inspection, which occurred every evening. He drew his wrist out of the doctor's hold, and turned the conversation abruptly to a new subject.

"There are a number of papers which I cannot find," he said, almost sharply, to Dora, with a meaning which immediately seemed to make the air tingle. He had recovered his usual looks in a remarkable degree, and had even a little colour in his cheek. His head was not drooping, nor his eye dim. The stoop of a man occupied all day among books seemed to have disappeared. He leaned back in his chair a little, perhaps, but not forward, as is the habit of weakness, and was not afraid to look the doctor in the face. Dora stood near him, alarmed, in the attitude of one about to flee. She was eager to leave him with the doctor, of whom he could ask no such difficult questions.

"Papers, father? What papers?" she said, with an air of innocence which perhaps was a little overdone.

"My business affairs are not so extensive," he said, with a faint smile; "and both you, doctor, who really are the author of the extravagance, and Dora, who is too young to meddle with such matters, know all about them. My bills!—Heaven knows they are enough to scare a poor man: but they must be found. They were all there a few days ago, now I can't find them. Bring them, Dora. I must make a composition with my creditors," he said, again, with that forced and uncomfortable smile. Then he added, with some impatience: "My dear, do what I tell you, and do it at once."

It was an emergency which Dora had been looking forward to, but that did not make it less terrible when it came. She stood very upright, holding by the table.

"The bills? I don't know where to find them," she said, growing suddenly very red, and then very pale.

"Dora!" cried her father, in a warning tone. Then he added, with an attempt at banter: "Never mind the doctor. The doctor is in it; he ought to pay half. We will take his advice. How small a dividend will content our creditors for the present? Make haste, and do not lose any more time."

Dora stood her ground without wavering. "I cannot find them, father," she said.

"You cannot find them? Nonsense! This is for my good, I suppose, lest I should not be able to bear it. My dear, your father declines to be managed for his good."

"I have not got them," said Dora firmly, but very pale. "I don't know where to find them; I don't want to find them, if I must say it, father,—not to manage you, but on my own account."

He raised himself upright too, and looked at her. Their eyes shone with the same glow; the two faces bore a strange resemblance,—his, the lines refined and softened by his illness; hers, every curve straightened and strengthened by force of passionate feeling.

"Father," said Dora almost fiercely, "I am not a child!"

"You are not a child?" A faint smile came over his face. "You are curiously like one," he said; "but what has that got to do with it?"

"Mannering, she is quite right. You ought to let her have her own way."

A cloud crossed Mr. Mannering's face. He was a mild man, but he did not easily brook interference. He made a slight gesture, as if throwing the intruder off.

"Father," said Dora again, "I have been the mistress of everything while you have been ill. You may say the doctor has done it, or Miss Bethune has done it,—they were very kind friends, and told me what to do,—but it was only your own child that had the right to do things for you, and the real person was me. I was a little girl when you began to be ill, but I am not so now. I've had to act for myself, father," the girl cried, the colour flaming back into her pale cheeks, "I've had to be responsible for a great many things; you can't take that from me, for it had to be. And you have not got a bill in the world."

He sat staring at her, half angry, half admiring, amazed by the change, the development; and yet to find her in her impulsive, childish vehemence exactly the same.

"They're all gone," cried Dora, with that dreadful womanish inclination to cry; which spoils so many a fine climax. "I had a right to them—they were mine all through, and not yours. Father, even Fiddler! I've given you a present of that big book, which I almost broke my arm (if it had not been for Harry Gordon) carrying back. And now I know it's quarter day, and you're quite well off. Father, now I'm your little girl again, to do what you like and go where you like, and never, never hear a word of this more," cried Dora, flinging herself upon his shoulder, with her arms round his neck, in a paroxysm of tenderness and tears.

What was the man to do or say? He had uttered a cry of pain and shame, and something like fury; but with the girl clinging round his neck, sobbing, flung upon his mercy, he was helpless. He looked over Dora's bright head at Dr. Roland with, notwithstanding his impatience of interference, a sort of appeal for help. However keen the pang was both to his heart and his pride, he could not throw off his only child from her shelter in his arms. After a moment his hand instinctively came upon her hair, smoothing it down, soothing her, though half against his will. The other arm, with which he had half put her away, stole round her with a softer pressure. His child, his only child, all of his, belonging to no one but him, and weeping her heart out upon his neck, altogether thrown upon him to be excused and pardoned for having given him all the tendance and care and help which it was in her to give. He looked at Roland with a half appeal, yet with that unconscious pride of superiority in the man who has, towards the man who has not.

"She has the right," said the doctor, himself moved, but not perhaps with any sense of inferiority, for though he was nearly as old as Mr. Mannering, the beatitude of having a daughter had not yet become an ideal bliss to him—"she has the right; if anybody in the world has it, she has it, Mannering, and though she is a child, she has a heart and judgment as good as any of us. You'll have to let her do in certain matters what seemeth good in her own eyes."

Mr. Mannering shook his head, and then bent it in reluctant acquiescence with a sigh.

CHAPTER XXV.

The house in Bloomsbury became vacant and silent.

The people who had given it interest and importance were dispersed and gone. Dr. Roland only remained, solitary and discontented, feeling himself cast adrift in the world, angry at the stillness overhead, where the solid foot of Gilchrist no longer made the floor creak, or the lighter step of her mistress sent a thrill of energy and life through it; but still more angry when new lodgers came, and new steps sounded over the carpet, which, deprived of all Miss Bethune's rugs, was thin and poor. The doctor thought of changing his lodging himself, in the depression of that change; but it is a serious matter for a doctor to change his abode, and Janie's anæmia was becoming a serious case, and wanted more looking after than ever would be given to it were he out of the way. So he consented to the inevitable, and remained. Mrs. Simcox had to refurnish the second floor, when all Mr. Mannering's pretty furniture and his books were taken away, and did it very badly, as was natural, and got "a couple" for her lodgers, who were quite satisfied with second-hand mahogany and hair-cloth. Dr. Roland looked at the new lodgers when he met them with eyes blank, and a total absence of interest: but beginning soon to see that the stock market was telling upon the first floor, and that the lady on the second had a cough, he began to allow himself a little to be shaken out of his indifference. They might, however, be objects of professional interest, but no more. The Mannerings were abroad. After that great flash in the pan of a return to the Museum, Nature had reclaimed her rights, and Mr. Mannering had been obliged to apply for a prolonged leave, which by degrees led to retirement and a pension. Miss Bethune had returned to her native country, and to the old house near the Highland line which belonged to her. Vague rumours that she was not Miss Bethune at all, but a married lady all the time, had reached Bloomsbury; but nobody knew, as Mrs. Simcox said, what were the rights of the case.

In a genial autumn, some years after the above events, Dr. Roland, who had never ceased to keep a hold upon his former neighbours, whose departure had so much saddened his life, arrived on a visit at that Highland home. It was a rambling house, consisting of many additions and enlargements built on to the original fabric of a small, strait, and high semi-fortified dwelling-place, breathing that air of austere and watchful defence which lingers about some old houses, though the parlours of the eighteenth century, not to say the drawing-rooms of the nineteenth, with their broad open windows, accessible from the ground, were strangely unlike the pointed tall gable with its crow steps, and the high post of watchfulness up among the roofs, the little balcony or terrace which swept the horizon on every side. There Miss Bethune, still Miss Bethune, abode in the fulness of a life which sought no further expansion, among her own people. She had called to her a few of the most ancient and trusted friends of the family on her first arrival there, and had disclosed to them her secret story, and asked their advice. She had never borne her husband's name. There had been no break, so far as any living person except Gilchrist was aware, in the continuity of her life. The old servants were dead, and the old minister, who had been coaxed and frightened into performing a furtive ceremony. No one except Gilchrist was aware of any of those strange events which had gone on in the maze of little rooms and crooked passages. Miss Bethune was strong in the idea of disclosing everything when she returned home. She meant to publish her strange and painful story among her friends and to the world at large, and to acknowledge and put in his right place, as she said, her son. A small knot of grave county gentlemen sat upon the matter, and had all the evidence placed before them in order to decide this question.

Harry Gordon himself was the first to let them know that his claims were more than doubtful—that they were, in fact, contradicted by his own recollections and everything he really knew about himself; and Mr. Templar brought his report, which made it altogether impossible to believe in the relationship. But Miss Bethune's neighbourssoon came to perceive that these were nothing to her own fervid conviction, which they only made stronger the oftener the objections were repeated. She would not believe that part of Mr. Templar's story which concerned the child; there was no documentary proof. The husband's death could be proved, but it was not even known where that of the unfortunate baby had taken place, and nothing could be ascertained about it. She took no notice of the fact that her husband and Harry Gordon's father had neither died at the same place nor at the same time. As it actually happened, there was sufficient analogy between time and place to make it possible to imagine, had there been no definite information, that they were the same person. And this was more than enough for Miss Bethune. She was persuaded at last, however, by the unanimous judgment of the friends she trusted, to depart from her first intention, to make no scandal in the countryside by changing her name, and to leave her property to Harry, describing him as a relation by the mother's side. "It came to you by will, not in direct inheritance," the chief of these gentlemen of the county said. "Let it go to him in the same way. We all respect the voice of nature, and you are not a silly woman, my dear Janet, to believe a thing that is not: but the evidence would not bear investigation in a court of law. He is a fine young fellow, and has spoken out like a gentleman."

"As he has a good right—the last of the Bethunes, as well as a Gordon of no mean name!"

"Just so," said the convener of the county; "there is nobody here that will not give him his hand. But you have kept the secret so long, it is my opinion you should keep it still. We all know— all that are worth considering—and what is the use of making a scandal and an outcry among all the silly auld wives of the countryside? And leave him your land by will, as the nearest relation you care to acknowledge on his mother's side."

This was the decision that was finally come to; and Miss Bethune was not less a happy mother, nor Harry Gordon the less a good son, that the relationship between them was quite beyond the reach of proof, and existed really in the settled conviction of one brain alone. The delusion made her happy, and it gave him a generous reason for acquiescing in the change so much to his advantage which took place in his life.

The Mannerings arrived at Beaton Castle shortly after the doctor, on their return from the Continent. Dora was now completely woman-grown, and had gradually and tacitly taken the command of her father and all his ways. He had been happy in the certainty that when he left off work and consented to take that long rest, it was his own income upon which they set out—an income no longer encumbered with any debts to pay, even for old books. He had gone on happily upon that conviction ever since; they had travelled a great deal together, and he had completely recovered his health, and in a great degree his interest, both in science and life. He had even taken up those studies which had been interrupted by the shipwreck of his happiness, and the breaking up of his existence, and had recently published some of the results of them, with a sudden lighting up once again of the fame of the more youthful Mannering, from whom such great things had been expected. The more he had become interested in work and the pursuits of knowledge, the less he had known or thought of external affairs; and for a long time Dora had acted very much as she pleased, increasing such luxuries as he liked, and encouraging every one of the extravagances into which, when left to himself, he naturally fell. Sometimes still he would pause over an expensive book, with a half hesitation, half apology.

"But perhaps we cannot afford it. I ought not to give myself so many indulgences, Dora."

"You know how little we spend, father," Dora would say,— "no house going on at home to swallow up the money. We live for next to nothing here." And he received her statement with implicit faith.

Thus both the elder personages of this history were deceived, and found a great part of their happiness in it. Was it a false foundation of happiness, and wrong in every way, as Dr. Roland maintained? He took these two young people into the woods, and read them the severest of lessons.

"You are two lies," he said; "you are deceiving two people who are of more moral worth than either of you. It is probably not your fault, but that of some wicked grandmother; but you ought to be told it, all the same. And I don't say that I blame you. I daresay I should do it also in your case. But it's a shame, all the same."

"In the case of my—mistress, my friend, my all but mother," said young Gordon, with some emotion, "the deceit is all her own. I have said all I could say, and so have her friends. We have proved to her that it could not be I, everything has been put before her; and if she determines, after all that, that I am the man, what can I do? I return her affection for affection cordially, for who was ever so good to any one as she is to me? And I serve her as her son might do. I am of use to her actually, though you may not think it. And why should I try to wound her heart, by reasserting that I am not what she thinks, and that she is deceived? I do my best to satisfy, not to deceive her. Therefore, do not say it; I am no lie."

"All very well and very plausible," said the doctor, "but in no wise altering my opinion. And, Miss Dora, what have you got to say?"

"I say nothing," said Dora; "there is no deceit at all. If you only knew how particular I am! Father's income suffices for himself; he is not in debt to any one. He has a good income—a very good income—four hundred a year, enough for any single man. Don't you think so? I have gone over it a great many times, and I am sure he does not spend more than that—not so much; the calculation is all on paper. Do you remember teaching me to do accounts long ago? I am very good at it now. Father is not bound to keep me, when there are other people who will keep on sending me money: and he has quite enough—too much for himself; then where is the deceit, or shame either? My conscience is quite clear."

"You are two special pleaders," the doctor said; "you are too many for me when you are together. I'll get you apart, and convince you of your sin. And what," he cried suddenly, taking them by surprise, "my fine young sir and madam, would happen if either one or other of you took it into your heads to marry? That is what I should like to know."

They looked at each other for a moment as it were in a flash of crimson light, which seemed to fly instantaneously from one to another. They looked first at him, and then exchanged one lightning glance, and then each turned a little aside on either side of the doctor. Was it to hide that something which was nothing, that spontaneous, involuntary momentary interchange of looks, from his curious eyes? Dr. Roland was struck as by that harmless lightning. He, the expert, had forgotten what contagion there might be in the air. They were both tall, both fair, two slim figures in their youthful grace, embodiments of all that was hopeful, strong, and lifelike. The doctor had not taken into consideration certain effects known to all men which are not in the books. "Whew-ew!" he breathed in a long whistle of astonishment, and said no more.

THE END.